Believe in love

DISTRACTION

The Underground Kings Series

Aurora Rose Reynolds

Terry xoxo

Dedication

To those who are strong because they have no other choice.

Table of Contents

Prologue

Sven, age ten

WALKING DOWN THE dimly lit hallway to my dad's home office, I stop just outside the door, watching him pull off his glasses and rub his eyes. I hate bothering him, but I really need my permission slip signed for my field trip tomorrow, and I can't go to my mom because I know she'll freak. She's always freaking out about something these days. Pulling the folded up form out of my back pocket, I step through the door then pause, feeling my stomach turn and get upset when I see my mom asleep on the couch under the window behind the door.

"What's up, bud?" Pulling my eyes from my mom, I look at my dad and take a step backward. "She's asleep. It's okay," he says softly, studying me.

"I can come back," I whisper, swinging my eyes to my mom to make sure she didn't wake when I spoke.

"I gave her her sleeping pills. She'll be out for awhile," he says gently, and I ball my hands into fists, crushing the paper in my grip. It sucks that I'm afraid of my own mother.

Licking my lips, I pull my eyes from her on the couch, move swiftly to the side of my dad's desk, and unfold the paper, placing it on top of the stack of paperwork sitting in front of him. "We have a field trip tomorrow and I need this signed," I tell him quietly, moving my eyes to my mom once more as fear makes my hands shake.

"Where are you guys going?" he asks, uncapping one of his fancy pens, one of the few Grandma got him for Christmas. One of the hundred he has, because she always buys him pens, the same way she always buys me socks. Her gifts suck, but she never fails to bring peanut butter cookies with Hershey Kisses on top that she bakes fresh, which makes her lame gifts worth it when she comes to visit.

"Um…some museum," I tell him, licking my lips again then feeling my heart stop when my mom moans and rolls over on the couch to face the back of it.

"That sounds fun." He chuckles. I wish I could laugh with him, but I can't breathe as I wait anxiously for him to sign the paper so I can leave. "Did you get something to eat?" he asks, placing the pen to the paper.

"Yes," I lie. When I got off the bus from school, I went right to my room, did my homework, and stayed there until now, because I didn't want to accidently run into my mom who I knew was home because her car was parked out front, half on the drive way and half on the grass, like she was in a hurry when she pulled up.

"I know things haven't been easy, bud, but I promise they're going to get better," he says, and my eyes meet his. I wish he was telling the truth, but I know he's lying. No matter how many times my mom comes to my school and embarrasses me, or how many times the police come here when she's freaking out, he still acts like nothing's wrong. He always just says things will get better, but they never do.

"I know," I lie back, watching his eyes flash with something before dropping to the paper and signing his name across the bottom.

"Do you need any money for tomorrow?" he inquires, shifting to the side, shoving his hand in his pocket, and pulling out a large wad of money before I can tell him yes or no. "You may want to buy a souvenir or get something to eat," he murmurs, pulling off two twenties from the wad, wrapping them in the permission slip, and handing it back to me.

"Thanks."

"Go get some sleep. I'll take you to school in the morning so you can sleep in."

"I can catch the bus," I rush out, knowing that if I don't, I will have to see my mom in the morning, and nowadays, I do everything within my power to avoid any kind of contact with her.

"We need to talk about something, so I'll drive you."

"Sure," I agree as his hand comes up to rest on my shoulder, giving it a squeeze before letting me go.

"Night, bud."

"Night," I mutter, rushing out of his office and down the hall to my room. Unfolding the paper, taking both twenties to my desk, and opening the top drawer, I add them to the pile of money I already have. My dad is always giving me money, whether I want it or not. I think he uses it as a way to not feel guilty for how crappy things have been lately.

At first I thought it was cool because I was able to get whatever I wanted, but not now. Now, I hate it. Closing the drawer, I go to my backpack and shove the permission slip inside one of the pockets then dig to the bottom of the bag until I find the candy bar I bought from the vending machine at school. I scarf it down, hating the way my chest hurts as I remember the times we used to have dinner like a normal family.

Jumping out of my sleep, my heart starts to pound. I don't know what woke me, but fear rushes through me as I turn to look at my bedroom door and see the hall is dark through the crack along the bottom. Closing my eyes, I do what I always do when this happens and play funny cartoons in my head, trying to get my heart to calm and get back to sleep.

Hearing a strange noise, my eyes spring open and my heart pounds hard once more. Getting out of bed quietly, I open my door and peek each way before tiptoeing as quickly and as silently as I can down the hall, through the living room, and toward my parents' bedroom on the other side of the house, wondering if they heard the noise too.

When I reach the hall to their room, some of the fear in me leaves. Their light is on, and I can hear murmurings coming from inside, letting me know they are awake and I'm not alone. Taking a step toward their door, which is open an inch, I feel warm wetness soak the front of my pajama bottoms. When I look through the crack, my mom is standing over my dad with a knife in her hands, her arms and the front of her nightgown covered in blood. Covering my mouth with my hand, I stumble away from the door, fall on my bottom, and then roll over, taking off and crying out in fear when light floods the hall. I hear my mom yell something behind me.

Running to the kitchen, I grab the phone that sits on the counter and a knife from the butcher block. I go to my room, not hearing anything behind me as I scurry into the back of my closet and hide in the crawlspace where I used to play when I was little. Breathing heavily, I dial nine-one-one on the phone and wait only one ring for the operator to pick up.

"Nine-one-one, what's your emergency?"

Clutching the knife to my chest, my voice chokes as I whisper, "My mom just killed my dad."

Chapter 1

Sven

You're a Lint-Licker

"**G**ET ON YOUR knees," I tell the blonde in front of me. One thing the women who want me to fuck them learn right away is that I don't say anything twice. Watching her eyes flare, she drops to her knees and her hands go behind her back. Her thighs spread, showing off her bare pussy.

"Open your mouth," I murmur, running my hand softly along her jaw in approval. When her head lifts and she looks up, I feed her my dick inch by inch until it hits the back of her throat. Hearing her gag, I pull back, only to surge forward again. "Lick it, just the tip," I command, watching her tongue swirl around the crown then press into her mouth, letting my head fall back as she bobs up and down along my length until I feel that familiar rush in my spine.

"Stop," I growl, pulling her to her feet, turning her to face my desk and bending her over the top. Hearing her moan I kick her feet apart and roll the condom on. My hands slide around her waist, one cupping her breasts and the other zeroing in on her clit, skimming over it as her hips tip back and I slide in. This is only about one thing; it's only *ever* about one thing. Stroking in and out of her, I feel her walls begin to spasm as I plant myself to the hilt and drop forward, coming hard. I take a second to catch my breath, and I can still feel her shaking in my arms as I pull out and step back.

"You can go," I tell her, pulling off the condom and tying it off before walking into the adjoining bathroom, tossing it in the toilet, and then washing my hands and dick.

"I can go?" she repeats, not moving away from my desk or adjusting her dress that is still up around her waist. Turning to look at her, I'm sure she's someone's daughter or sister; she may even be a nice girl, but she means nothing to me. Like all the other women that my security asks to come up here, they come without knowing anything about me except what the rumors are.

"Yes, you can go," I tell her, tucking myself back in and adjusting my shirt before walking over to my desk and taking a seat.

"You're a prick," she mumbles, wiggling her dress back down over her ass and stomping in her heels across the carpet to her bag that she dropped on the couch when she came in.

"You got what you wanted," I remind her as she angrily shoves her arm through the strap of her bag. I may be a dick, but I didn't fill her head with false expectations before fucking her and telling her to get out. She knew what was going to happen before she walked her ass up the stairs to my office, or at least she had a good idea of what was going to occur, and I sure as hell didn't force her to her knees to suck me off.

"Whatever," she says, looking at me once more, and I know from the look in her eyes that all I'd have to do is call her back and she would come. Annoyed by that, I look down at the spreadsheet in front of me, hearing the door slam hard.

Turning my chair, I look out over the club through the large window. There are hundreds of people below and some nights, like tonight, I'll scan the floor and tell my security which woman I want. They'll approach her and give her the choice to come to me or not. I have never had a woman say no, and most of the time they leave happy. But then there are times they leave pissed, because they think their pussy is made of gold and I should ask for seconds or drop a ring on their finger. Scanning the club, a flash of light catches my attention, and my eyes land on a woman who is between two guys with her phone in her hand. She is pointing at them then her cell phone. Normally, I wouldn't think much about it, but something in the woman's eyes isn't right. Picking the phone up off my desk, I dial two.

"Already on it," Zack, the head of my security, states and hangs up. Moving back to the window, I watch Zack and Lane approach her through the crowd then frown. She's not dressed like she's out for a night of fun with her friends; she looks like she's wearing pajamas, and not even the sexy kind. Living in Sin City, you see a lot of shit, and chicks show up to the club in the strangest outfits, especially if they are having a bachelorette party.

Once Zack reaches her, he shoves one of the guys toward Lane then bends his face toward the woman, who lifts her phone to him. Squinting, I try to make out what's on the screen, but the distance and lighting in the club makes it difficult to see anything. Shaking his head, the woman points at the phone again, and Zack touches his ear as my desk phone rings.

"Yeah?"

"She's looking for someone who drugged her sister," Zack says over the music and the crowd downstairs.

"Drugged and beat the crap out of my sister, at this club," the woman screams into the mic.

"Bring her up," I snarl, hanging up the phone, lifting my jacket from the back of my chair, slipping it on, and then straightening my tie. I don't need this shit—not right now, not while all this other shit is going on around me. Over the last few months, a multitude of women have been drugged while partying here, but no one has ever gotten hurt—no one I'm aware of anyway.

"Put me down right now!" the woman yells, kicking her feet and hitting Zack in the back as she enters my office over his shoulder. Lowering her to the ground, he grunts as she pokes him in his chest and yells, "I'm not paying for your chiropractor bills, you giant, overgrown jerk."

"Miss, can you please have a seat?" I ask, and her head turns toward me, her big honey-colored eyes catching me off guard. Seeing the look in her gaze does some shit to my chest that makes me uncomfortable.

Pulling my eyes from hers, I sweep them down the length of her body.

I have no fucking idea how she got into the club wearing pajamas, but she did. The blue plaid bottoms that are about four sizes too big are dragging under her flip-flops. The thin, tight, white tank top she has on allows a glimpse of her breasts and dark nipples. I wouldn't say she's fat; she's all curves, with large breasts and wide hips. Her long, dark hair is in a low ponytail, and her face is round and soft, almost innocent-looking. She's beautiful in a way I'm not accustomed to.

"How did you get in here?" I ask when my eyes meet hers once more.

"I paid the guy at the front a hundred dollars to let me in," she says, glaring at me and crossing her arms over her chest, accentuating her cleavage. Looking over the top of her head, my eyes meet Zack's and he nods before stepping out of the office, closing the door behind him.

"Do you want to tell me why you're here?" I ask, taking a seat and motioning for her to do the same across from me.

"My sister was here earlier tonight," she says, reaching into the top of her tank top, pulling out a cellphone that must be twenty years old, flipping it open, and shoving it across the desk. Picking the phone up, the grainy image of a smiling woman who looks similar to the one across from me is on the screen. She's much slimmer than her sister, so slim she looks ill.

"You told Zack she was drugged here and beat up. If you don't mind me asking, why aren't the police here instead of you?" I query, watching her face close down almost instantly. "If this is some kind of ploy to get money, it won't work," I tell her, pushing the cell phone back across the top of the desk.

"A ploy to get money? Do you mean like blackmail?" she growls, grabbing the phone and clasping it tightly in her hand.

"That's exactly what I mean." I nod, watching her stand.

"You're a...you're a real lint-licker, you know that?" She paces in front of my desk, lifting her hand and pulling out her hair tie, allowing her mane to cascade down her back and over her shoulders.

"Lint-licker," I repeat, trying not to smile as I watch her.

"Lint-licker." She nods then stops pacing and turns to look at me. "I don't want money. The police won't come, because my sister isn't healthy. She has a drug problem, and they don't care what happens to her. She's just one more faceless druggie in a sea of fricking druggies. But I love her. She's my sister, so I want to find the scum buckets who did what they did and turn them in myself," she says, and my hackles instantly rise.

"You're never coming back here again," I snarl, standing and placing my hands on the top of my desk, leaning onto them.

"You can't stop me." She shrugs, and just like that, she turns her back on me and leaves my office before I can even comprehend what just happened. Following after her, I run downstairs through the crowded club. Once I reach the front entrance, I catch a glimpse of her right before she gets into a car the size of my desk and takes off down the street.

"Everything okay, Boss?" Turning my head to look over my shoulder, I glance at Zack and shake my head.

"She's gonna be a problem," I warn him, rubbing my chest as I head back inside.

"Boss, she's here again." Glaring at Teo, who just stepped into my office, I turn to search through the large glass window that looks out over the club floor below. Spotting her sitting at the bar with a drink in front of her, I know it's cranberry juice, the only thing she ever orders.

"Who the fuck let her in this time?" I ask turning around, watching Lane shrug and a smile with a twitch in his lips.

"Zack said he was going to ask Maggie if she wanted a job." He smiles.

"Who the hell is Maggie?"

"The girl…that's her name. Maggie."

"You guys are on a first name basis now?" I ask, leaning back in my chair and tilting my head back, feeling a headache coming on.

"Well, she's here everyday. It would be rude not to know her name."

"This shit's getting ridiculous," I mutter to the ceiling. The damn woman has shown up every night over the last two weeks. She gets here when the club opens and stays 'til closing. She no longer asks people if they know her sister, but she does inspect drinks, and talks to the women at the bar about making sure they are being safe. She is driving me fucking crazy.

"She's kinda cute." Lowering my head, I look at Teo and narrow my eyes, watching him raise his hands in front of him. "But she has a boyfriend," he adds with a smile.

"Who?" I ask without thinking.

"Don't know." He shrugs, walking over to the window, looking down toward the bar.

"Well, the guy is obviously a piece of shit if he lets his woman out of the house every night to come to a club alone," I mutter under my breath.

"What are you going to do about her?" he questions, turning to look at me.

"Give her a job," I half joke. She's persistent as fuck, and if things keep going the way they have been, she's going to end up causing trouble, and I don't need anymore trouble. *At least, that's the lie I'm telling myself.*

"You do need a new assistant."

"Fuck no," I snap, loosening my tie. The last assistant I had ended up being a clusterfuck. The woman was pissed that I wouldn't fuck her. I finally had to fire her ass when she brought another woman up to my office and proceeded to try and get me to join them on my couch when I walked in on them half naked. Work is work. Yes, I might invite women up to fuck, but never anyone I work with.

"It's not like she's your type," he says, and I feel my jaw tick. "Besides, if she's up here with you, she'll stop harassing the women down there." He nods toward where she's sitting and my eyes follow the movement, seeing her talking to a girl who looks a little startled by whatever it is Maggie is telling her.

"It's not happening. You guys need to keep her out of the club," I tell him, turning away from the window.

"Just saying it would be a good way to keep an eye on her," he gripes, patting my shoulder before leaving my office and closing the door behind him.

Letting out a frustrated breath, I turn away from the window and try to focus on all the shit I need to get done.

"Yeah," I pick up my desk phone when it beeps and looking at the clock, seeing that an hour has passed since Teo left.

"Look out your window," Zack says, and I spin my chair around and scan the floor, wondering what he wants me to see. Then I spot Maggie with a man's head tucked under her arm as she leads him toward the front of the club, with Lane and Zack following closely behind them.

"What the fuck is going on?"

"That guy tried to put something in some chick's drink, and Maggie saw him and went postal on his ass," he explains almost proudly.

"Jesus Christ, what the fuck do I pay you for?" I gripe.

"I saw the whole thing. I was getting ready to step in when she stood up on her barstool, jumped on the guy's back, and then did some fucking ninja shit, wrapping her arm around the guy's head and forcing him to his knees. She won't let him go. She said she wants to ask him some questions."

"I'm on my way down," I say, slamming down the phone and jerking open the door to my office, taking the stairs two at a time. Reaching the front of the club, I see Zack holding the guy and Lane's arms wrapped around Maggie's waist, trying to drag her away. What the fuck is going on?" I roar, and all eyes come to me except Maggie's, who takes the opportunity to grab the man's ear and twist, making him drop hard to the ground on his knees.

"You think it's funny to drug innocent women, you flaming turd bucket?" she yells, hitting the top of the guy's bald head, and Zack chuckles along with Lane, but I don't see one damn thing that's funny about this shit.

"Maggie, let him go and come here," I growl, and she raises her eyes to meet mine, looking startled.

"He—"

"I said get your ass over here now!" I yell, cutting her off and feeling the vein in my neck bulge as I point to the ground at my feet.

"Fine." She pouts, letting the guy go, walking sullenly toward me as Zack pulls the man to his feet, taking him with him around the corner, with Lane following behind them with his phone to his ear. I'm sure they are going to have a talk and wait for the cops.

"Let's go," I say, wrapping my hand around the back of her neck, leading her through the club and up the stairs to my office. Sitting her in the chair in front of my desk, I walk over to the cabinets where I keep my personal bottle of scotch and pull out the cap. I then lift the bottle to my lips, taking a swig while trying to calm down.

"Alcohol isn't good for you," she informs me as I take a seat behind my desk.

"Do I look like I give a fuck about that?" I ask her, taking another swig.

"You might not care about what it can do to your body right now, but you may want to know that it lowers sperm count and stamina in the long run."

"Jesus." I shake my head and rub my eyes in aggravation.

"Just saying it's not good for you," she mutters, dropping her eyes to her lap.

"What happened downstairs isn't okay, Mags."

"Maggie," she corrects, still not looking at me.

"Whatever," I drone, taking another swig. "You could have gotten hurt."

"I have a black belt—"

"Look at me," I demand, cutting her off and slamming the bottle down on the top of the desk, waiting for her eyes to meet mine. "You could have gotten hurt or worse. Do you understand that? He could have had a weapon on him."

"You don't understand," she whispers as tears fill her eyes, but I harden myself against them, needing her to understand this isn't a fucking movie. This is real life, and there are bad—*really* fucking bad—people in this world.

"You're not allowed on the club floor anymore," I state firmly.

"I'm going to find the guys who hurt my sister," she states, and I see the determination in her eyes that make me proud and pissed at the same time.

"If you come, you come to my office, and if something happens down there"—I point to the club floor over my shoulder—"you'll be the first to know."

"Why would I come to your office? I need to be at the bar where I can see what's going on."

"You just got the job as my new assistant," I tell her, watching her frown while wondering what the fuck I'm doing. This chick is a distraction I do not need right now, or ever for that matter.

"I already have a job," she says as her frown grows deeper.

"Well, quit. You're here every night, Mags, and you don't leave 'til the club closes at one. I can tell by the bags under your eyes that you're exhausted."

"Why would you want me to work here?" Now, isn't that the million dollar question?

"Either take me up on my offer, or I'm going to have a restraining order placed against you and you won't be allowed within a few hundred feet of the club." I shrug like it's all the same to me.

"You know this is malarkey, right?" she stands and I take her in fully for the first time tonight. Her loose, sheer, black dress is cinched with a thin belt emphasizing the dip in her waist between her full hips and breasts. Her hair is down in a mass of messy waves, and her makeup is subtle but still draws attention to her eyes, which look even more golden now that she's standing in front of me looking pissed off.

"I'm not messing around with you anymore either. You take me up on my deal, or I'll call the police and have them escort you off the premises," I tell her, ignoring the fact I'm getting hard just looking at her.

"This is total crap," she mumbles, looking around before meeting my eyes again.

"Take it or leave it."

"Jeez, can I have a second to think?" she cries, and I feel my lips twitch, so I rub my hand down over my mouth to hide it.

"Ten," I state, watching her eyes narrow. "Nine…eight…seven…" I continue counting, watching as she looks at me like she's ready to kill me. "Six," I raise a brow. "Five…"

"Fine!" she yells when I open my mouth to finish my countdown.

"Thought so," I say triumphantly.

"You're such a…you're such a bigasterd," she growls.

"A what?" I ask, and I can't help it, I laugh at that one.

"When do I start?" she asks, ignoring my question while red spreads across her cheeks and down her neck.

"Tomorrow. Be here at five, and I'll show you around the club and tell you your responsibilities."

"Fine."

"Now, let's go. I have shit to do," I tell her, standing and putting on my suit jacket.

"What?" she asks, backing up.

"I'm taking you to your car," I tell her, walking past her toward the door.

"I can walk myself," she says as her brows pull inward.

"Yeah, and I know you are your own brand of chaos, so I can't leave you alone in the club until we build up the trust between us."

"That is so…so stupid," she mutters looking adorable.

"Now," I tell her, swinging the door open and motioning her out ahead of me.

"Lint-licker," she murmurs under her breath as she passes and then stomps down the stairs in front of me, giving me a view of her ass and legs that will be burned into my brain for years. Once we reach the club floor, I wrap my hand around the back of her neck, gaining a glare from her that I ignore as I lead her through the crowd.

Passing Teo, who is manning the front door, I give him a chin lift, watching his eyes dart between Maggie and me.

"You good?" I hear him ask, thinking he's talking to me. I look at him like, *Why the fuck are you asking that?* Then I see his eyes are on Maggie.

"Yeah, thanks, Teo. Have a good night," she says softly, smiling at him, which pisses me off.

"Where's your car?" Her eyes fly to me, losing the softness instantly and she try's to pull away.

"Down two blocks. I can walk myself. We're outside, so you don't have to worry about me causing any problems."

"Come on." I ignore her and take her hand, feeling the softness of it against my palm, and then tighten my fingers when she tries to pull away again.

Walking the two blocks, I try to understand what's going on in my head. I have never let a woman effect me, but this woman has done just that without even realizing it, and I have no idea what the hell I'm going to do about it.

"This is my car," she tells me, forcefully tugging her hand free of mine.

Looking at the car, my anger comes back tenfold. The thing looks like I could pick it up and toss it with one hand tied behind my back. It sure as hell doesn't look safe for anyone to drive, especially in this town.

"What the hell is this?" I ask, watching her pull a key out of her bra—where I'm thinking she must keep everything, since the last time I was with her, that's where her phone was.

"It's a car." She rolls her eyes.

"This is a death trap, Mags. One little bump in this piece of shit and you're done," I say, running a hand through my hair.

"It's Maggie, M-A-G-G-I-E, Sven, and it's safe. Plus, it's good for the environment."

"Yeah, because it kills people off, so there is one less person on Earth to fuck it up."

"You're very dramatic and you curse a lot," she says, pushing me back a step, getting in behind the wheel, and slamming the door. Once the car is on, she rolls down the window. "See you tomorrow, Boss."

"Drive carefully, and call the club when you get home," I tell her, knowing she doesn't have my cell number, which I'm going to have to fix tomorrow. Plus, I'll get her a phone that isn't from the dark ages and tell her it's for work, because I know she won't take it any other way.

"Yeah, I'm not calling you, but I'll see you tomorrow," she retorts and then pulls out of the small space, narrowly missing a car that's passing by. Letting out an annoyed sigh, I turn and walk back to the club, mumbling under my breath the whole way, asking myself what the fuck am I doing?

Chapter 2

Maggie

Show Me the Money

LOOKING AT MYSELF in my full-length mirror, I turn to the side and make sure I look okay. Since I'm working with Sven, who I've seen wear nothing but suits, I chose to wear my sheer black sleeveless dress shirt with a high collar that ties with a bow at my neck. My cream-colored high-waisted skirt fits snugly against my curves leaving my legs bare, showcasing one of my favorite pairs of leopard-print heels that have a pointy toe and a thin, spiked heel.

I left my long hair down except for my bangs, which I swept to the side and pinned back away from my face. I kept my makeup minimal, with just mascara and a little blush, not really in the mood to do a full face of makeup. Picking up my bag from my bed, I head into the living room where I find my sister, Morgan, sitting on the couch, watching TV. She has healed a lot over the last couple weeks, but she's still carrying bruises that remind me of what could have happened, that I could have lost her.

"Are you going to work?" she asks, pressing pause on the show she's watching.

"Yeah, there are leftovers in the fridge if you get hungry. I'm not sure what time I'll be home, but if you need me, I have my cell on me," I tell her as I pick up my car keys from the counter in the kitchen.

"I can take care of myself," she grumbles, picking up a bag of Cheetos from the coffee table.

"I know," I agree, not wanting to point out that she's done a horrible job of taking care of herself so far.

"I may go out tonight," she says casually as she un-pauses the show she's watching.

"Where?" I ask while my tightly controlled facade slips.

"I don't know. Amy called and said I needed to get out of the house, and I agreed with her."

I hate my sister's best friend. I've never trusted her, and anytime Morgan has gotten in trouble, Amy has been involved in one way or another. "You still have bruises from the last time you went out with her," I point out hoping she will see for herself the kind of friend Amy really is.

"It's not fair for you to make what happened seem like Amy's fault."

"Will you call and tell me where you're going?" I ask, knowing it's completely pointless to argue with her about her relationship with Amy. I don't think she will ever see how being friends with her is affecting her.

"I'll call," she says absently while shoving her hand into the bag of Cheetos on her lap and looking at the TV.

"Love you," I tell her, getting a nod in return before heading out the front door and down the stairs to my car.

Walking into Sven's office, I fight the instinct to turn around and run right back out when I see he's on the phone. I have no idea what I was thinking agreeing to come work for him, but then again, my life has been a series of events just like this one.

"Hold on, Mags," he says, startling me.

Pulling his phone away from his ear, he motions for me to take a seat in one of the two dark blue, velvet high-back chairs in front of his large oak desk. Rolling my eyes at him, I take a seat, watching the corner of his mouth lift before he covers it with his hand. I hate that he calls me Mags—or that's what I'm telling myself, anyway. But then again, it's better than the nickname my parents gave me at my spirit ceremony, when they called down the moon goddess while standing naked in the middle of a field on my tenth birthday. I think I'm still traumatized by that experience.

Crossing one leg over the other I pull in a breath while I study him. Sven is gorgeous in a way that is completely unfair to the rest of the men on Earth. He's tall enough that I could wear my six-inch heels and he would still tower over me. His body is lean, with just the right amount of muscle. His dark blond hair is overgrown on top and little shorter on the sides, giving him an unkempt, sexy look. His eyes are a startling blue that look green when he's angry, and the long, dark lashes that surround them make them appear that much more enticing.

His nose is straight, his cheekbones are high, and his lips are full and are surrounded by a five o'clock shadow that takes his hotness up a few notches. He looks like he could be on the cover of GQ—hell, for all I know, he *has* been on the cover. The few nights I sat down at the bar, I heard women talk about him, and from what I gathered most of the female population of Vegas knows who he is. I swear every single leggy blonde, redhead, and brunette knew exactly who he was by name, and judging by the way they spoke about him, they probably screamed it a few times.

"Nice of you to show up, Mags," he says, pulling me out of my perusal and setting his phone on top of the desk. Sitting up a little taller, I narrow my eyes and watch as he walks around the desk toward me, unbuttoning his suit jacket and taking a seat on top of the wooden surface, leaning a little closer than necessary.

"You said be here at five it's five." I hold up my hand when it looks like he's going to say something else. "And we need to discuss my salary," I state, uncrossing my legs then re-crossing them in the other direction, ignoring the way his eyes watch the movement and change color.

"Salary?" He frowns, and I can't help the smile that forms on my lips at the confusion on his face.

"Yes, my salary. I mean, you didn't actually think I was going to come work for you for free, did you?" I ask, raising my brow.

"Of course not. I'll start you off at thirty-five thousand—"

"Yeah, that's not going to work for me. At my old job, the one I just quit to come work for you, I made one hundred and seventy-five thousand a year, with four weeks paid vacation and one week sick pay," I say, cutting him off. I actually make much more than that modeling, but he doesn't need to know that.

"Where the hell did you work?" he growls, making my girly parts tingle.

Ignoring my body's reaction to him, I wave my hand around in front of me and continue, "That doesn't matter now, so since I'm just starting out here, I'll take one hundred and fifty thousand, but I want the same for paid days off, including sick days."

"*No.*"

"Yes."

"Jesus, what the fuck was I thinking?" he asks, tilting his head back and looking toward the ceiling for an answer to his question.

"You're thinking you just got yourself the best assistant money can buy," I retort then press my lips together to keep from smiling at the look of gloom on his face when his eyes meet mine.

Running his hand through his hair, his eyes scan me over and he shakes his head. "Fine, but you're at my beck and call. That means twenty-four hours a day, seven days a week, if I call, you come running."

"I don't work weekends." I smirk then wonder why the hell I love fighting with him so much.

His eyes study me for a long time, so long that I fight the urge to squirm in my seat. "Fine, but five days a week, you're mine twenty-four seven."

"Sure." I shrug, knowing he has no idea what he's in for. "So what do you want me to do today?" I ask looking around his office, noticing it's tidy. The top of his desk is clean with his top of the line computer and a neat stack of papers. The upper and lower cabinets to the right of his desk with a counter between are bare, only a crystal decanter that is half full of dark liquid and two glasses sitting on top. The leather couch behind me with the round, rustic wooden coffee table is clean with a stack of books on top, which I'm certain no one has ever read and is there just for show.

Everything seems to have a specific spot, but there is nothing overly personal in the space. Not a single picture of family or friends, no mementos of places he's gone. It looks like a magazine ad for a man's office. The little devil, who has taken up a place on my shoulder since meeting Sven, is begging me to move stuff around just to see what will happen if I do, while the angel on the other side is shaking her head in disapproval.

Frowning, he looks at me then glances around as well before bringing his gaze back to mine. "There are some orders that need to be filled. You can watch me do that, and then I'll take you down, show you around the club, and introduce you to everyone."

"It's your show, Boss." I smile and watch him take off his suit jacket and lay it neatly over the edge of the desk, and then I scoot back in my chair as he walks toward me so he can pick up the chair next to mine. Carrying the chair around the desk, he sets it down next to his on the opposite side.

"You can sit here...unless you want to sit on my lap?" He smirks while nodding to the chair he placed next to his.

"Does shizzle like that actually work for you?" I ask him, standing from the chair I'm currently sitting in and walking around to take the seat.

"Do you ever curse?" he counters, ignoring my question, and I feel his knee lean against my thigh.

"Yes." I shrug. I may not curse with the same words he does, but the meaning is the same.

"Say 'fuck,'" he challenges me with a raise of his brow.

"Frick." I smile, pulling my leg away from his when it seems he's not going to move.

"That's not the same thing."

"Says who? Everyday, words are added to the English language. Who's to say that 'frick' won't mean the word you said in a few years?"

"You're something else," he mutters under his breath while his eyes stay locked on mine.

"Are you going to show me what I need to know, or stare at me all day?" I question, pointing to the screen, needing him to look away, because him looking at me is causing a range of emotions I'm not comfortable with to run through me.

"I'm definitely going to show you something," he grunts, pulling his eyes from mine. Sitting back, I ignore the warm feeling in my lower belly and watch for an hour as he shows me how to use the computer system to place orders for the club. Then, I follow him down to the club floor, where he introduces me to everyone and shows me around.

"I'm going to order in some food. Would you like something?" I ask Sven, standing from the couch, where he told me to sit three hours ago after handing me one of the most boring books in the world about Vegas night club codes and policies.

Stretching, I look at him and frown, noticing he hasn't moved. "Sven," I repeat, walking toward his desk. "Hey." I snap my fingers close to his ear, making him jump.

"Are you okay?" he asks, running his hands through his hair.

"I need food. Would you like anything?" I repeat, looking at the clock on the wall and seeing it's a little after eleven.

"Sure," he mutters, reaching into his back pocket, pulling out his wallet, and holding it out toward me.

"Do you have any preference?" I ask, ignoring his outstretched hand.

"I'll have whatever you're having," he says, taking a hundred dollar bill from his wallet, attempting to hand it to me instead.

"Are you sure you want to eat what I'm eating?" I inquire as he frowns, studying me then the money in his hand.

Shaking his hand, he shoves the money toward me again. "I'm sure, now take the money."

"I can buy my own food." I grab my cell phone from the top of his desk, where I plugged it in to charge.

"You're not paying," he states, standing.

Ignoring him, I turn on my heel and leave the office, hearing his curse as I head to the bottom of the stairs, where I make a call to one of my favorite Indian restaurants before heading through the club to wait outside for the delivery.

"Does Boss Man know you're out here?" Teo asks me as I step through the doors and to the side, smiling at a group of men who say hi as they pass me on their way inside the club.

"He knows I'm getting food," I tell him, wrapping my arms around myself as the night air moves across my exposed skin, sending a chill through me. I met Teo the first night I showed up here after my sister was attacked. He took a hundred dollars from me and let me into the club. The second time I came back, he took another hundred from me, but on the third he gave me all my money back.

"Didn't jump anyone on your way out?" he questions with a grin before taking money from a couple in line.

"Ha, ha. Very funny," I mutter, but feel my cheeks burn at the thought of what happened yesterday when I was here.

"Just asking." He laughs as I lean back against the wall, cringing when three women step to the front of the line wearing what looks like skimpy lingerie. This is Vegas, so their choice of attire doesn't really surprise me, but as a woman, I will never understand the need to wear clothes that leave nothing to the imagination.

"Did that guy get arrested?" I ask quietly as the women head into the club.

"He got arrested and is still waiting bond."

"That's good," I say, letting out a relieved breath that at least one creep is off the streets for now.

"How's your sister?" he asks, folding his large body in half as he sits on a small metal stool that looks ready to give out under his weight.

"She's doing better," I respond softly, leaning my head back to look up at the night sky.

"Here."

I look down at his extended hand and the card he's holding out to me. "What's this?" I ask, taking the card from him. The front is blank, and the back only has a phone number.

"If your sister wants help, I know some people who can give it to her," he says quietly, and I study him for a long-time, wondering how he knows. Tears fill my eyes as I nod holding the card tightly in my hand, wishing it were as easy as making a phone call.

"Sometimes, you don't have a choice and you have to let go," he mutters, but lucky for me, I don't have to respond because the delivery driver for the food I ordered pulls up just in time. Paying for the food with a fifty, I tell the driver to keep the change then walk past Teo, giving him a short wave as I head back into the building and around the packed club floor. Spotting Zack, Sven's head of security, at the bottom of the stairs that lead to his office, I feel a smile form on my lips as his eyes lock on mine.

"Hey, Maggie," he greets softly, leaning in to press a light kiss to my cheek. Zack is a beautiful black man, with large, bulky muscles, dark, creamy skin, a bald head, and soft, soulful eyes. He is the kind of man I normally find myself dating, and is the opposite of my current boyfriend of seven months, Wyatt.

I met Wyatt on a photo shoot we did together when I was working on an ad campaign for one of my favorite plus-size brands. Wyatt is the boy-next-door type, with sun kissed skin, dark blond hair, and blue eyes. He's not much taller than me, and I can never wear heels when we go out, but his smile and gentle manner make being with him easy.

"You okay?"

"Great."

I smile then feel my spine stiffen when a woman asks in a squeaky voice, "Is Sven upstairs?" Looking at her I notice she's one of the women from outside wearing lingerie. Grinning, her friends come to stand on either side of her.

"Sorry, doll. He's not accepting company at this time," Zack says, and something in my chest pinches.

"Well, I brought my friends this time. Can't you call and ask him to look down here? Maybe he'll change his mind when he sees us," she says with a pout.

"I'm gonna head up," I say softly, getting a soft look and a nod from Zack as I head up the stairs as quickly as my heels will take me. Getting to the door at the top, I take a deep breath push it open and step inside.

"Is it safe to walk barefoot in here?" I ask Sven, who stands from behind his desk as I turn to shut the door behind me.

"Why are you asking that?" he questions, walking toward me.

"I don't know how much DNA is on the floor, and my heels are killing me," I tell him as he takes the bags from my hands.

"DNA?" He frowns, placing the bags on the coffee table, then turns toward me crossing his arms over his chest. I notice that while I was gone, he lost his tie and unbuttoned the top two buttons of his shirt, exposing his tan neck.

"Well, a group of women—who obviously don't understand that it's called Victoria's *Secret* for a reason—are downstairs. They're asking to come up to play with you, because their friend was up here a couple weeks ago, and now they want to see if it's all hype."

"Jesus," he mutters, rubbing his jaw and looking toward the door like he expects them to break it down.

"Don't worry, Zack is down there standing guard. But can I take my shoes off, or should I leave them on?"

"Take off your damn shoes, Mags," he prowls past me to the door, slamming it behind him as he leaves.

"Alrighty then," I mumble to the empty office as I kick off my shoes off by the door. Going to the couch, I pause and then turn around, going to the bathroom I grab the can of Lysol to spray the couch and the floor.

"What the hell are you doing?" Sven asks, making me jump. I was so caught up in disinfecting that I didn't even hear him come in.

"Disinfecting," I tell him with a wave of the Lysol can, which he grabs away from me and takes back to the bathroom, coming back a second later looking annoyed as he waves his hand in front of his face. "If you want, I can leave for a little while and come back when you're done with playtime and in a better mood," I offer, watching as a smile twitches his lips.

"Stop being a smartass and feed me," he mutters, unbuttoning the cuffs of his shirt and rolling them up, giving me a glimpse at tattoos I never would have guessed he had. "Earth to Mags."

Untying the bow at my neck that has suddenly gotten too tight, I take a seat on the couch, noticing he hasn't moved.

"Do you have drinks? I didn't even think about ordering any," I add, ignoring whatever look it is he's giving me.

"What would you like?" he asks gruffly before clearing his throat.

"Do you have any juice?" I question as I pull the food out of the bag and set it on the coffee table.

"Sure." He grabs two bottles of orange juice from the fridge then takes a seat next to me on the couch. "What did you order?" he asks, opening the Styrofoam containers and sniffing the contents.

"Vegetable korma, tikka masala, and cheese nan," I say as I hand him a napkin and a fork. Then, I dish out rice on two plates and hand him one.

"Where's the meat?" he questions with a frown as I add vegetable korma to my plate.

"You said you would eat what I was eating," I remind him, taking the plate I handed him out of his hand, spooning out the tikka masala onto the rice, and then handing it back to him.

"Is this tofu?" He pokes one of the chunks of tofu with his fork while his face scrunches up like a little boy who was told he had to eat his vegetables.

"It's good. Try it," I encourage him while scooping up some with my fork and holding it near his mouth like I used to do with the kids I babysat.

"Are you seriously trying to feed me right now?" he asks as his eyes shine with amusement.

"Sorry," I mumble, and begin to pull away the fork, but before I can, his mouth closes around the fork and my eyes lock onto his lips, feeling my core clench. I watch him chew, and then laugh when he grimaces.

"That's awful."

"Try this." I scoop up some of the korma from my plate and hold it out toward him. This time, his eyes lock on mine as his mouth closes around the fork. The look in their blue-green depths has my pulse singing in my ears. Swallowing, I pull the utensil away then drop my eyes from his to his mouth.

"Better," he says roughly as his warm hand comes up and wraps around my lower jaw. Startled, my gaze meets his for a moment before his eyes drop to my mouth and he begins to lean in.

"Let's eat before it gets cold," I blurt, turning my head so his hand is forced to let me go. "You can have this, since you don't like the tikka," I tell him, handing him my plate and fork and taking his off his lap while avoiding looking at him. Settling back into the couch, I stuff my mouth with a piece of nan and chew slowly so I don't do something absolutely dumb, like push him back onto the couch, rip off his shirt, and see if he's hiding anymore tattoos.

"So either you're a vegetarian, or you're testing me," he says, and I chew then swallow before looking at him.

"I'm a vegetarian," I agree, watching him sit back and place his ankle to his knee.

"Why?"

"Why what?" I frown.

"Why are you a vegetarian?"

"It's just something I've always done. My parents are vegetarians, and they raised me to be one."

"Have you ever tried meat?"

"Once, when I was in high school. There was never much on the lunch menu for vegetarians. I'm a big girl and was starving to death most days, so I attempted to eat meatloaf. That was the first…and last time," I add with a smile as his eyes rake over me.

"You're not big," he states, almost like he's offended on my behalf.

"I love my body and have accepted it for what it is. I have a pooch, hips, and an ass. When I was young, I would get teased, but now I know I have the body of a woman and I'm okay with who I am."

"You should be. You're beautiful," he responds immediately, the sincerity of his words and the look in his eyes making my belly warm.

Wow. I don't know what to say to that, since most men who look like him wouldn't even glance in my direction. "Where's your boy-friend?" he asks, catching me off guard while he leans forward and takes a piece of nan out of the foil on the table.

"Who told you I have a boyfriend?" I frown.

"The guys said you mentioned him."

"Oh," I mumble, lifting my feet to the couch and resting my plate on top of my knees. "He lives in Seattle, but is here in town most weekends."

"How does he feel about you working here?"

"He's okay with it." I shrug. Wyatt doesn't really have strong opin-ions about anything. I know he cares about me, but he's not the kind of man to say, '*No, you can't do this or that.*' He's much too passive for that.

"Really?" he asks with a tone laced with disbelief.

"Yeah." I shrug again.

"So you only see him when he's in town…like you're a booty call?" he questions, making my cheeks heat in embarrassment and my spine stiffen in annoyance.

"Wyatt is a perfect gentlemen," I hiss, setting my feet to the floor. No way will I tell him that I'm saving my virginity until I find the man I know I will spend the rest of my life with. Since I was a little girl, I have watched my parents, their friends, and my sister sleep around like sex means nothing to them. Hell, when I was sixteen, my mom and dad told me that I was free to have sex with whoever I wanted, and even invited me to one of their free love parties. I just couldn't do it. And yes, I tried at other times, but every time things got to the point where sex was imminent, I would close down.

"It's just a question," he says low, like that should make me feel better about him being an intrusive jerk.

"How often do you sleep with women you meet in this club?" I ask, and his jaw tics. "What? It's just a question." I get up from the couch and take my plate to the garbage can, shoving it in with a little more force than necessary.

"Come sit down, Mags."

"No."

"I won't bring up Wyatt again," he says, spitting Wyatt's name out like it tastes bad.

"Good, my relationship is none of your business," I tell him firmly, crossing my arms over my chest.

"For now."

"What is that supposed to mean?" I cry, throwing my arms in the air.

"He's bound to come up eventually, Mags. You work here, remember?"

"So you're telling me that I have the right to ask you about the women you're spending time with outside of the time we're working together?" I ask, watching his nostrils flare and his eyes dilate in anger. "I didn't think so. I expect the same respect I'm showing you," I tell him, slipping on my shoes.

"Where the fuck do you think you're going?" he asks, watching my every move.

"I'm using one of my sick days. I suddenly don't feel so great," I retort, grabbing my purse from the hook near the door and swinging it over my shoulder. Giving him one last look, I leave the office before he can stop me. The moment I get downstairs, I spot Zack coming toward me with his hand on his ear, and I know he's speaking with Sven.

"I'll walk you."

"I'll walk myself." I shake off his hand and rush through the club and out the front door.

"You okay?" Teo asks when he spots me.

"Fine, have a good night," I say, giving him a shaky smile as I hurry past him to my car. I know it seems like I'm running, but I don't like the feelings Sven evokes in me, even if it's because it's the first time I've felt them in a long time.

Chapter 3

Maggie

Her Name's Maggie, Not Mags

"**S**O HOW LONG is it going to be until you talk to me?" Sven asks as soon as I open the office door and step inside. Carrying my cup of coffee in one hand and a stack of folders in the other, I balance them carefully as I turn and use my foot to kick the door closed. It's been three days since our blow up, and in those three days we haven't spoken...or I should say *I* haven't spoken to *him* unless it has to do with work. No one has ever set me off the way he had, and that alone gave me pause when dealing with him.

"I talk to you everyday," I murmur as I place the stack of folders on his desk then use my coffee as an excuse to avoid looking at him directly.

"You ask me what you need to do, but avoid any kind of communication otherwise," he says, sounding frustrated, and when my eyes meet his, I grudgingly notice the lavender shirt he has on today makes them even more gorgeous.

"If you're finding me lacking, you can fire me." I shrug, watching his eyes narrow and turn a darker shade of blue-green.

"I think I'll keep you," he replies in a tone that sounds like a threat, but it does something strange to my belly making it dip.

"So what did you need me to do today?" I ask ignoring my body's reaction to him.

"I have to meet with a friend to discuss business and would like you to come along," he says as I take a seat across from him.

"Oh." Looking down at my black jeans, I run my finger over one of the rips in the material, trying to think of a way to get out of going, then raise my eyes to his. "Is it necessary for me to be there?" I finally ask, and a small smile twitches the corner of his mouth.

"Are you my assistant? The best assistant money can buy?" He raises a brow in a silent dare.

"Touché," I mutter under my breath, dropping my eyes again when I see him smile his gorgeous smile.

"Give me five and I'll meet you downstairs."

"Alrighty then." Taking my coffee with me, I leave the office without a backward glance and head down to the floor below. Walking through the empty club, I make my way toward the bar when I see Eva standing behind it, wiping out empty glasses.

"Hey, girly," she greets when she spots me.

"How are things?" I ask, climbing up onto one of the barstools, setting my bag and coffee on the countertop.

"Busy as ever." She smiles, setting down one glass and picking up another.

"How's school going?" I question as I take in her tired eyes. Eva, like most women who work behind bars in Vegas, is beautiful. Looking at her, I can see her Native American heritage and can picture her dressed in custom tribal attire with bright clothing that would accentuate her caramel skin, and braids with feathers in her hair dark.

"Thank God I only have a few months left," she sighs, setting yet another glass down.

"Then you'll take the Bar exam?" I ask, knowing she is studying to be a lawyer.

"Yep."

"You don't seem too happy about that," I note quietly.

"I'm happy about finishing school, but my whole future from then on out is completely mapped out for me. I know when I pass my bar exam, I'll work for my father and our tribe, I'll marry someone I've probably known my whole life, and then I'll have two kids. All I can hope is, somewhere in there, I'm happy."

"You can always make your own way," I say quietly as I study her somber expression.

"I wish it was that easy," she mutters then nods behind me, and I turn to look over my shoulder at Sven, who is walking—no, *prowling*—across the empty club floor. He's looking more handsome than I've ever seen him, in jeans and a plain tee with Converse on his feet. "Please be careful with him," Eva whispers, and I pull my eyes from everything that is Sven to look at her.

"You don't have to worry about me, honey," I whisper back with a smile as I slip off the barstool.

"Ready?" Sven asks, nodding at Eva behind the bar once he reaches my side.

"Yep," I agree then ask, "Am I overdressed?" as we step outside.

"We'll stop and get you some sneakers," he says absently, typing into his phone.

"I have shoes in my car," I tell him, half tempted to take the phone out of his hand and toss it into the street. He's always on his phone or looking at his computer and as much as I hate to admit it I like when his attention is on me. Walking away from him, I head to my car and grab my own Converse from the trunk. "I thought you said we were meeting with a friend of yours to discuss business," I mutter as I exchange my heels for my sneakers.

"We are."

"What's that supposed to mean?" I ask, folding up the bottom of my jeans so my look is more casual, then stand and unbutton my dress shirt.

"Leave the shirt."

"What?" I question, turning to face him.

"Fuck." He frowns as his eyes move from my breasts up to my face. "This guy loves women, so just do me a favor and leave the shirt on."

"This tank covers the girls," I say, looking down. Yes, I have cleavage, but it's not too extreme, and it sure as heck is less than a lot of women show, especially here in Vegas.

"I know they're covered, but please, for my sanity, wear the shirt."

Rolling my eyes, I take off the shirt and toss it into the trunk along with my heels.

"You're such a pain in the ass," he gripes.

"Yeah, and you're Mr. Perfect," I mutter as I head across the parking lot to his SUV, before coming to a halt when he grabs my hand and leads me toward the street. "Are we walking to your friend's?" I ask, taking my hand from his.

"No, my driver is taking us."

"You have a driver?"

"Yep," he says, distracted by his phone dinging in his hand. Grabbing the stupid thing, I shove it in my back pocket and then walk backward away from him.

"Mags, give me my phone."

"I'll give it back to you when you stop being rude and look at me when you're talking to me," I tell him, jumping away from him when he lunges for me.

"Maggie, stop fucking around."

"Promise you'll stop being rude, and I'll give you your phone." I dodge him once more.

"Seems you've got your hands full, boy'o," an older gentleman, who is standing next to the open backdoor of a Town Car, says as I duck Sven again.

"Tell me about it, Ken," Sven says as he glares at me.

"I told you I'd give you your phone back when you promise to look at me when you're speaking to me." I shrug.

"Fine." He holds out his hand.

Taking his phone out of my pocket, I hold it above his hand then move it before he has a chance to wrap his fingers around it.

"Mags," he sighs, fighting a smile.

Giving in, I hand him his phone, but then squeal when he lunges, wraps his arms around me, and lifts me off the ground. "Put me down!" I yell as he spins me in circles.

"Are you going to behave?" He laughs.

"Probably not," I tell him honestly just as my feet find purchase on the sidewalk.

"You're lucky I like you just the way you are," he whispers against my ear, causing heat to flood my body before he takes a step back and embraces Ken with a one-armed hug.

How's Ann?" Sven inquires as he takes a step back toward me.

"She's sent her love and an invite to dinner."

"I'll send her a message this week. I need a good home-cooked meal," Sven replies with a grin.

"She'd like that," Ken remarks with a warm smile that reminds me of my grandfather, and then his eyes move to me and he asks, "And who's this?"

"Maggie, I'd like you to meet Ken. He's been putting up with me ever since I moved to Vegas."

"Nice to meet you, Ken." I smile as he wraps his hand around mine and uses his free one to cover both our hands.

"You too, dear, and don't let this boy get away with too much." He winks.

"I won't," I promise, looking at Sven and smiling, and then I stick out my tongue.

Shaking his head at me, he mutters, "We need to get on the road if we're going to make it in time."

"It shouldn't take long once we get to the highway," Ken assures him with a shake of his head as he drops my hand.

"Why aren't you driving?" I ask curiously as Ken steps away from the open backdoor.

"I need to work, and I can't do that if I'm driving," Sven replies as he motions for me to get into the car.

"Where are we going?"

"I think it's best I don't tell you," he mumbles, sounding distracted as I crawl across the wide backseat. Looking over my shoulder, I expect to find his eyes on his phone. Instead, I find them locked firmly on my upturned rear. Feeling my cheeks heat, I fall to my bottom and scoot close to the opposite door so he can get in next to me.

"I don't like surprises, so I'd rather you tell me where we're going," I grouch as the door is closed and the interior of the town car goes dark.

"Do you trust me?"

"No," I answer immediately, but then feel bad when his jaw jerks. "Don't take it personally. I don't trust anyone, not even my family," I add quietly.

"Trust me this once. I won't let anything happen to you." Studying his expression, I try to figure out what the look in his eyes means and why this moment seems so important. I have been let down by my sister and the people who raised me more times than I would like to admit, and they have made me wary of trusting anyone. "Promise," he quietly states, and I nod before turning to look out the window, feeling my throat grow tight.

Feeling a light touch down my cheek, I hear Sven's voice break through my unconsciousness, stating, "We're here."

I groan and ask, "Where's here?" without lifting my head or opening my eyes.

Chuckling, he mutters, "Open your eyes and see."

Opening one eye then the other, I pull my face away from the door, where I rested it and apparently fell asleep, and then feel my heart lodge itself in my throat as I look out the window. I see the words *Kip's Skydiving* proudly written in bold letters from nose to tail on a small plane.

"Um...why are we here?" I ask, though I'm not sure the words are loud enough to be heard over the pounding of my heart.

"We're going skydiving."

"You mean *you're* going skydiving," I reply, pulling my eyes from the window to look at him and glare.

So much for the whole trusting thing.

"No, *we're* going skydiving." He grins as Ken opens the back door, allowing light to fill the car.

"I think I'll just wait here," I tell him, scooting as far away from the open door as I can possibly get while wishing I were a chameleon so I could blend in with the leather of the car.

"You told me you would trust me."

"That was before I knew you wanted to strap a piece of fabric to my back and hurl me from a moving plane at hundreds of miles per hour toward the Earth, where I'm likely to splatter into a bazillion pieces," I breathe out in a rush.

"You're going to be strapped to me." He smiles like that makes it all okay.

"That's not making me feel any better," I cry then try to tug my arm free from his hold as he pulls me across the seat. Getting away, I grab onto the door handle and hold on for dear life as he grabs both my feet and pulls. "Sven, let me go!" I yell, and then my body stiffens as an all too familiar deep baritone voice calls, "Maggie?"

"No," I whisper, letting go of the door to look over my shoulder.

"How do you know Mags?" Sven growls, letting my feet go so he can stand to his full height, which only slightly towers over Ace, a man I dated on and off for a few months. A man who makes Sven's womanizing ways look like child's play.

"We dated." He frowns then looks between Sven and me before asking, "How do you know Maggie?"

"I work for him," I state as I get out of the car and adjust my clothes.

"Oh." Ace grins, showing off his perfect teeth and dimple, which is made even more adorable by his dark skin.

Jerk.

"You dated him?" Sven asks from my side, and I turn to look at him.

"I know. Big, huge, *giant* mistake."

"It wasn't that bad," Ace mutters as three blondes who all look almost identical walk up to our group, giggling.

"Yeah, it was that bad," I tell him as Sven stiffens at my side when one of the blondes stands next to him.

"Why are you working for Sven? I thought you were still modeling?"

"Modeling?" Sven asks, and the three women begin to giggle louder, like they can't believe their ears.

"I thought we were skydiving," I state, changing the subject, because at this time, I would much rather be falling to my death than in the middle of this situation.

"Who's your friend?" the blonde standing at Sven's side asks, raking her eyes over him.

"Sorry, ladies. This is my friend, Sven, and this is Maggie." He smiles, nodding toward me.

"And you dated her?" a different blonde questions, looking between Ace and me with a puzzled look on her (sadly) beautiful face.

"I did." Ace nods, still smiling.

"But she's fat," she mutters, looking me over.

"Pardon?" Sven snarls as Ace growls, "Crystal."

"Sorry," she whispers, taking a step back toward the safety of her friends.

"Let's go." Grabbing my hand and not giving me a choice, Sven pulls me away from the group and leads me toward the building, swinging his arm over my shoulders, asking, "Are you okay?"

"I'm fine. It's not the first time someone has called me fat."

"I mean with Ace."

"Oh, him? Yeah." I shrug.

"Really?"

"Of course, we dated casually for a few months. It wasn't serious. Like you, I don't think he will ever settle down with one woman."

"What the fuck does that mean?" he snaps, sounding insulted as he pulls his arm from me like I just burned him.

"Hey, don't be offended. There are two types of men in this world: the kind who want a family, and the kind who want to have a good time. As long as you're okay with who you are, nothing else matters."

"Who said I don't want a family?"

"When have you ever had a serious relationship?" I ask, and his face closes down. "Exactly," I mumble as we step out of the hot sun and into the cool interior of the building.

"So what, you and Ace just hooked up?"

"No." I shake my head then whisper so Ace, who is following close behind, can't hear. "I think I caught him during a time he believed he wanted something more, only he didn't really want the pressure or the fidelity of a real relationship." Just then, thankfully, a tall, older gentleman who Sven introduces to me as Kip, the owner, comes out to greet us and takes us back to the hangar.

"Since I have more jumps under my belt, I think Mags should jump with me," Ace says as I put on the jumpsuit the instructor just gave me.

"She's jumping with me, and her name is Maggie, not Mags," Sven grumbles from my side as he reads over some paperwork Kip gave him.

"You call her Mags?" Ace states, crossing his arms over his chest with an amused grin.

"She's mine."

"I'm not a thing. I'm a human, and I'm not yours." I roll my eyes at Sven then look at Ace. "I'm not jumping with you. Take Dumb, Dumber, or Dumbest," I say with a nod to the three blondes, who are each looking confused as the instructors attempt to help them get into their gear.

"Is that jealousy I hear in your tone, Maggie?"

"No, I just don't want to be close to you."

"If I recall correctly, you used to like being close to me," he says quietly enough for just me to hear.

"I also used to like strawberries until I found out they were the cause for the hives I kept getting," I mutter, and he chuckles.

"You always did make me laugh," he says softly.

"That's me, always good for a laugh," I grumble, turning away·from him.

"Will you be okay while I go talk with Ace for a few minutes?" Sven asks, placing his fingers under my chin, forcing my eyes to meet his.

"Of course," I whisper, wishing in that moment he would kiss me, which is absolutely ridiculous.

"I'll be just a couple minutes," he whispers back searching my gaze then shakes his head, drops his hand, and turns placing his hand on Ace's shoulder leading him away. Watching them, I wonder what kind of business they need to talk about. Ace is a poker player who first made a name for himself in online gambling, but has since grown into one of the biggest names in Vegas. I haven't seen Ace since the day I told him I couldn't see him anymore two years ago. He was always searching for the next adrenalin rush, while I was searching for a happily ever after. It looks like we're both still looking. Ignoring the sadness that thought makes me feel, I finish getting ready, take a seat, and wait for Sven to come back.

"ARE YOU READY?" Sven asks close to my ear, so I can hear him over the loud roar of the plane's engines. Shaking my head, I squeeze my eyes closed then grab onto both his thighs when the plane bounces. "I promise nothing will happen to you," he says gently, giving my waist a squeeze, pulling me closer to him, which seems impossible since I'm literally sitting on his lap.

"We're at diving altitude," the pilot announces over the loud speakers that run the length of the interior of the plane. Opening my eyes, I watch one of the instructors unlatch the door and pull it open, causing the interior to fill with cool air.

"We'll jump last," Sven yells.

I nod then call back, "If I die, I'm going to come back and haunt you." It only serves to make him laugh so hard that my body, which is strapped to his, shakes with it.

"See you below!" Ace hollers as he heads past us with one of the blondes strapped to his front.

"Good riddance," I grumble then feel Sven's body shake under mine once more. Watching Ace jump from the plane, followed by his other two girlfriends who are strapped to instructors, I feel a surge of adrenalin rush through my system.

"Let's go, babe," Sven says standing up, leaving me no choice but to go with him toward the open door. Looking down, my eyes fill with tears. I have taken plane trips a lot over the years, and I have always loved when I'm able to get the window seat so I can look out over the world as we fly above it. But knowing I'm going to be falling toward the quilted-looking ground below is a different feeling altogether.

"Cross your arms over your chest, baby," Sven instructs, lightly taking my wrists in his hands and placing them across my front.

"I hate you."

"On three. One, two…"

And then we're falling.

"You motherfucking asshole, son of a bitch!" I gulp as air rushes toward me so fast that my mouth opens and fills, causing my cheeks to expand. Forcing my mouth closed, I grab onto the straps near my shoulders and hold on for dear life, even though I know they can do nothing to save me. Squeezing my eyes closed, we twist and turn as my stomach dips and drops.

"I'm gonna open the 'chute."

"Good idea," I yell, and our bodies are jerked backward and my eyes spring open.

"See? Not so bad, is it?" Sven laughs, and I look over my shoulder and notice he looks happy, really happy right now. The stress he normally carries around his eyes is gone and is replaced by laugh lines that make him even more beautiful.

"We still have to land," I tell him, and his smile broadens.

"But until then, just feel and watch."

Pulling my eyes reluctantly from his happy ones, I look around and then below. I hate to admit it, but this is one of the most amazing experiences I've ever had. Floating through the air, the view of the land below and the sky above, leave me in awe. The feeling of freedom as we fall. Sven against my back, his arm around my waist, making me feel safe in a way I've never felt safe before. As we get closer to the ground, I tuck my knees up toward my chest and close my eyes, not wanting to see the ground coming swiftly at me. As quickly as it began, it's over and I feel the ground under my bottom and my eyes open slowly.

"That was awesome!" I laugh, looking over my shoulder at Sven as two men come running up to us and help us get out of our gear.

"I knew you would love it." Sven smiles as we stand.

"I didn't love it," I lie, and he smiles, muttering, "Liar." While wrapping his arm around my shoulder and leading me toward the truck that will take us back to the hanger.

As soon as we arrive back to the hanger, Sven leaves to talk with Ace who got back before us, so I head inside to get a bottle of water then notice they have pictures available from our jump.

"I would like two of this one," I tell the girl working behind the desk inside Kip's as I point at a picture of the two of us smiling at each other after Sven opened the parachute.

"Would you like to add the commemorative frame for twenty dollars more?" she asks, pointing at a glass picture frame with the Kip's Skydiving logo and a small plane painted on it that is sitting on a shelf behind her.

"Can I get two of them?"

"Sure." She smiles before disappearing through a door behind her. Turning around to make sure Sven is still distracted, I spot him and Ace standing next to the town car, while all three of Ace's girlfriends lounge in the sun on a picnic table a few feet away. All three of them have taken the opportunity to take their shirts off leaving them in different color bikini tops.

"That will be sixty-two dollars," the girl says, pulling my attention from the window, as she places a bag on the countertop.

Pulling a hundred dollar bill out of my bra, I hand it to the girl, take the bag and pictures from her along with my change, and then make my way out toward Sven, planning to wait in the car until he's ready to go. But the minute he spots me, he gives me a smile that has my steps faltering.

"I hope you didn't pay for those things," he says as soon as I'm standing next to him.

"Why wouldn't I pay?"

"Me and Ace gave Kip the money to start up this place a few years ago. In return, we don't pay when we want to jump, and *you* don't have to pay if you want a souvenir."

"Well, I'm happy to pay," I mutter, and he swings his arm over my shoulders, shaking his head, then looks at Ace, who is looking at us with a knowing smile on his face. What he thinks he knows I have no idea.

"We'll talk in a few days," Sven tells him as he opens the door for me to get into the idling car.

"Thanks, man." He shakes Sven's hand then drops his eyes to me. "You still have my number. Call me."

Snorting at that, I mutter, "Goodbye," and get into the car, hearing both guys laugh behind me.

"Did you have fun, dear?" Ken asks as his eyes connect with mine in the rearview mirror and I slide across the back seat.

"Don't tell anyone, but it was amazing." I grin, and he chuckles then mutters, "Your secret is safe with me."

"What secret?" Sven asks, getting into the car and shutting the door behind him.

"Nothing," Ken and I say in unison.

"Did you have fun?" Sven inquires, and I look at Ken in the mirror briefly before looking at Sven.

"If you consider being afraid that you're going to pee yourself while watching your life passing before your eyes fun, then sure, I had fun," I state with a straight face, hearing Ken in the front seat laugh out.

"You loved it," Sven mutters before pulling his phone out of his pocket. Looking out the window, I smile to myself then glance at Ken, whose eyes are on me, and I wink.

"You cursed."

Pulling my eyes from the view going by quickly as we drive back toward Vegas, I look at Sven and frown, asking, "Pardon?"

"When we jumped, you cursed like a sailor." He grins.

"I thought I was going to die," I explain, not denying it. I don't even know what came over me, but every bad word I have ever thought of came tumbling out.

"It was cute," he mutters quietly before going back to work on his phone. Pulling my old cell phone out of the front pocket of my jeans, I flip it open and frown. The screen has turned completely black. Closing it again, I flip it open once more then tap the numbers and they light up. "What's wrong?" Sven asks, and I turn to look at him and hold my phone up.

"It's not working."

"Let me see." Taking the phone from my hand, he pulls the battery off the back then puts it back in place and presses the on button. "I think it's time for you to get a phone that's not from 1999."

"I've had that phone since I was twenty," I mumble, taking the phone from him and pressing the buttons once more. "It's always been trusty."

"Well, it seems to me that it's finally kicked the bucket."

"I wonder if I can have it fixed," I grumble, tapping the screen again.

"We can stop and pick you up a new phone."

"But this has all my numbers in it," I complain, pressing buttons, hoping something will happen and the screen with magically light up, but all that happens is one of the numbers presses in and sticks.

"Sorry, babe."

Narrowing my eyes, I look at him. "You don't sound sorry."

"That phone is old, and I can't imagine it was reliable. You need something that will work when you need it to work, and I need you to have a phone so I can reach you." He shrugs then tells Ken to stop at one of the local cell service stores.

By the time we are done picking me up a new phone and having dinner at a small diner, we make it back to the club a little after eleven, and the line outside is already stretched around the building. Walking down the street and past the waiting line, Sven stops when a group of women, who obviously know him, call him over. Waiting a few feet away, I pull out my new phone and power up the screen. I have no idea what the heck I'm going to do with a phone that seems smarter than me and that didn't even come with an instruction manual.

"Ready?" Sven asks, making me jump. Looking over my shoulder as he leads me down the sidewalk, I see the group of women all watching us with sneers on their faces.

"Sven," someone called, and he places his hand on my lower back.

"Give me a minute, babe. Just wait here," he mutters as he walks toward another group of women, who all smile and laugh as he heads toward them.

Watching him from a distance, I can't hear what the women are saying, but their body language screams everything loud and clear. Something ugly shifts through me as I watch him smile, and I find myself walking away alone toward the club entrance, not wanting to witness any more than I need to. Smiling at Teo when I reach the front of the line, he grins back and lifts the red rope, allowing me to slide under his arm. Feeling a body press against me and hands wrap around my hips, pulling me back into a hard erection, I look over my shoulder, ready to tell whoever it is not to touch me, when Sven shoves his way between people and pulls the guy off me, tossing him to Teo.

"Get the fuck out of here," he roars as Teo shoves the kid toward the sidewalk.

"I was just fucking around, man," the kid grumbles, looking nervously between Sven and Teo.

"Go inside, Maggie, and straight to the office," Sven demands without taking his eyes off the kid.

Hating that I'm following orders like a dog, but not really having a choice, I stomp into the club and stop when I see the stage. The DJ spinning tonight is well-known and has thousands of followers who trek to whatever club he's playing to watch him spin. The crowd on the dance floor is going crazy, and the music is so loud I can feel my bones vibrating with the beat.

Moving around the dance floor, I push my way through the people gathered around the edge chatting, and head upstairs to Sven's office. Shutting the door behind me, I move to the couch, set down the bag with the pictures from today, take out my new cell phone, and press the button so the screen lights up. I sent Morgan a message earlier on Facebook, letting her know I got a new phone and to text me from her number so I can store it, but she still hasn't messaged me back, and that has me worried. Jumping when the door slams, my pulse skitters as Sven storms toward me with a look of fury in his eyes.

"I told you to give me a minute. I told you to wait for me, but you didn't listen and you could have gotten yourself hurt."

"Um..." I breathe, unsure what to say or why he looks ready to strangle me.

"*Um?*" he snarls as his face twists with rage. "No, Maggie, not *um*. Fucking listen to me when I tell you to do something," he roars, making me flinch, and I hate myself for showing fear to him.

"Stand back," I tell him, but then lean forward when he doesn't budge and yell in his face, "Stand the heck back, Sven, before I punch you in your stupid face!"

"Those kids down there are all high." He points to the floor. "Who knows what would have happened if I didn't see what was happening to you.

"'Cause I'm weak, right?" I tilt my head to the side. "I'm just a girl, and I can't take care of myself?" I ask sweetly in a little girl's voice, and the muscle in his cheek starts to twitch rapidly. Raising myself a bare inch from the couch, just enough that I have a little bit of leverage, but not enough for him to notice. I ask again, "Do you think I'm weak, Sven?"

"You're a woman, Maggie."

Yeah, wrong answer.

I use the leverage I gained moments ago and propel myself forward, shoving my shoulder into his waist while my hands wrap around the back of his thigh. His thud hitting the ground makes the glasses on the shelf near the bar rattle. Putting my foot against his groin, I dare him to say anything else.

"Oh, did you fall?" I ask sweetly as he blinks up at me in shock.

"You need to be more careful, Sven. You never know what might happen to you," I tell him, pressing my foot down as a reminder.

"Mags."

"Do not *ever* doubt that I have the ability to take care of myself, Sven. I may be a woman, but I have been taking care of myself since I was a little girl," I whisper the last part then take a step back.

"I was worried." He gets up from the ground with his nostrils flaring and the pulse in his neck working so hard it can be seen from where I'm standing near the door.

"Well next time, instead of coming at me like a crazy person, maybe you could say that instead," I suggest, going back to the couch and taking a seat.

"Sorry," he mutters, but I pretend I don't hear him as I pull the frames out of the bag, along with the pictures of us skydiving. "I was worried."

"Yeah, you said that," I mumble, not looking at him as he takes a seat on the couch next to me. Finishing placing the picture in the frame and closing it up, I tip it upright and look at the image. "Here." I hand him the frame as I take the other one out of its box and open the back. Putting together the one I got for myself, I place it back in the box it came in then rest it on the coffee table, chancing a look at Sven. His eyes are on the picture of us in his hands.

"You," he whispers under his breath so quietly I almost miss it.

"Me what?"

His head lifts when our eyes meet. This time they're full of a sadness I don't understand. "I like you, Mags, but I'm no good for you."

His words hurt more than they should, so I do what I always do, and joke. "It sounds like you're trying to break up with me."

Shaking his head, his hand suddenly strikes out and wraps around the back of my neck as he pulls me to him. Pressing his lips to my forehead briefly, I feel their sting as his arms wrap around me in an embrace that has tears pooling in my eyes. He says he's no good for me, but I think it's the other way around. I'm no good for him.

Chapter 4

Maggie

Are you crazy?

"YOU OKAY?" Looking up from my cell phone, my eyes lock with Sven's. I shrug in response, and his eyes go soft as he sets his phone down on top of his desk then walks around to where I'm sitting. He takes the seat next to me, placing his elbows on his knees, getting even closer.

"You still haven't heard from her?" he guesses softly, and I pull my bottom lip between my teeth and shake my head as anxiety and worry washes over me. Morgan disappeared the day Sven and I went skydiving, and since then, I haven't heard from her. Feeling my heart constrict in my chest, I fight back tears. I love my sister, but I hate the person she's become. Her drug problem has gotten progressively worse over the last three years, and I don't know what to do anymore. It kills me that I can't fix this for her, because she doesn't want help.

"I thought she would change," I tell him weakly. I thought for sure she would change when the police called me in the middle of the night to tell me that she was in the hospital. I remember thinking, *This is it. This is her wake up call. She will finally understand she is putting her life at risk.*

I was crushed walking into the ICU, seeing her hooked up to machines, covered in large black and blue bruises. When she told the police and me what happened at Sven's club, I demanded they do something, but they refused. They told me that even though she was beat up badly, her story didn't add up. They believed she probably tried to steal from a dealer and her injuries were a result of that. That's when I decided to take matters into my own hands and go to Sven's club to see if I could find anything out. Looking back now, I honestly don't know if I believe her story from that night. I don't know what to believe when it comes to her anymore.

I don't even know who she is anymore.

"It's going to be okay." His arm wraps around my shoulders and he pulls me into his side. Turning my face, I press my nose to his neck, allowing myself a brief moment to escape the turmoil going on inside me and accept comfort from him before pulling away.

"Did you need anything else?" I question as I stand and adjust my skirt. His eyes scan my face for a long moment then his hands clench into fists as he stands to his full height, which towers over me even in my heels.

"Mags, if she—"

"She'll be back," I cut him off, speaking with more conviction than I feel, wanting so badly to believe my own lie. His hand wraps around the side of my neck and his thumb runs down the column of my throat as his eyes soften further.

Prior to Morgan moving in with me, it wasn't abnormal for her to disappear for days at a time before turning up strung out, wearing the same clothes she disappeared in. Even though I know deep down this time it's something different, there's nothing I can do. When I went to the police, they were hesitant to even fill out a missing person report, because they know her history. They know she has a drug problem, and to them, she was just one more druggie in a long line of missing drug users.

"I'm here for you," he says gently, moving his thumb in soothing strokes that cause me to lean into his touch instead of pull away like I should. I want to believe him, but I know people. I know you can only really depend on people until they get what they want, and then they turn their backs on you. My family is a shining example of that. My whole life, I have been the person my family turns to when they need something. I have always been the adult, always the responsible one, and always the one left holding the bag when they get what they want and walk away.

"Thanks," I choke out, feeling that pressure in my chest press in on my lungs, making it hard to breathe.

"It will be okay," he says, leaning in, pressing his lips to my forehead, and letting them linger there until the feel of them is imprinted on my skin. Then, he pulls back enough to catch my eye. "Why don't you have dinner with me tonight?" he asks softly, searching my face.

"I think I'm just going to go home and get to bed early," I tell him, taking a step back before I can say something stupid, like 'yes.' I like Sven way too much, and the more time I spend with him, the *more* I like him.

"Sure." He nods. "Get some rest." Seeing the brief flash of disappointment in his eyes right before he turns his back on me makes me waiver in my decision to keep my distance, but then I remember what has happened every time I let someone in.

"I'll see you tomorrow," I murmur as I step out of his office, taking the stairs down to the main floor. I walk through the empty club, waving at Eva, who's on the phone behind the bar, as I pass her on the way to the door.

"You heading home already?" Teo asks when I step outside.

"Yep, Sven had me up early to run errands, so I'm off now."

"I'll walk you to your car." He stands from the small metal stool he was sitting on and tosses a half smoked cigarette into the street.

"You don't have to do that," I assure him, motioning for him to sit back down.

"Sorry, I mean I *am* walking you to your car." He grins, wrapping his giant hand around my bicep.

"Fine," I sigh, knowing there is no point in arguing with him. Since I started working here, there has never been a time I have gone to my car alone. Even in the middle of the day, someone is with me.

"You know Sven doesn't like you leaving the club alone," he says, leading me around the side of the building to the parking lot. Ignoring his comment and the way it makes me feel, I try to keep up with his long stride in my heels as we walk past Sven's giant SUV to my car that is about ten times smaller in size.

"Sven doesn't like much of anything," I say under my breath, hearing him chuckle.

"One day, this shit's gonna go nuclear."

"What?" I ask, tilting my head back to peer up at him as we stop at the back of my car.

"Nothing." He shakes his head as a small smile forms on his lips.

"If you say so." I frown as his eyes study me, running over my hair and face then down over my body before stopping on my shoes, moving back up to meet my eyes once more.

"Fucking nuclear." He shakes his head, and his smile broadens, confusing me even more.

"Um…"

"Get home safe," he rumbles, opening the door to my car.

Giving up on understanding him, I lean up on my heels to give him a quick peck on the cheek. "See you tomorrow."

Nodding, he steps back, allowing me to slide behind the wheel. Starting my hybrid, I check the battery and make sure I have enough of a charge to make it home before backing up and waving at Teo as I pass him.

Getting home, I head up the stairs that lead to my apartment and unlock the door, silently praying that Morgan will be inside, but she's not. The place is quiet and is exactly the same as I left it this morning before I went to run errands for Sven.

Heading to my room, I slip off my heels and toss them onto the pile of shoes in the bottom of my closet. My bedroom is my favorite room. After my first modeling job, I splurged and bought a bedroom suite that was made for a princess. The white, four-poster canopy bed with sheer curtains that hang down around the sides remind me of a bed from *Sleeping Beauty*. The white matching dressers, one tall, the other long, have etched glass mirrors on the front of each drawer, with shiny silver handles. The side tables match the dressers, and each has a blown glass lamp on top; the Tiffany blue color matches the duvet on my bed.

Walking to my long dresser, the one covered in frames of different sizes, I pick up a picture of Morgan and me. I must have been about six at the time, and Morgan was around four. We were sitting outside my parents' house on the wooden steps that lead to their front door. My arm was wrapped around her shoulders, and we were naked, wearing nothing but rain boots and covered in mud. We were happy. *She* was happy. Picking up another picture of us from around four years ago, I run my finger over her face, wondering where her light went. There was a time her smile lit up the room; people would gravitate toward her without even knowing they were doing it. I don't know what happened to take away her light.

"What happened to you?" I whisper, gaining no answer. I set down the picture and put my hands behind me to unzip my skirt then slip out of my blouse, tossing both items toward the bathroom, where the washer and dryer is located. Then, I slip off my bra and go to the laundry basket next to my bed that is full of clothes I need to put away. I find a pair of sweats and a shirt and put both on and then head down the short hallway, past the guest bath and Morgan's room, which used to be my office. Stopping in the living room, I turn on the stereo, allowing Adele to fill the silence, and then toss the remote on the sectional across from the television.

Heading toward the kitchen, a letter sitting on top of the stack of mail I brought inside yesterday catches my eye when I see my mom's swirly handwriting. Sliding my finger under the edge of the envelope, I pull out the folded up letter and read it quickly. My parents don't have phones or internet, so my mom keeps in contact with letters, and this one is just like the rest: a short update about her and my dad and an invite to come visit when I can.

Sitting down in one of my dining chairs, I write a quick note telling her that Morgan has once again disappeared and that I probably won't be able to visit for awhile, but will send a letter when I can. I know my mom will be concerned about Morgan, but she will say what she always says: *This is your life, so you have to make your own decisions.* Shoving the letter into an envelope, I place it in my purse so I can mail it tomorrow. I get up and go to the kitchen, pulling out a pot to boil water.

I was raised in a small community outside of Phoenix, where they didn't believe in the government or in most modern amenities. When I was ten, my parents offered me the opportunity to join public school and I accepted. That was when I figured out how different we were from everyone, and how much my parents had prevented me from learning. My first year of public school was really difficult, and I ended up being held back a year so that I could catch up with everyone else. After that first year, I excelled, and by graduation, I was top of my class.

I don't regret how I grew up, but I still resent my parents for not being parents. Most of my major life decisions were ones I made for myself, even before I should have been allowed to, and if there was ever a problem, I knew I would have to find a solution on my own without the help of the two people who should have been there to guide me.

Shaking the depressing thoughts about my parents out of my head, I toss some angel hair pasta in the boiling water and pull down a bowl from my cabinet then go to the fridge to grab the butter and a bottle of orange juice. Once the pasta is soft, I strain it and put it in the bowl along with some butter, salt, and pepper then pour myself a cup of orange juice, taking both to the living room.

LOOKING FROM THE door to the clock on the cable box, the bright red numbers read 11:36. Looking at the door again, I feel my eyebrows pull tight as the door handle jiggles like it did moments ago. Getting off the couch, where I planted myself a few hours ago to watch TV, I walk slowly to the door, feeling something strange slide down my spine as I get up on my tiptoes and press my hand to the wood to look through the peephole. The porch light is off, but the light from the streetlamp near my building has cast a glow around two men on the other side of the door.

Backing away slowly, my heart pounds so hard in my chest that the sound of my blood pumping fills my ears. Moving as quickly and as silently as I can down the hall to my bedroom, I shut my door, whimpering when I realize there is no lock. Scurrying around the bed, I grab my phone off the charger then run to the bathroom in the hall, knowing there's a lock on that door and if someone breaks in, he will have to break down that door, which will give me a few more seconds. Getting into the tub and pulling the curtain around me, I fumble with the phone as I dial and place it to my ear.

"911, what's your emergency?" the dispatcher answers as I hear footsteps sound somewhere in the apartment.

"I'm at 267 Hemming Way, apartment 17. Someone is in my apartment," I whisper then scream as the bathroom door crashes open and the shower curtain is shoved aside.

"Help!" I shout as hands grab me by my hair, pulling me up from the tub. Dropping the phone, I fight back, elbowing the guy in the stomach, then turn and bring my hand down hard on his shoulder, which causes him to drop to the ground instantly.

Click, click.

My body freezes and fear rushes over me as I look up, coming face-to-face with the barrel of a gun. Raising my hands in front of me, I'm not prepared for the blow to my stomach that has me doubling over, gasping for air.

"You fucking cunt," the guy I took down moments ago says, back-handing me so hard I hit the wall. Wrapping his hands around my hair, he drags me stumbling out of the bathroom, down the hall behind him to the living room, where he shoves me to my knees.

"Where is your sister?" the man holding the gun roars, smacking me with the butt of his weapon across my face so hard that my head flies to the side and I taste blood in my mouth.

"I don't know," I tell him, lifting my eyes and trying to focus on his face.

"Don't lie, bitch," he says, pressing the gun into my forehead.

"I don't know," I whimper in fear as the guy behind me uses my ponytail to pull me up off the floor.

"Your cunt sister stole ten grand from me," the one holding the gun says as his face comes close to mine…so close I can smell the scent of mint on his breath.

"I can give you the money," I sob as I feel my hair being ripped out of my scalp when I'm jerked back and forth.

"Do you really think it's that fucking simple?" he asks, wrapping his hand around my throat. "No one fucking takes from me. No one!" he snarls, squeezing my throat tighter as stars blur my vision.

"Cops," the guy behind me says as the sound of sirens off in the distance gets louder.

"Tell your sister I'm coming for her."

Falling to my knees, I gasp for air then roll into a ball as his booted foot connects with my side. Watching them run out of my apartment. I don't know how long I lay there but I eventually pull up enough energy to get to my feet and stumble toward the door.

"Freeze."

My head lifts and I swallow as tears stream out of my eyes, seeing two uniformed police officers standing at the top landing in front of my apartment. "They're gone," I croak through the soreness of my throat, leaning into the door.

"You know which way they went?" one of the officers questions while taking a step toward me.

"No," I say then shake my head when the words aren't loud enough to be heard.

"I'll stay with her. You go and check around and let me know if you find anything," the cop before me says, putting his gun away as the other takes off back down the stairs. "Come on, honey," he instructs gently as he takes my arm. He leads me over to my couch, where he helps me sit before getting down in front of me and pushing my hair away from my face. "You got some ice?"

"Peas," I murmur, watching him get up and go to the kitchen, coming back a few seconds later with a bag of frozen peas in his hand. Taking it from him, I press it to my throat then to my face, blinking rapidly, trying to control the tears I feel filling my eyes.

"Would you like to call someone?"

How pathetic is it that my answer was, "Not really"? But that was the truth, wasn't it? I have no one, no one I can depend on, no one I can count on when I need anything. My parents don't even have a telephone I can call them on if there's an emergency. *Like now,* I think bitterly. Then, my sister, seeing how she's the reason I was in this mess. I knew that even if I were able to get ahold of her she wouldn't be able to help me. Hell, she would probably run away when she found out the guys she stole from were looking for her. Wyatt is out of the question, since I broke up with him yesterday after realizing it was pointless to be in a relationship with someone who lives hundreds of miles away. My mind flashes to Sven, but I don't want him to worry...or at least that's what I'm telling myself right now. "No, I don't want to call anyone."

"I'm gonna call an ambulance and have them come look you over."

"That's not necessary," I whisper through the soreness of my throat.

"Honey, I'd really like to make sure you don't have a concussion."

"I don't think I do," I tell him, dropping my eyes to his badge. "Officer Jenkins."

"Not sure you would know that." He smiles.

Sighing, I give up and mutter, "Fine," and he smiles bigger then pats my knee. He puts his hand to his chest and leans down, telling dispatch to send an ambulance.

"Do you know who broke in?" he asks as soon as he gets the conformation that the ambulance is in route.

"No, they were looking for my sister."

"Did they say what they wanted with her?" he asks, moving to sit next to me on the couch.

Shaking my head, I start to lie then squeeze my eyes closed and open them back up. "They said she stole money and they were going to pay her back."

"I see." He nods, and I fight the urge to defend her, even though I know she has gone too far this time.

"None of the neighbors heard anything, and I didn't see anyone on the street," the other officer says, walking through the open front door, followed by two paramedics who come directly to me. It doesn't surprise me that no one heard anything. My two closest neighbors are older; one uses a hearing aid most of the time, and the other usually has the television on so high that he wouldn't hear it if the world was coming to an end outside his door.

"As soon as they check her over, we'll go over the details of what happened," I hear Officer Jenkins say to his partner as the paramedics begin to examine me. When they're done, they tell me to take some Advil for the pain, but assure me I will be fine. Officer Jenkins takes the seat next to me on the couch once more as the other officer, Lent, leads the paramedics to the door and closes it behind them, coming back a second later, grabbing one of the chairs from my dining room table, and sitting on it across from me.

"I already explained to Officer Lent that the men who broke in were looking for your sister," Officer Jenkins says as he pulls out a pen from the pocket of his shirt. "Can you tell me anything else about them?"

Pressing my lips together, I try to remember any details about the two men, but my mind comes up empty. "It all happened so fast. They were both white, and dressed similar in black t-shirts, jeans, and boots, but I didn't get a good look at either of them."

"Do you know where your sister is?" Officer Lent asks, sitting forward and studying me.

"No, I filed a missing person report on her. I haven't heard from her in two days," I tell him, and his eyes scan my face and I know he sees I'm holding something back.

"What are you not telling us?" he asks gently, and that's when the dam breaks and tears begin to fall silently from my eyes, down my cheeks, and onto my shirt.

"She has a drug problem. She was doing really well for a few weeks, and I thought this time she was going to stick with it and go into rehab, but she lost her way again, and now this happened." Covering my face with my hands, I try to get myself back under control. Crying like a baby won't solve anything right now, even though that is exactly what I want to do. Sitting up straight, I look between the two policemen and ask, "What do I need to do now?"

"There isn't much we can do at this time. We don't exactly know who we're looking for, and I doubt your sister is going to show up and tell us who she stole from," Officer Lent says softly like he regrets his words.

"I'd really like you to stay somewhere else tonight," Officer Jenkins says quietly after a moment, and my eyes go to him.

"I'll go to a hotel. I wouldn't be able to sleep here if I wanted to, not while knowing there is a possibility those guys might come back."

"I don't think they'll come back tonight, but I'd rather you be safe somewhere else, at least for a few days. You also need to have your locks changed and a deadbolt put in before you do stay here. The guys who broke in were able to pick your lock easily, and to be honest, you're a woman living alone. You should have some form of protection."

"I'll call a locksmith tomorrow and have them put in new locks," I agree, instantly ignoring his 'you're a woman' comment, 'cause all that does is annoy me, even if he is right. But then again, there was a gun involved, and if not for that, I probably could have kicked butt...or at least that's what I'm going to tell myself.

"Go get your stuff, honey, and we'll follow you to the hotel," he replies, looking as if he wants to say something else but thinking better of it. If this had been any other time, I would have taken an extra moment to appreciate how handsome he is. But now is not that time, so I get off the couch, walk back to my bedroom, pull out my large duffle bag from my closet, and stuff it full with enough clothes to last me a few days. Once I'm done, I drag it into the hall behind me.

"This is my card. If you think of anything or need anything, just give me a call," Officer Jenkins says as he picks up my bag then turns his attention to Officer Lent. "I'm gonna take this down and phone into the station to let them know we're following her to the hotel and getting her checked in."

"I'll help her lock up then we'll be down," he replies as I go into the kitchen and turn out the light then to the living room to do the same and turn off the TV before heading for the front door.

"I shouldn't be telling you this, but I have a sister your age, and I know if something like this ever happened to her I would want her to have whatever protection she could get her hands on," Officer Lent says quietly as I step outside with him and lock my front door. "Every other week at Lawson's, I teach a class on gun safety, and I would be happy to have you in my next class." He hands me a card, and I look at it then back up at him. "Guns can be dangerous, but they can also save your life, and in my class, I'll teach you how to be comfortable handling a gun and what to do in different situations. You don't have to buy a gun if you don't want to, but you can come to the class and find out for yourself if that is something you want to do or not."

"Thank you," I tell him sincerely as I place both cards in my bag. I've never thought about owning a gun, but after tonight, it might not be a bad idea to have one.

"WHAT THE FUCK happened to your face?"

Jumping in surprise, I lift my eyes from the computer screen in front of me and my gaze collides with Sven's blue ones. I didn't even hear him come into the office.

"Nothing," I tell him then lean back when his hands go to the top of the desk and his body looms over until his face is just inches from mine.

"That bruise on your face doesn't look like nothing. Wanna try again?" he taunts as his face twist in anger.

"Not particularly," I mumble sitting further back in my chair.

"Too bad. What happened?" he rumbles, lifting one hand, touching my cheek gently.

"My sister stole money from some guy," I say, and then regret it instantly when his energy changes and wraps around me so tight that my breath comes out in a rush.

"He put his hands on you?" His words are soft, but the angry, vibrating energy I feel coming off of him grates against my skin. "Tell me everything."

"Sven," His body leans even closer to me as he snarls, "Now."

"Sheesh, fine." I take a deep breath and let it out then tell him about hearing someone at the door and thinking that my sister was home but that she lost her key. Then I tell him about the guys breaking in and the police showing up. I only stop talking when I tell him that I stayed at a hotel last night and he roars.

"You didn't call me?"

"I knew you were probably busy." I shrug, trying to make it seem like it's not a big deal.

"I wasn't. Goddammit, Mags! You should have fucking called me." He paces back and forth in front of the desk then goes to the window behind me and looks out over the club. "You're staying with me until your sister cleans her fucking mess up."

"N... No, I'm not," I choke out in distress at the idea.

"You are, and if you even think about going anywhere but my penthouse, I will track your ass down and drag you back with me."

"Sven, don't be stupid." His penthouse is nice, really nice, but it only has one bedroom, and his couch isn't even one you would want to sleep on if left with no choice. It's modern and edgy, but in no way does it say 'come sleep on me'.

"Do we need to go to your place to get some stuff?" he asks, ignoring me.

"I'm not staying with you," I repeat.

"You are," he says, storming out of his office. Digging my compact out of my bag, I look at myself in the mirror. I thought I had done a good job covering up the bruises, but apparently I hadn't.

"Mags."

"What?" I huff, looking up from the computer once more when he storms back into the office.

"Get up. We're meeting with a realtor in thirty minutes."

"Pardon?"

"You're right. My place now doesn't really have space," he grits out as he walks over to the bathroom and shuts the door halfway then continues talking through the small gap. "We're going to look at a few houses," he says, and I can hear him flush then the water turn on before the door opens and he steps out. "Do you need anything before we head out?"

"Are you crazy?" I ask, frowning and standing from the chair I'm sitting in.

"Nope," he denies, walking toward me. Taking my elbow, he stops at the door and grabs my bag then pulls me with him out of his office, down the stairs, and through the club. He then leads me to his SUV and sets me inside, yelling for me to put my belt on as he slams the door.

"Put your seatbelt on," I mimic under my breath as I slide it around me, locking it in place.

CROSSING MY ARMS over my chest, I glare out the windshield. Five hours ago, we met up with a guy named Don, who I learned moments after meeting him was a realtor. Don seems like a nice enough guy, but since meeting up with him, we have seen ten houses—okay, not houses, *mansions*—and now we're on our way to view another.

"You haven't even attempted to appreciate any of them," Sven grumbles, and I turn my head and transfer my glare to him.

"Do you know how crazy it is to buy a house that you don't even want?" I ask, really wondering if he understands how ridiculous this is.

"I want a house," he says, shifting in his seat, suddenly looking uncomfortable.

"For what, Sven?" I ask, holding up my hand and ticking off my fingers one at a time. "You're single, you don't have a wife or kids, and you don't need more space." I sigh, placing my hand back in my lap. "You're talking about spending millions of dollars just so I have a room to sleep in for a few days. That is the definition of crazy."

"Do you want to sleep in my bed with me?" he asks, and this time it's me who shifts uncomfortably. If I was to ever be honest with myself, I would like to sleep next to him, but what red-blooded woman wouldn't want that?

"Let's just go buy a comfortable couch if it's that important to you, and I'll sleep on it," I tell him, but then stop talking altogether when we pull down a street with kids outside playing on sidewalks and front laws, and families talking and visiting with their neighbors. Spotting a for sale sign in one of the yards, I feel a smile on my face for the first time in hours. The two-story terracotta stone house with curved windows and doors, and a wooden shingle roof, looks like something out of a fairy tale and is my dream home.

"You like that house?"

Looking from the house to Sven, a feeling of disappointment hits me as we drive past it. "It's a cute house," I murmur, looking over my shoulder one more time as he turns onto another road then another until we're pulling up in front of a house that looks like all the others we have seen today.

Completely atrocious.

"Wait here." Getting out of the car, he walks toward Don, who is standing on the front porch. They talk for a brief moment before Sven walks back toward me.

"What's going on?" I ask when he gets in behind the wheel.

"We're skipping this one," he mutters, looking over his shoulder to the street behind us.

"Bummer," I say sarcastically, watching as his lips twitch as he backs out of the driveway. Looking out the window, I realize we are heading back toward the neighborhood we drove through earlier, and when we pull into the driveway of the terracotta house, I sit up a little taller in my seat.

"You like this house?" he asks, surprised, looking at the house in front of us. It's not a mansion, but it is a really beautiful house in the perfect little neighborhood. The kind of house I wish I had grown up in.

"Some people strive for normal," I say, getting out of the car and walking through the thick grass in the front yard then up to the large bay window, where I put my hands to the glass and press my forehead close so I can see inside.

"Mags, you don't need to peep through the window. We're going to go inside," Sven says, and I feel his warmth at my back and his fingers curve around my waist.

"You want to view this house?" I ask doubtfully.

Ignoring my question, he pulls me from the window and leads me toward the front of the house, where Don is unlocking the box attached to the door handle. Pushing the door open, he motions for us to go inside. The moment I step into the foyer, I'm in awe. It's beautiful, with high ceilings and natural light. To the left is a large library, and the right, a sunken living room with comfortable couches that make you want to kick off your shoes, grab a book, and hang out awhile. The kitchen is in the back of the house, with a long island, and a breakfast nook that is surrounded by windows. Upstairs are five bedrooms, including a master with a walk-in closet and a bathroom bigger than my bedroom at home, plus a bonus room the pervious owners set up like a theater.

"You'd be happy in a house like this, wouldn't you?" Sven asks, and his eyes go from where he's looking outside to sweeping over me as he shakes his head. "Most women want bigger, Mags, and then there's you."

"I don't want to be like most women," I tell him, feeling like I need to defend myself.

"I know," he says quietly, stepping away from the window and coming to stand in front of me. "I fucking hate these bruises." He whispers running his eyes over them before meeting my gaze again. Looking into his eyes, my body leans into his as his fingers wrap around my jaw and his lips touch my forehead in a spot that I've decided is his. Closing my eyes, I only open them back up when I hear his voice in the distance yell, "Come on, Mags. We have a house to buy."

"What's happening to me?" I ask the empty room, but gaining no answer from it, I follow him down to the first floor, where the realtor is waiting.

Wrapping his arm around my waist as soon as I reach his side, he tells Don, "We'll take it."

"Are you sure? This is kind of small." Don frowns looking around.

I have no idea in what world five-thousand square feet is small, but the way he's looking at me and Sven gives me the impression he really believed this house was far too small for anyone to live in.

"How long until we can close?" Sven asks, ignoring Don's comment and pulling me closer to him as I struggle with his fingers, attempting to remove them from my waist.

"The average closing time is about a month right now."

"See if we can rent it from them until closing. Also let them know that if they agree to my terms and can close within the next week I will add ten-grand on top of asking price."

"Sven," I hiss, swinging my gaze up to his.

"You love this house, Mags."

"You can't just throw money around, Sven."

"Sure I can." He shrugs then turns me with him toward the front door. "Send the offer and get back to me by the end of the day," he tells Don while leading me out of the house.

"I'm pretty sure you may be insane," I tell him as we drive back toward downtown.

"The most important thing my father taught me is you never let an opportunity pass you by, and this is one opportunity I wouldn't dream of missing out on."

"That makes no sense," I tell him, studying his profile.

"One day, Mags, I guarantee you that it will," he says quietly, pulling on a pair of sunglasses and turning up the stereo.

Looking from him to the windshield, I wonder why I feel so relaxed, why I'm not stressed about this, and why I actually feel happy.

Chapter 5

Maggie

The morning after

I'M PRETTY SURE *he's trying to torture me*, I think as Sven comes into the kitchen, using his T-shirt to wipe the sweat from his face and chest. Tearing my eyes from him, I wait for my toast to pop up while silently praying he puts the shirt on. It's been three weeks since we moved in together, and every day feels like torture. Not that things have been bad. Things have actually been really great. But working together, having meals together, and seeing Sven half dressed in the mornings and at night is messing with my head.

"Morning," I hear him say, but I don't turn to look at him as I reply quietly,

"Morning," while staring at the toaster, hoping I can make it through one morning where I don't drool all over him.

God, give me strength.

"How'd you sleep?"

"Good."

"Are you mad?" he asks sounding concerned.

Tugging my eyes from the toaster, I look at him then regret it when my belly dips and my mouth floods with saliva. Sven in a suit is a sight to behold. Sven in jeans and a tee is mouthwatering. But Sven shirtless, his hair mussed from sleep, and his eyes soft on me is completely unhinging.

"No, why?"

"Just wondering." He grins then takes a step toward me and places his thumb on the corner of my mouth and swipes it under my bottom lip. Watching his eyes grow darker, I feel my pulse speed up. "Toothpaste," he grunts, dropping his hand away from me but staying in my space.

Licking my bottom lip, I take a step back and wipe my mouth, feeling my cheeks heat. "Thanks."

"I have a couple friends coming into town tonight. Do you mind picking up some groceries?"

"Not at all."

"Meat, Mags, not tofu." He smiles, and my belly does that dip-drop thing again and gets warm.

"I already know that," I grumble back, rolling my eyes at him. Then I turn back toward the toaster and take my bread out, pulling down the peanut butter and slathering both slices. Taking my plate with me, I go to the table in the breakfast nook to sit down then take a moment to appreciate him while he moves around the kitchen.

"Do you want coffee?"

Feeling my cheeks heat, I pull my gaze from his abs and raise them to meet his eyes.

Busted again.

"Orange juice," I mumble, covering my hand with my mouth as I chew. Nodding, he pours me a glass of juice then comes to sit across from me, holding his cup of coffee in his hand.

"Thanks."

"No problem," he replies, studying me, and then runs his hand over his jaw. "So tell me about your modeling. Why did you stop?"

Great. This is something I had hoped he forgot about since he never asked me about it after Ace brought it up. Apparently, I couldn't be so lucky.

"My first job was actually for a friend of mine, who designed her own clothing line when she was in college. She asked if I would do some pictures wearing her clothes for her website. Two months after she launched her line, I got a call from an agency and they wanted to represent me. I really didn't take it seriously at first, but then I got my first paid job, and like they say, the rest is history." I take another bite of my toast.

"Why did you stop modeling?"

"I didn't exactly stop. I just haven't had a job in a few months. When things happened with Morgan, I knew I couldn't risk leaving her alone, so I told my agency that if the job was out of town to pass it on to someone else."

"Did you enjoy it?" he questions, taking one of the slices of toast off my plate, taking a bite, and then setting it back down.

"It was fun. When I was younger, I loved it because it gave me a chance to travel, but I don't think I would have done it for much longer. Staying in hotels and being away from home was getting old."

"Do you have any of your pictures?"

"A few, but not really. I'm sure you could Google me and see some." I shrug then watch horrified as he pulls out his cell phone from the pocket of his sweats.

"What name did you use? I tried searching before, but nothing ever came up."

"You tried looking me up before?" I whisper.

"Yes." He raises a brow smirking.

Sighing, I mutter, "Star Laurence, my middle name and my grand-mother's name." Typing into his phone, his hand holds the cell tight in his grasp as he swipes his finger across the screen.

"Jesus," he sits back in the chair then looks me over.

"What?"

"You're half naked."

"What?" I ask, grabbing his phone from his hand then paling when I see that he's come across some of the photos for a plus-size lingerie line I did a year ago. Feeling suddenly embarrassed, I exit out of the web browser, set his phone down on the table, and then take my plate to the sink. "I'm gonna go get ready. What time are you leaving?" I ask while avoiding looking at him.

"Mags, you looked beautiful."

Looking up at the sound of his quiet words, I wonder what I should say.

"Honestly, beautiful," he says earnestly.

"Thanks," I whisper, dropping my eyes from his, focusing all my attention on scrubbing my plate.

Putting some more soap on the sponge in my hand, I wash out my cup then jump when I feel his arm slide past me so he can set his mug in the sink. "I'm gonna leave for the airport in about an hour."

"Okay, I'll see you later," I tell him, or tell the sink, when I pick up his cup and wash it out as well. His lips touch the top of my head then he's gone. Letting out a breath, I set the dishes in the drainer then head up to my room and plop myself down onto my bed, covering my face with my hands. I don't have body issues. I'm totally comfortable in my skin. My parents may not have been the best parents, but there was never a time I was made to feel less beautiful than my sister, even though I was a few sizes bigger than her. We were taught there was beauty in all shapes and sizes, but Sven seeing me half naked wearing close to nothing isn't something I'm exactly okay with, especially when I didn't have the courage to look into his eyes to see what he thought. Groaning against my palms, I get up and go to the bathroom in my room and get into the shower, figuring I can beat myself up about it later after I go to the grocery store.

PUTTING AWAY THE groceries I picked up, I hear the door open and boots hit the marble in the entryway, and I know Sven is home. By the time I got out of the shower, Sven was already gone and had taken my car keys, something he had started doing recently so I wouldn't drive it. Without any other option, I took his SUV to the store and got the items on the list I made yesterday, along with a few steaks for him.

While I was out, I also called Eva to see how things were going at the club, since neither Sven nor I would be there tonight. After talking for a few minutes, she asked if I had plans for the evening. I explained to her about Sven's friends coming in to town, but then she shocked me and said she had a friend she thought I should meet and asked if tonight was a good night to have dinner with him. My first response was to say no, but the more I thought about it, the more I wondered, *Why not?*

I haven't dated anyone since my breakup with Wyatt, and my feelings for Sven were starting to confuse me. Living with him and working with him meant we spent most of our time together, and I was starting to more than like him, meaning the lines of our relationship were beginning to blur, and that wasn't good. Even though he gets on my nerves and has a tendency to piss me off, the good outweighed the bad. He is the kind of man a girl could fall in love with, without ever knowing she was doing it. And that's the exact reason I agreed to go on a date tonight.

"Oh good, you're here. I got all the crap you asked for," I tell him, shutting the door to the fridge as he walks into the kitchen.

"Meat is not crap, Mags," he replies with a smile.

"Stop calling me Mags. It's Maggie for the millionth time," I say, then regret it when I see his smile leaves, but I need to keep strong. I need to separate. "And meat is gross." I shake my head then turn to look at who just walked in.

Holy cow.

Sven is gorgeous, but the man who is standing in the kitchen right now looks like some kind of Hawaiian warrior, and the whole scary look definitely works for him in a big, big way. "You have zero manners," I say, turning to look at Sven then back to the man, only to realize there is another older gentleman with him wearing a bright Hawaiian shirt and a lot of, probably too much, gold jewelry around his neck and on every one of his fingers.

"He's rude. Sorry about that. I'm Maggie, this guy's assistant. Nice to meet you guys." I take the big man's hand, noticing he doesn't return his name, then place my hand out for the other guy, who takes my outstretched hand and pulls me closer.

"Nice to meet you, Maggie," he says, lowering his lips and brushing them over the back of my hand.

"Aww, you're so cute." I pat his cheek then step back and look at Sven. "I'm going to head out. I have a date tonight," I tell him, ignoring the way his jaw tics and the shake of his head.

"You need to work tonight," he grits out, narrowing his eyes.

"I don't work weekends." I laugh, trying to cover up the nausea I feel turning in my stomach. "Nice meeting you guys," I tell the two men, who are both looking at me curiously, then walk over to the counter, pick up my bag and my key Sven dropped when he came in, and head out of the kitchen before he can say anything else. Shutting the door behind me, I make it down the stairs, only to hear a loud bang that has me spinning around.

"You go on a date tonight and you're fired, Maggie."

"Wh...what?" I stutter out as he prowls toward me, eating up the distance separating us.

"You heard me. Go to the club. I'll let Teo know you're on your way."

"You can't be serious." I whisper taking a step back.

"Deadly," he snarls. If his tone didn't tell me he was serious, his body language would have spelled it out for me. I have seen Sven mad before, but right now, he is completely enraged. I just don't understand what set him off.

"Fine, you win," I breathe out, feeling my throat get tight but fighting it, not wanting to cry in front of him.

"I'll see you tomorrow."

"Sure," I agree then watch his jaw clench again before he turns away from me and walks back toward the house. Standing in the driveway, I look up at the house and pull out my cell phone.

"Maggie, what's up?" Eva asks on the second ring.

"I need to work tonight, can you please tell your friend I'm sorry, maybe we can meet another time."

"You we're supposed to be off."

"I know," I whisper, dropping my eyes to the concrete below my feet as I swipe a tear off my cheek.

"Are you okay?"

"I'm fine."

"Sven," she whispers, and I lift my head and look up at the house, my fairytale house, the house I would have picked if I ever got married, the house I would want to raise kids in.

"He's a jerk," I tell her then turn and head for my car.

"It will be okay, Maggie."

"Yeah," I agree, "I'll see you in a bit."

"See you," she says, hanging up. Getting into my car, I drop my phone in the cup holder then my forehead to the steering wheel for a moment before turning on my car and backing out of the driveway heading toward the club.

I WAKE UP with my head pounding, the feel of a bare hairy leg over the top of mine, and a hand wrapped around my breast. I open one eye and close it immediately when I see dark golden hair, a nose, and lips I know too well.

Sven.

I try to recall last night, but my whole memory is blank. My heart starts to beat more rapidly as I notice I'm completely naked—and so is the man asleep on top of me.

"What have I done?" I whisper as I recognize the space between my legs is sore.

Tears fill my eyes as I realize the thing I promised myself I would only give to my husband has been given to a man who has had more partners in and out of his bed than he can even count. And the worst part is I don't remember anything.

"Why are you crying?" Sven asks, pulling his hand from my breast and moving it to my face, where his fingers slide over my cheek, swiping away a tear.

"What happened?" I ask, opening my eyes as he gets up on his elbow, his eyes travel from mine to my breasts, and I pull the sheet up, covering myself.

"What do you mean what happened?" he asks, looking confused.

"Why are we naked in bed together?" I ask, already knowing the answer.

"That's not funny, Mags," he says as his eyes slide over my face again.

"Sven," I whisper, clutching the sheet tighter against my chest.

"Jesus, you have to be shitting me right now, Mags." He jumps from the bed and begins pacing along the side of it. Sitting up, I watch as his naked form moves back and forth in front of me. "I made love to you." His voice is anguished as he runs his hands over his head then down over his face.

"I…"

"You told me you love me," he groans, holding his hand to his chest like the words cause him pain.

"Oh, God," I whimper. I'm in love with Sven, but I would never tell him that. I would never trust him with that information. I also would never risk what I have with him.

"I fucking knew it," he stops next to the bed to look down at me. "I fucking knew I should have followed my gut."

Okay, that didn't feel good. In fact, those words cut something deep inside me—something I didn't even realize was vulnerable when it came to him.

"Goddammit," he roars then storms to the bathroom, slamming the door, leaving me sitting cross-legged in the middle of his bed, naked, confused, and hurt.

Getting up quickly, I look around for my clothes that are nowhere to be found then wrap the sheet around myself, leaving the room to go to mine, which is right next to his. I pull on a pair of panties and a bra then find a pair of shorts and a tank top, slipping on my flip-flops, then rush to the stairs and stop dead. From the bottom landing to the top stair, our clothes are scattered. Whimpering, I stumble down the steps, picking up the pieces of my discarded clothes along the way until my hands are full. I grab my bag and keys from the table near the door, rush out of the house, throw the clothes into my back seat, and then back out of the driveway.

Biting my lip to keep from crying, I drive faster.

"What have I done?" I whisper to my windshield as I pull up in front of my apartment. Sven didn't want me to keep it, but when I was moving in with him, I left my sister a note on the kitchen counter, explaining what happened with the guys that came and how she could get ahold of me. I honestly didn't think she would ever come back, at least not alive. The next time I stopped by to check the mail, I found a note from her telling me that she was okay, but she was trying to find a way to fix her mess. After that, I decided to keep the apartment; that way, she would have a place to crash if she needed it.

Getting into the apartment, I shut and lock the door with the three extra locks I purchased after the break-in and head directly to my old room, stripping off my clothes. Catching a glimpse of myself in the mirror, I inhale sharply. My nipples are darker than I have ever seen them and are surrounded by tiny hickeys.

"Stop marking me." I laugh as his head lowers, pulling my nipple into his mouth, making my back arch. Lifting his head above mine, he smiles softly and I run my fingers through his hair.

"I like knowing you're carrying my mark around under your clothes," he whispers before stealing my breath with a kiss.

Stumbling back, I sit on the edge of the tub and lower my face into my hands. I have no idea if that's a real memory or just something my subconscious made up.

Reaching over, I start up the shower and get in to stand under the running water. Making quick work I wash my hair and body then get out and wrap my hair in a towel. Going into my room, I put back on the clothes I arrived in, since everything else is at Sven's house, and head for the living room, thankful that I left the couch.

Grabbing a Diet Coke, one of the only things in the fridge, I wander into the living room and take a seat on my couch, setting my Coke on the floor. Holding my phone in my hand, I try to decide what to do. I press my hand to my forehead and replay the events from last night in my head. After I got to the club, Teo escorted me straight to the office, where I stayed until around one. Instead of leaving and going home, I decided to sit at the bar and talk to Eva, since we didn't have a chance to chat earlier. I remember she asked me if I wanted a drink, but like always, I chose cranberry juice, since I knew I had to drive. After she poured me a glass, we chatted between customers. After that,

Nothing

My mind is blank.

Pressing the button on my cell phone, the screen lights up and I see there are twenty-seven phone calls and ten text messages from Sven. I don't read any of the messages as I type quickly.

SVEN: *I'm okay. I just need the night to think.*

I press send then sit back on the couch, close my eyes, and before I know it, I'm asleep.

"I'm never letting you go."

Waking suddenly, I pant looking around in the darkness then squeeze my eyes closed, trying to calm my breathing and rid my mind of the image of Sven above me, his muscles tight as he fills me. Opening my eyes again, it's pitch black, and my neck hurts from the awkward angle it's bent at. I hold my phone away from my face and press the button, seeing it's after midnight.

Groaning, I sit up and rest my head in my hands for a moment while I go over all the variables for the conversation that will happen between Sven and I. Worst-case scenario, I lose Sven forever. Best-case, we pretend like nothing ever happened. Neither of those scenarios makes me feel good, but I need to understand what happened last night, and judging by Sven's reaction to me not remembering, he needs to know too.

Knowing Sven is probably at the club and I have a couple hours to figure out what to say to him when I see him, I pull the pepper spray out of my bag and make my way to my car. Taking the long way home I pull into the driveway at a little after one. Not recognizing the car parked in the driveway it takes me a second to remember Sven has friends in town. Feeling embarrassment hit me, I shut off my engine, and stare at the house until I finally build up the courage to get out and head inside. I don't even register the sound of the car door slamming behind me. The only thing I'm thinking about when I open the front door is the smell of a woman's perfume as I step into the house.

"It took you long enough."

Turning on the foyer light, my heart falls into my stomach as a woman wearing nothing but a pair of shear panties and heels walks around the corner out of the living room. My blood starts to pump so fast and so loud that I can't even hear what she's saying as she gets closer. But I know she's speaking to me as I watch her lips move and a snarl form on her pouty mouth.

"What the fuck are you doing here?" Sven roars from behind me, and I swing my head around to look at him and stumble back, caught off-guard by the anger in his voice and the look in his eyes.

"I—"

"Get out now," he thunders, and I follow his eyes to the woman standing naked in the entryway of the house. Her arms cross over her chest and she looks at Sven then me and back again.

"Whatever." She turns on her heels and heads back into the living room, grabbing a coat off the couch and putting it on, tying the waist. "Your friend still owes me," she says as she passes by Sven, who is holding open the front door. As soon as she clears the door, Sven slams it closed and presses his hand to the wood, dropping his head forward to hang between his shoulders.

"I was waiting outside of your apartment. I must have fallen asleep, 'cause when I woke up, your car was gone. Do you know how fucking scared I was?" He turns to face me and pins me in place with the look in his eyes. "First, you run out on me, and then you send me a message saying that you need time to think." He shakes his head, running his hand over his stubble-covered jaw. "What you need to think about, I have no fucking clue, because you have no idea what I'm feeling."

"Sven," I whisper as tears clog my throat.

"No, Mags, I've given you time. I've done everything but write it in the sky, and you still do not understand I'm in love with you. I loved you before I even understood the pain you caused in my chest." He steps toward me then pauses as his eyes sweep over me and go soft.

"Then you gave yourself to me last night, gave me a gift that I know I'm not worthy of, but I took it anyway, only to wake up this morning in a fucking nightmare," he says, and my heart that had been soaring begins to crash to the ground in a fiery ball of flames. "I'm at a loss, baby. For the first time in my life, I feel lost on what to do. I love you, but if this isn't what you want, I need you to just leave, because I don't have the strength to do this anymore."

Tears begin streaming down my cheeks and I try to swipe them away, but they are coming so quickly that I don't have time to catch them all. There is no way I can walk away from Sven, but the idea of being with him scares me.

"Why?" I shake my head, not sure what I'm asking. Why does he love me? Why is he telling me this now? Why is he doing this to me? Why am I not jumping for joy?

"Why?" he repeats, taking another step toward me and I nod. "I'm not sure. I wasn't even looking, but then one day you were there and I knew you were it."

"I'm not even your type," I point out on a quiet sob as I cover my mouth.

"What type would that be?" he asks tenderly, pulling me up against his body, where I go willingly, melting into him. "The beautiful, sassy, smart type?" he questions, wrapping his arms tighter around me.

"You're my boss."

"Yeah, and if you're *mine*..." He smiles a smile I've never seen before then dips his face closer to mine. "I'll finally be able to do what I've wanted to do every time you've pranced around my office in those tight skirts and tights with the sweet little designs on them." I feel heat hit my cheeks then duck my head so he can't see how his words affect me. I have always been attracted to Sven, but to know he feels the same thing for me is overwhelming.

"We have to talk about last night." I swallow and pull away, needing to put some distance between us so I can think clearly.

"Let's go sit down." His tone has my eyes flying up to meet his. Long gone is the sweet smile, and in its place is rage.

Leading me over to the couch, he sits then pulls me down onto his lap.

"Maybe I should sit over there." I point to the chair that sits catty-corner to the couch.

"No, I need you right here when we talk about last night."

Searching his gaze, I agree with a quiet, "Okay."

"What do you remember about last night?" he asks, pushing some hair behind my ear as his eyes run over me.

"Nothing," I say, feeling a chill slide down my spine.

"Nothing," he repeats as his hand on my thigh moves in soothing strokes. "What was your last memory from yesterday?"

"I didn't want to come home, so I went down to the bar to hang with Eva for awhile. When I got there, she still had customers, so she poured me a cranberry juice and we talked a bit, but she was busy." I end letting my words hang in the air between us.

Leaning back, he pulls his hand from my thigh and runs it over his face. "When I got to the club, you were laughing and having a good time, but you weren't blitzed."

"I don't know. I don't remember anything. I don't even remember seeing you."

"Jesus," he groans, wrapping his arms around me, burying his face in my neck. "You had to have been roofied and I didn't even think about it. I just knew you were finally opening up to me and that was all I saw, so I took my shot."

"Wouldn't I have been passed out or something?" I whisper.

"I would never have gone there if I believed for one second that was the case, Mags. You have to believe that."

I do actually believe he wouldn't take advantage of me. I know deep down that if he thought for one second I had been drugged, I would have been in the hospital, not in his bed doing whatever it is we did last night.

"I believe you," I tell him, running my hand through his hair. When his face comes out of my neck, the worry in his eyes is still there. I hate that look on him, but I have no idea how I can fix it.

"Where do we go from here?" he asks so quietly I'm not even sure those are the exact words.

"What do you mean?"

"You told me last night you were in love with me. Was that real? Do we even have a shot at fixing this?"

"You're my best friend. I don't want to lose that," I tell him my deepest fear. Before Sven, I didn't have anyone to lean on, anyone to protect me. I wasn't sure I could trust what he was asking of me, but I also knew in my heart I would be stupid not to find out.

"What exactly are you looking for?"

"Forever," he says immediately, catching me off-guard.

"I'm barely accepting the fact you would want to be with me. I mean, there was a woman in the house naked when I came home tonight." *A woman who looked like she could have been on the cover of* Maxim, *for God's sake,* I think but leave out. I know I'm pretty. I have been told that my whole life. I have no qualms about my size-twelve shape, but I have curves that take a lot more to cover.

"I have no idea who she was or how she got inside. I haven't touched another woman since the night we met. I want you, Mags, and no one else."

"You haven't been with anyone sin…since we met?" I breathe out, searching his face for any sign of deceit.

"No one."

I swear I feel my eyes pop out of my head at that comment. Sven is young, wealthy, and attractive. I know for a fact women throw themselves at him all the time. I have been there on more then one occasion when it's happened, but if I really think about it, he's not lying. I have not seen him return any of the advances he's received. I don't even see his phone light up constantly like it used to when I first started working for him, with names like Bambie and Lexus. I haven't heard of him hooking up with anyone at the club.

"I'm no good at relationships," I admit.

"I've never been in a relationship, so my standards are pretty low." He smiles and I shake my head, wrapping my fingers around the side of his neck, needing him to understand how serious I am.

"After I broke up with Wyatt, I did some soul searching," I say, ignoring the way his nostrils flare at the mention of my ex. "I realized I've constantly picked men who couldn't let me down, because I didn't have any expectations for them to live up to. Like Ace—I knew he wasn't looking for anything serious, or Wyatt, who lived hundreds of miles away. I wasn't invested in them, because I didn't have to be."

"Don't put me in the same category as them," he flips me to my back, making me squeak as he moves his face above mine. "This is me and you. I'm invested in us, and I expect you to be, too. I won't let you off the hook or let you downplay what we have between us."

"I wasn't—"

"It sounded like you were making excuses for why this won't work," he cuts me off, holding my face in his hands. Crap, that's exactly what I was doing, reassuring him that when things come to an end that it won't be his fault, that it's me who isn't good at relationships. "I'm not saying things are going to be perfect, but the idea of not having you, all of you, isn't going to work for me anymore. I tried to ignore what I'm feeling, but you got under my skin, permanently branded yourself there without me even knowing it."

Tears fill my eyes and slide down into my hair at his confession. "This is a lot to take in," I sob as his fingers slide under my eyes.

"This has been happening for a long time, baby," he says, gently brushing his lips across mine.

"I know," I agree, crying harder while clutching onto him. Rolling us to our sides with me tucked into the back of the couch, he presses my face into his chest, holding one hand behind my head, the other wrapped tightly around me. "I love you, too," I whisper. His body stills and his arms tighten before he lets out a long breath.

"I know, baby." Feeling his lips at the top of my head, I lean my head back to look at him.

"Are your friends still here?"

"No they caught a flight out before I went to the club last night."

"That was a short visit."

"It was just business," he mutters then searches my face. "Did you sleep?" he asks studying me.

"Yes." I nod, pressing my forehead into his chest.

"Did you eat?"

"No, I had a Diet Coke," I say, cuddling deeper into him, feeling myself relax.

"You need to eat, and then I want to take you to the hospital."

"Why do I need to go to the hospital?" I ask, feeling my muscles grow tight.

"I want them to take some blood so we know what you were drugged with."

"Oh," I whisper, tilting my head back to look at him. "You have a camera over the bar."

"I do. Zack sent over the video, but it didn't capture anything out of the ordinary. The only person who poured your drinks was Eva—"

"She wouldn't drug me," I say, cutting him off, and his lips brush over mine.

"I know she's your friend, baby, but everyone is a suspect right now." He's right, and that sucks. I like Eva a lot, but she is the only one I remember giving me a drink, and knowing me, I never would have left that drink unattended. "We'll face that bridge when we come to it, but for now, I want you to eat something so we can go to the hospital."

"Okay," I agree as he rolls us off of the couch and takes me to the kitchen, making me sit as he makes me a peanut butter and jelly sandwich. Then he sits with me as I eat it before putting me in his SUV and taking me to the hospital.

"ARE YOU ON any kind of birth control?" the nurse asks as another woman places the needle in my arm.

"No," I tell her, absently noticing the way Sven's body has gone tight next to mine.

"Are you on any medication?"

"No," I repeat, watching the woman in front of me place a small cylinder on the end of the needle then let out a ragged breath as the tube fills with blood.

"Have you taken any drugs in the last twenty-four hours that your aware of?"

"No."

"We should have the results for this test back in the next week. If the drug is still in your system, we will let you know what we find."

"Thanks," I tell her then watch her and the other woman leave the room. After putting on my sweater, Sven takes my hand and leads me out of the hospital to the SUV and helps me inside, making sure I'm buckled before going around the front to get behind the wheel. Once we're halfway home, I look over at him, realizing he hasn't spoken.

"Are you okay?" Lifting my hand to his lips, he kisses my fingers then says something against them I can't make out as he drops our entwined hands to his thigh. "What was that?" I ask, studying his profile.

"We didn't use protection."

Blinking, I wonder if I heard him correctly then blink again as his fingers tighten around mine. "It sounded like you just said we didn't use protection."

"I did."

"As in condoms?" I ask, and his face turns toward me as he pulls up to a stop sign. "Holy crap."

"I assumed."

"You assumed," I repeat, because apparently that's all I can do as I study him.

"Fuck."

"Ditto," I whisper back then blabber, "The chance of getting pregnant from having sex once is like almost nonexistent right? I mean, that kind of thing doesn't happen like ev—"

"Four times."

"What?" I breathe, looking over at him.

"It was four times, not once." He clarifies.

"Four?"

"Four," he repeats, turning onto our block.

And I don't remember even one time. "Was it even good?" I ask without thinking.

"The best I've ever had," he says immediately.

"I was a virgin," I whisper, wondering how the heck I could possibly be the best he ever had when I had never done it before.

"I know, and it kills me that you don't remember."

"Well," I mutter, having no clue what to say now.

"I guarantee you will remember the next time," he says as he pulls into the driveway and shuts down the engine.

Oh wow, okay.

Without another word, he gets out, comes around to help me down, and then leads me inside and upstairs. Pulling his hand when we reach the top landing, his eyes come to me. "That's my room," I tell him with a nod of my head toward my door.

"You're sleeping with me."

"Um..."

"Sleep, Mags."

"I..." I mutter trying to come up with something to say.

"Let's go." He tugs my hand. I follow him past my door and into his room then into his bathroom where he set's up his toothbrush for me. Without a word I brush my teeth while watching him watch me in the mirror. When I finish I watch as he uses his toothbrush. When he's done, he takes my hand again, letting it go when I'm standing at the side of the bed. I watch him kick off his shoes and pull his shirt off over his head. "Come here." He takes a seat on the side of the bed then drags me to stand between his spread thighs.

"What are you doing?" I ask as he unbuttons my shorts and slides them down over my hips, letting them fall to the floor leaving me in a pair of cotton boy shorts.

"You need sleep," he mutters, pulling my sweater off my shoulders, letting it join my shorts, and then he runs his hands up my back, under my tank, unhooking my bra.

"Sven," I whisper to the top of his head.

"Just sleep, I promise, baby." He kisses my stomach then reaches under the strap of my tank top to slide my bra straps down my arms. He pulls each of my hands out gently before coasting his up my stomach, under my tank, making my muscles tense as he grasp the front of my bra and pulls it out, dropping it to the ground.

Okay, that was hot...seriously hot, I think, as the space between my legs tingles.

Standing, he puts his fingers to the button of his jeans then pushes them down and kicks them to the side. My eyes automatically go to his waist then drop to his very aroused manhood.

Holy cow.

"Not tonight."

Lifting my eyes to his, I swallow then squeak as he pulls me down with him into the bed and adjusts us until my head his pillowed against his chest. Tugging the blankets over us, he then reaches over, picks up the remote for the light, and hits the button, turning the room dark.

"Sleep, baby."

I want to tell him I'm not tired or that there is no possible way I will be able to sleep, but my eyes grow heavy, and before I know it, I'm asleep exactly where I want to be.

Chapter 6

Sven

Truth be told

LYING WITH MAGGIE in my arms, her soft breathing letting me know she's asleep, I squeeze my eyes closed. It's not safe for her to be with me right now, but the idea of her being anywhere else is enough to drive me mad. Paulie Amidio, the mob boss for Lacamo, is sure to put two and two together with Kai's sudden return to life and Paulie's son being dead. Regardless of the fact his son was going to take him out, he will want revenge for his death. I trust Kai and Kenton. I know both men want to put an end to Paulie's rein of terror, but until he's taken out and his power extinguished, no one is safe, including Maggie. And that's not okay with me, which means I need to take every precaution necessary to make sure she stays safe.

Pulling her closer to me, her warmth settles into my skin helping me drift off to sleep.

WAKING TO THE soft, warm woman in my arms, her ass cradled against my thighs, my hands full of her curves, and the scent of her in my nose, I regret that I have to get up soon. All I really want to do is roll her to her back and listen to her breath hitch, like it did every time I slid into her. I wasn't lying when I said she's the best I've ever had. Her body alone is enough to bring me to my knees, but the way she looks at me, the way she says my name, and the feel of her skin against mine all give me something I didn't know I was missing when it came to sex. Something I didn't care about before her, an intimacy that made being with her almost unbearable.

My possessiveness when it comes to her is an emotion I never expected to experience firsthand, and nothing could have ever prepared me for it. I knew I wanted Maggie when I first met her, but after feeling my first bite of jealousy, I knew what I was feeling for her was more than just infatuation and lust. I knew I would do everything within my power to make sure she never looked at or touched another man again. I knew I would do whatever necessary to make sure she was mine. I just didn't realize the walls I thought I built up around myself were nothing compared to the walls she has around her. She guards herself so closely, never allowing herself to be vulnerable for anyone. But I won't accept anything less than all of her. I want her—no, *need* her—to feel for me what I feel for her.

Turning in my arms, her face goes into my chest and my eyes drop down to see if she's awake, only to find her eyes closed, her dark lashes resting against her cheeks, her mouth in a soft pout. Kissing her forehead, I wrap my arms tighter around her and rest my chin on top of her head. I'm not happy about the shit I have to do today, but knowing what could've happened had I not shown up at the club when I did has had me on edge since yesterday afternoon when I woke with her in my bed with tears of confusion and horror in her beautiful eyes.

Regardless of the fact things worked out in my favor, someone is going to pay for what's been done. Then I have the issue of figuring out who the fuck the chick was in my house last night, how she got in, and who sent her. If Maggie wasn't Maggie, that whole fucked up situation could have lead me to losing her before she ever realized she's mine, and that is not okay with me.

Hearing her moan my name as her legs move restlessly against the sheet, I pull my head back to look down at her and watch as her nipples press against her tank top and her legs twitch again. Running my hand down her side and over the curve of her hip, I pull her closer, hearing her moan once more.

"Baby," I whisper against her ear, only to have her whimper. Then her body stills and my head dips, finding her eyes open on me, a deeper honey color than I've ever seen, giving me an inkling of what she was dreaming of. "You were dreaming."

"I…" She squeezes her eyes closed and her chest heaves.

Rolling her to her back, I wrap my hand around her calf and pull it up around my hip. Kissing her mouth, her cheek, and then her ear, I whisper, "What were you dreaming about?"

"I don't remember," she murmurs her lie as her hands slide up my sides and her head dips back into the pillow, allowing me access to the curve of her throat.

"You do," I tell her, dragging my tongue up her throat, and then ask, "Was I doing that?"

"No," she moans, and I grind my erection against her.

"Hmm, what about this?" I coast my hand up her thigh, along the curve of her waist, and cup her breast, running my thumb across her nipple. Her back arches off the bed and her eyes open to meet mine.

"I…I don't remember," she whimpers, raising her hands to my shoulders then one smoothly up the side of my neck, into the back of my hair. Lowering my mouth down onto hers, I kiss her bottom lip then slide my tongue across the seam of her mouth as I pinch her nipple between two fingers. I use her gasp to slip my tongue between her lips, touching hers. Moaning into my mouth, I side my hand up then down under her tank and cup her breast in my palm.

"Oh, God," she cries into my mouth as I roll her nipple.

Kissing down her throat, I bend my head and pull her nipple into my mouth, sucking hard, loving that my marks are still there. Her legs lift and wrap around my ass, and my free hand moves between her legs, sliding over her panties, feeling the wetness on the material as my fingers pass over it. Pressing my cock into the bed, I raise my head to look at her then slide along the inner seam of her underwear, and groan when my fingers slip through her slick heat.

"You're so wet, Mags, so fucking wet for me," I praise, gliding my finger around her clit, causing her hips to buck.

"Sven."

"I'm right here." I pull her nipple back into my mouth then move to her other breast and do the same.

"Please," she cries while my fingers glide down, one then two, entering her and feeling her clamp down on them like a vise. "So tight, so fucking hot." I rise up, taking her mouth again, freeing my cock from my boxers, and move her panties to the side to slide the tip over her clit then down, putting just the head inside. Pulling back, I watch her eyes go half-mast and listen to her breath hitch as I press fully into her, gritting my teeth against the exquisite pleasure of having her wrapped around me. Leaning back on my knees, I pull her forward to tug her top off over her head then lean forward again, pulling out then sinking back in.

"Jesus, fucking, heaven." Wrapping my fist around her hair, I tilt her head back and take her mouth again.

"What...?" she whimpers as I pull out of her and sit back on my calves.

"Shhh," I hush, sliding her panties over her hips and down her thighs, dropping them to the bed. I kick off my shorts and move between her legs again, wrapping them over my arms, then dip my face to pull her nipple into my mouth, sliding into her at the same time. Releasing her nipple with a pop, her hands wrap around my shoulders and her head falls back onto the bed while her eyes slide closed.

"Look at me, Maggie," I demand, and her head tips down, her eyes meeting mine. "So beautiful, baby, you're so fucking gorgeous taking my cock, taking all of me," I praise her, sliding out then back in slowly.

"Faster, please," she whispers, running her hand down my chest and over my abs.

"Just like this," I whisper back, focusing on her face.

I swallow when her hand wraps around the side of my neck and her gaze locks on mine while her eyes fill with tears. "Don't cry." I drop her legs then my forehead to hers, never losing eye contact as I sink into her slowly, sliding my cock along her walls, feeling them ripple and tighten around me.

"Oh…" she whimpers, bringing her legs higher around my hips, forcing me impossibly deeper.

It takes everything in me not to slam into her, but I want this moment, I want her to have a memory of what it was like our first time. I want her to know without words how much she means to me. "Let yourself go, baby." I kiss away the tears as they fall from her eyes. "Give yourself to me completely, Mags."

"I…I don't know if I can," she whispers, and I know she's talking about more than just this moment, but I'm not willing to accept anything less than all of her.

"You can. Trust me and let go," I tell her softly, watching again as tears fill her beautiful eyes, eyes that hold me captive as she loses herself, clutching her arms and legs tighter around me as she rides out her orgasm. Burying my face in her hair, I lose myself deep inside her.

Mine! My mind screams as I roll to my back, taking her with me, never losing our connection as she falls limply against my chest. Roaming my hands over her smooth skin, I kiss the top of her head and close my eyes trying to get my heart rate and breathing under control.

"I get flashes. I'm not sure if they are real or not," she says quietly, and my hands still. "I remember laughing when you…when you were marking me."

"That happened," I tell her, moving my hands again.

"I…" She lets out a long, deep breath then raises her head to rest her chin on my chest. "I hate that I don't remember."

Running my fingers down her jaw, I watch her eyes slide half closed. "We'll make new memories," I assure her, adjusting my hips, leaving her warmth, but then dragging the blanket over us.

"We'll also make a baby if I don't get on birth control," she mutters, looking over my shoulder at the pillow. Feeling my mouth lift, I run my fingers along her bottom lip, gaining her eyes again. I could think of worse things than her having my child, but she was right; we don't need a baby, at least not yet. "I'll make sure we're more careful from now on."

"Thanks," she whispers, and I study her beautiful face then ask the question that has been plaguing me.

"How were you still a virgin?" I didn't know there were such thing as virgins, at least not in this day and age, not women older than nineteen at most. If she hadn't told me she was before I slid into her, I wouldn't have known. She is far too beautiful and far too seductive; hell, looking at her, all you can think about is sex.

"I didn't have sex," she says, pressing her lips together to keep from smiling. Tugging a piece of her hair, I wait for her to answer my question. "I don't know. I guess it has a lot to do with my parents." Feeling my body turn to granite, she shakes her head. "They never did anything to me. They just…" She pauses then searches my face for a moment.

"Sex was never made to seem like a big deal. When I was sixteen, they told me I was free to make my own choices about my body and what I did with it. They made it so casual that it scared me. My parents have both had relationships outside of their marriage. I mean, I know they love each other and they were honest about what they were or are doing, but I didn't understand. I still don't understand how they made it seem like it wasn't a big deal to share a piece of themselves with someone they didn't or don't care about." She pauses, pulling in a breath.

"The few times I've been close to losing control, something in me couldn't let go and I would pull away. I know it's stupid and unrealistic this day and age, but after a while, I got it in my head that I would only ever give myself completely to the man I planned on marrying," she says as her cheeks grow pink and her bottom lip goes between her teeth.

"You didn't close down with me," I tell her, not even referring to the first time, but to this time.

"No, even my subconscious knows what you are to me," she says softly, raising her hand to my jaw.

"And what's that?" I ask gently, studying her features as they move over mine.

"I'm not sure. Important. Vital. Even if we don't last, I know I'll never regret giving myself to you," she says, and my chest aches because I know I'm not worthy of her, not even close. But she needs to know that what she has given me means something to me.

"Sex has never meant anything to me. It's always been just a release, a way to get rid of pent-up energy. I never knew it could be more," I tell her, watching her eyes grow soft. "Being with you is something different, a completely different experience, one that takes sex to a whole new level. Makes me feel connected to you in a way that transcends time."

"What?" she whispers in awe, and her face softens in a way I have never seen before.

"I didn't wait for you, baby, but you have a piece of me no one else does." I take her hand, resting it over my heart.

"Sven." Her forehead drops to my chest, and I wrap my arms around her and roll her to her side.

Holding her, I look at the clock and let out a frustrated breath. "I wish I didn't need to get up, but I need to go to the club."

"I'll go with you," she says, starting to pull away.

"No, you're staying home."

"Sven…"

Before she can say anything, I roll her to her back, smooth her hair out of her face, and settle my hands under her jaw. "I need to know you're safe. This isn't something that's up for debate. Until I've discussed what happened yesterday with Zack, Lane, and Teo and get their feedback about the situation, I'm not willing to let you step foot in the club."

"I can take care of myself," she growls, and I drop a kiss to her pouty lips then lean back and grin.

"I didn't say you couldn't take care of yourself, Maggie. I know you're a fighter." I smile then shake my head. "I don't want you to have to fight, and I don't want something to happen to you that I can prevent. Last night, you were drugged. I know we're good now, but this situation could have been completely different had I not shown up at the club when I did." My gut twists and I pull in a breath. "I fucking hate thinking about it like this, baby, but I took you when you didn't know what you were doing."

"Sven," she whispers, bringing her hand up running her fingers along my jaw.

Turning my head, I press a kiss to her palm. "It's true, baby. Fucked up, but true."

"Okay, I'll stay home," she agrees, and I can tell she doesn't want to, but is doing it for me.

"Good, now kiss me. I gotta shower," I tell her, watching her eyes heat in a way that makes me groan and my cock grow hard once more. Pulling her toward me, I wrap a fist in her hair and force her head to the side, kissing her until she's breathing heavy and clawing at my chest. Slowing down, I pull away with once last nibble to her lips. "While I'm gone, I want you thinking about what I'm going to do to you when I get home," I growl, pulling her breast into my mouth, leaving another hickey before reluctantly leaving her in bed.

As soon as I walk through the door of the club, all eyes come to me. Seeing the concern on the faces of my employees, I walk toward their small huddle around the bar.

"Where's Maggie?" Eva asks, looking toward the door.

"Home, she won't be in today," I tell her, and her hands wring together in front of her as her eyes fill with worry when they lift to meet mine.

"I called, but she didn't answer," she whispers.

"She was getting in the shower when I left. I'm sure she'll call you back when she checks her phone," I assure, not positive if I'm lying. I know Maggie wants to believe Eva is her friend, but after last night, she has doubts about who she can trust. And as fucked up as it is, that works for me. Between what happened with Maggie and things coming to a head with Paulie and his crew, the list of people I know I can trust is small, and growing smaller by the second.

"If she doesn't, will you tell her I'm worried about her?" she asks, straightening her shoulders.

"I'll let her know," I mutter then look at Zack, Teo, and Lane. "We need to talk," I tell them, leaving the bar, knowing they're following without looking. Getting to my office, I slip off my jacket and toss it on the couch then wait for all of them to enter. As soon as the door is closed, the vibe in the room changes.

"Is Maggie okay?" Lane asks first, breaking the silence. Studying him, I notice his eyes are full of worry, a worry that matches Zack's and Teo's. My woman has made an impression with these guys, and I know the concern I see is out of care for her, but the jealousy in the pit of my stomach still bubbles to the surface.

"She's home in our bed, resting," I tell him, letting the words speak for themselves.

"Fucking told you," Teo mutters, looking at Lane and Zack.

"Told them what?" I question, crossing my arms over my chest and raising a brow.

"You said *our* bed, meaning a bed you share. I told these fucks that you and her were together. I knew." He grins then mutters, "You fucks owe me a hundred each."

Pressing my fingers to the bridge of my nose, I let out a breath then lift my eyes to Teo and narrow them. "As entertaining as it is to know you're betting on my relationship, we need to talk about Maggie and what happened," I growl, and the energy in the room instantly shifts once more. "I looked over the tapes and didn't come across anything out of the ordinary. I know from the timestamp that Maggie got to the bar a little after one, and she didn't move from her seat until I came in."

"She was at the bar the whole time. Lane and I made sure no one approached her while she was sitting there," Zack says, and I nod my thanks to him.

"No one even got close," Lane agrees, crossing his arms over his broad chest.

"Eva got close," I say, looking between the three of them.

"Why would she drug her?" Teo asks as his brows draw together in confusion.

"I don't know," I finally mutter, running my fingers through my hair.

"She's the only one who would've had a chance. I watched the tapes a hundred times. Marco was down at the opposite end of the bar the whole night. He didn't even acknowledge Maggie, except to give her a chin lift when she first sat down. No one else had an opportunity."

"I agree Eva is the only one who had the opportunity, but what would be her motive?" Teo asks the million-dollar question, the question that has been plaguing me since I saw the tapes.

"I'm not sure. That's what I need to find out."

"So what are we going to do until we find out?" Zack asks as I walk to the window that looks down over the club floor.

"Maggie isn't going to sit at home while I figure this shit out," I mutter to myself, hearing them chuckle behind me, and I can't help but smile, even though I'm annoyed. Regardless of her understanding this morning, there is no way she will be willing to sit at home until it's safe for her to come back here.

Turning around to face them once more, I study each of them. A friend of mine, Nico Mayson, knew Zack, Lane, and Teo from his bounty hunting days. He handpicked each of them to work for me after he found out my previously hired security was helping filter drugs into the club for Paulie, taking a cut from the sale of product and the recruitment of girls. Luckily, I caught that shit in the early stages before my club was overran and I was forced out, or worse—shut down. Being in Vegas means you're constantly watching your back; people are always trying to make money any way they can, and that includes using you when you don't even know your being used.

"I'm gonna put a call in to a friend of mine to see if he can dig up anything on Eva. In the meantime, I want you guys to keep an eye on her when she's here, and tell me if you notice anything out of the ordinary with her."

"No problem," they all agree as I take a seat in my chair, and they head for the door.

"And guys, if Maggie's here, make sure she doesn't get into any kind of trouble," I add, hearing them laugh as the door closes behind them.

Pulling my cell out of my pocket, I press send on Justin's number and wait for him to pick up. Justin is not only a friend of mine, but he's a computer guru who is somehow able to find shit out that I'm sure would scare our biggest government agencies. He not only works for Kenton, doing intel and searches; he also runs an online group called the Winds of the North, a group of online hackers and activists who help to shut down terrorists and extremists through their websites.

"Seven-Eleven," he greets after the second ring, making me chuckle, but his next words make me see red and cause my blood to boil. "You sent my gift away from your house without a word. What the fuck, man? She was paid for and everything."

"You motherfucker," I roar, feeling the pulse in my neck beat against the collar of my shirt.

"What?" he asks casually.

"How the fuck did she get into my house, Justin?"

"I let her in," he mutters like *duh*, which only serves to piss me off even more.

"Maggie is the one who opened the door and found her there," I whisper, because otherwise I'm going to blow the window out of my office. I swear if he was in front of me, I would kill him.

"Did you and Maggie sort your shit out?" he asks, and I pull the phone away from my ear and look at it, wondering how the fuck this guy is able to do the shit he does when he's obviously stupid as fuck.

"Me and Maggie are none of your fucking concern."

"I'm taking that as a yes. So you can just tell me thank you."

"Why the fuck would I tell you thank you, motherfucker?"

"I helped you guys get past your stupid issues, and now you're to-gether," he says, the smile evident in his voice.

"Maggie was roofied. I didn't know that shit, and we got together while she was drugged. The next morning, she took off on me and went to her old apartment. I waited outside her place and must have fallen asleep for a second, because when I opened my eyes, her car was gone. She got home before I did, and when she walked in, there was a random piece in our house. So please forgive me for not fucking telling you thanks for your fuck-up."

"What?" he whispers in distress.

"Yeah, now you're getting it," I growl, standing from my desk so I can pace the floor of my office.

"Fuck, man, is she okay? I saw her on the feed for her apartment, but I just thought you guys had a fight. I wanted to help, man. I swear I never would have done that shit otherwise." Hearing the genuine concern in his tone does a little to alleviate the anger I'm feeling, but just a little.

"She's fine now. Yesterday, fuck no she wasn't okay, and thank fuck she believed me when I said I didn't know who the chick was in the house or how she got there."

"I'll tell her it was me."

"What the fuck is that going to do?" I roll my eyes and rub my forehead.

"Okay, good point," he mutters under his breath.

"From now on, keep to your profession, 'cause your matchmaking skills are lacking severely."

"Got it," he agrees.

"You owe me, man, and I expect you to pay up," I tell him. Normally, I pay Justin for his services, but this one is going to be on him.

"Anything, just tell me what you need."

"I need you to find me whatever you can on Eva Locklear. She works the bar here at the club and—"

"You think she has something to do with your girl getting drugged?" he asks, cutting me off, and I hear him typing through the phone.

"They're friends, but she's the only one who would have had a chance to do it. I watched the tapes, and no one else had an opportuni-ty."

"Got it," he mutters, distracted.

"Have you found out anything new on Maggie's sister?" I question, sitting back down.

After the men broke into Maggie's apartment, looking for her sister, I put in a call to Justin to see if he could find out anything on her whereabouts. His search came up empty-handed; she didn't have any cards in her name and wasn't working, and her friend she hung out with was a dead end as well.

I couldn't honestly give a fuck about the woman, but until she turns up and cleans up her mess, Maggie is in danger. Plus, I know it's hurting my woman that her sister is in danger, and that's enough for me to put my own personal feelings aside to look for her.

"Nada, she's still ghost, and it's been two weeks since I've seen her on the camera I put up at the apartment."

"Fuck." I run a hand through my hair.

"I'm in Vegas, and I'll be here for a few days, so I'll see if I can find out anything on the street about her."

"I'd appreciate that."

"No problem, and I'm sorry about your girl."

"Thanks, man," I grumble. If Justin was anyone else, I would hunt his ass down, but I know him and know that in his fucked up way, he really thought he was helping.

"I'll message you what I find."

"Sounds good." I hang up and look at the clock. "It's gonna be a long fucking night."

WALKING INTO THE house, the light in the foyer is on, and I smile, knowing Maggie left it that way so it wouldn't be pitch black when I walked inside.

Walking toward the kitchen, I stop in my tracks when I find her asleep on the couch with a book held loosely in her grasp. Taking the book from her, I set it on the coffee table then sit on the edge of the couch and run my finger down her cheek. Her eyes open slowly, and she looks confused for a moment then smiles softly.

"Hey," she whispers, bringing her hand up to my jaw.

"Hey," I whisper back, taking her hand, kissing her fingers, which curl around mine.

"I fell asleep," she tells me and I grin.

"I see that. Did you eat?"

Rolling her eyes, she sits up and mutters, "Yes," and I lean forward, kissing her before pulling back and searching her face, loving the way her eyes soften every time my mouth leaves hers.

"I didn't eat. Do you want to hang in the kitchen with me while I find something?" I ask.

"I made dinner. It's in the oven on warm." She smiles, pushing my hands away as they make their way under the edge of her shirt.

"You made dinner?"

"I did, but it's vegetarian."

"Is it tofu?"

"No." She smiles, standing from the couch. "It's eggplant parmesan."

"I've never had it," I admit as she takes my hand and leads me toward the kitchen. Turning on the light, she leads me to the table then pushes me to take a seat, running away quickly when I try to pull her down on my lap.

"You need to eat. No funny business, mister."

"I missed you," I tell her as she goes to the stove and opens it. Her eyes come to me and go soft once more.

"I missed you, too," she grumbles like she shouldn't have missed me, which only makes me grin. Pulling a plate out of the oven, she then goes to the fridge and grabs a bowl, pulling a piece of saran wrap off of it before grabbing the plate and bringing both to me. "What would you like to drink?" she asks, going to step away after setting the plate and bowl in front of me.

Grabbing her hand, I stop her and pull her back to stand between my legs. "Kiss me," I demand, wrapping my hands around her waist. I wait for her to touch her mouth to mine then fist my hand in her hair at the back of her neck to keep her in place. I take over, nipping her lip until her mouth opens so my tongue can slide between her lips. The first touch of her tongue against mine and her taste flooding my mouth are enough to bring me from hard to painfully erect. I can't get enough of her taste, and the thought of eating her instead of food is sounding better by the second.

"You need to eat," she breathes against my mouth, trying to pull away.

"Come sit on the table and feed me then," I take her mouth again then adjust my legs, sliding one between hers while pulling her down so she's straddling my thigh. Feeling the heat of her pussy through my slacks drives me to take the kiss deeper.

"Sven!" she cries as I move us to the floor and slip her shirt off over her head.

"Shhhh." I grab both of her wrists and pull them up above her head. "Keep them there," I tell her, kissing her neck then down over the edge of her lace bra, over her stomach, then along the edge of her cotton shorts.

Grabbing the waist, I drag them down her ass and sit back long enough to pull them off her legs. Spreading her thighs wide, I take in the beauty of her body then duck my head to run my tongue up her center, collecting her sweet taste on my tongue. "Fuck, I could live off your essence alone and never go hungry."

"Oh, God." Looking up her body, I see her eyes are closed and her chest is rising and falling quickly. Licking up her center again and again, I build her up until I know she's right on the brink then slide two fingers into her and suck her clit into my mouth, pulling hard until she's screaming and flooding my mouth. Grabbing a condom out of my pocket, I make quick work of my pants and slide it on, adjusting her hips and burying myself deep within her.

Dropping my head forward, I breathe in through my nose, trying to control the urge to come. Her tight heat is still pulsing with her orgasm, squeezing my cock in rapid succession.

"Sven," she gasps, lifting her legs, wrapping them around my back.

"Fuck, baby, that's not helping. You wrapped around me, feeling your pussy gripping me like it never wants to let me go, is driving me to the brink of losing control," I confess on a groan, pulling out slowly as her walls try to grab and drag me back in. Grabbing her hands, I keep them above her, pressed to the floor.

As I rock in and out of her slowly at first, I then pick up the pace, dipping my head and rolling my tongue around her nipple, and then bite the tip and tug. Her core tightening and her loud moan have me kissing across her chest to her other nipple, rolling my tongue around it and biting the tip, tugging it, too. Her loud cries and the way her head starts to thrash tell me that she's close. Holding her wrists with one hand, I glide my fingers down her side then move them between her legs, strumming her clit.

Her scream fills the house and I slam my mouth down over hers, groaning down her throat as my own orgasm suddenly crashes over me. As I release her wrists, her arms wrap around my shoulders, and she lifts her head, burying her face against my neck.

"You okay, baby?" I question, turning my mouth toward her ear.

"Yeah," she breathes as I pull her face back so I can see her eyes.

"Good," I whisper softly, pulling out of her slowly, hearing her mewl of loss. Kissing her forehead then her lips, I help her up then smile when she turns and abruptly drops to her hands and knees, turning red as she looks around.

"What are you doing?"

"The blinds are open," she hisses, crawling toward her shirt on the floor. Groaning, I feel myself get hard once more as I watch her ass bounce. Grabbing her shirt, I hand it to her, slip off the condom, and adjust my pants. I go to the blinds in the dining room and close them while she puts on her shorts. "Your food is probably cold now." She frowns as I toss the condom in the garbage.

"It was worth it," I mutter, wrapping my arms around her waist when she brings my plate to the microwave. "Actually, I'm not even hungry anymore," I nip her neck, making her giggle a sound I don't think I've ever heard her make, a noise I love so much that I plan on making her make it more often.

"You're too much," she whispers, dipping her head as my mouth licks over her skin.

"You love it."

"Maybe a little," she agrees, turning in my arms and getting up on her tiptoes. Her hands run through my hair and I pause just to look at her. I never knew I could have this and feel content. The idea of loving anyone in the past would have sent me into a panic, but Maggie makes it easy. Everything about her makes being with her easy. "Why are you looking at me like that?" she asks quietly.

"You're perfect."

"Not even close," she murmurs with a shake of her head. Running her fingertips across my jaw, she whispers, "Perfect is unattainable and an unrealistic expectation. No one is perfect, and if you think they are, you will be let down when you see they are flawed, just like everyone else."

Studying her face and hearing her words, I know she's right, but she's also very fucking wrong. She's perfect for me. I just hope I can be the same for her.

Chapter 7
Maggie
Choices

MY STEP FLOUNDERS as I walk into the bathroom and see Sven wearing his loose basketball shorts, standing shirtless at the sink with his toothbrush in his mouth. Moving my eyes down his chest and abs, I feel a flutter in my lower belly and a tingle between my legs, reminding me of what he did to my body not fifteen minutes ago. Moving my eyes back up to his face, he smiles around the brush in his mouth, looking all too smug.

"Nice shirt," he mutters through the foam in his mouth as I slide up next to him, pulling out my toothbrush from the cup next to the sink.

Six weeks ago when we became an us, we moved all of my stuff into his room, a room that is now ours.

"Thanks." I fight my smile and a shiver when his eyes heat and rake over me. When I finally got up enough energy to pull myself out of bed, where he left me still panting for breath, I grabbed his shirt and slipped it on.

"I really like the lace," he tells me—something I already know, as his hand smoothes over my ass and I inhale at his touch. The lacy boy shorts I have on are the same ones I put on this morning, only to have them removed a few minutes later when Sven tossed *me* onto the bed then tossed *them* to the floor.

"You need to go to work," I remind him quietly, as he moves to stand behind me and slides his hands over his shirt around my waist then up under my breasts.

"I know." He frowns, running his hands down to settle on the curve of my waist. "You're not putting up much of a fight about staying home." He's right. I'm not. Him telling me I should take the day off fits with what I need to do today. Last night, I got a message from my sister asking me to meet her. I know if I tell him about the message, he will likely flip out and do something ridiculous like forbid me from going to see her. I don't want that, not right now, not when things seem to be going in a direction I like. *A lot.*

I know ignorance is not always bliss, but in this case, I have to believe that what Sven doesn't know can't hurt him, and judging by his previous comments regarding my sister, that's exactly what will happen if I tell him she contacted me and that I want to meet with her. Hell, when I told him I wanted to keep my old apartment in case she needed somewhere to stay, he was pissed. He didn't think I needed to do anything for her, not after what happened, but I can't turn my back on my sister; I just can't.

"I know you're worried about me and I don't want you to worry," I lie, and his eyes move across my face in the mirror then settle on mine. Fighting the urge to look away or squirm, I hold his gaze and my breath.

"Thanks, baby."

Guilt instantly washes over me at his words, and I drop my eyes and place my hands over his, mumbling a quiet, "You're welcome."

"Do you want to shower with me?"

Feeling my lips lift slightly, I shake my head then raise my eyes to look at him once more. "I better not. You're going to be late."

"You're right, but seeing how I'm the boss, I think I can make an excuse."

Rolling my eyes at that one, I turn in his arms and rest my hands against his abs. "Go shower. I'll make you coffee," I tell him, kissing the underside of his jaw, only to have him pull me back against him and kiss me properly before releasing me and dropping his shorts to the floor. Swallowing, I watch his cock bounce against his stomach.

"You're looking at me like you want to get wet with me." He smiles, and I take a step back then another, and then run out of the bathroom, leaving him laughing behind me.

HEADING ACROSS THE parking lot toward the Starbucks where I told my sister to meet me, I scan the lot, looking for anyone out of place. My stomach is a jumbled mess and my nerves are on edge from not only lying to Sven, but from knowing I'm about to see my sister for the first time in months. I know I shouldn't exactly trust her after what she's done in the past, but I really hope she's ready to tell me she wants to get some real help this time, the kind of help only a professional can give her.

Pulling open the door, the overpowering smell of coffee assaults me, making my stomach roll. Scanning the patrons, I spot Morgan sitting at a small round table in the back near the restrooms. I didn't think it was possible for her to lose any more weight, but she has. The black tank top she has on shows off her extremely thin arms, and the jean shorts she's wearing give me a view of her legs, which are so thin I can make out the bones of her knees and ankles.

Making my way toward her, I feel myself pale; she looks frail and sick. Her skin has lost its golden hue and is now a greyish color, and her hair is so thin I can see her scalp. Long gone is the beautiful girl who would turn heads as she walked down the sidewalk, and in her place is someone I don't even recognize.

"Maggie," she whispers, standing to greet me with a hug. Hugging her back, my arms can almost wrap around her twice and tears burn the back of my eyes. Releasing me, she takes a step back.

"God, you look awesome, Maggie, totally fucking awesome." She smiles, but I still catch the sadness and pain in her eyes as she speaks.

"Thanks," I mutter, feeling guilty for every ounce of happiness I've felt over the last few months—months she's obviously been slowly deteriorating.

"Do you want coffee?" she asks, taking a seat.

"No, thanks," I reply, sitting across from her. We both stare at each other for a long time, and I have no idea what to say. I want to yell at her for being selfish, but I also want to tell her I miss her so much. Not the Morgan she's become over the last few years, but the Morgan who helped me get even with my first boyfriend when I found out he kissed another girl, the Morgan I could tell anything to, the Morgan who was my best friend.

"Thanks for meeting with me," she says quietly and I nod. "I want to get help," she blurts loudly, so loudly that a few of the people around us stop to look at us.

"You want to get help?" I repeat quietly, not able to keep the surprise or doubt out of my voice.

"I know I've messed up."

"Yeah," I agree. I'm not going to coddle or sugarcoat things for her this time. I always do that, and it never, ever works. "You could have gotten me killed."

"I...I'm...I'm sorry. I wish I could change that," she whispers as my phone in my purse rings. Pulling it out, I look at the screen and see Sven's calling. Pressing the silence button, I squeeze the phone in my hand and feel my heart rate speed up. "If you need to take that, it's okay," she says, studying me. I really, really do not want to answer the phone. I really don't, but I also don't want Sven to worry. Sliding my finger across the screen, I place the phone to my ear.

"He—" I drop my eyes from my sister to my lap as he cuts me off.

"Where are you, Maggie?"

I can tell he's not asking like he needs to know. He's asking to see if I will lie about it. How he knows where I am, I have no idea, but I can tell he does.

"Starbucks," I reply, biting my lip when I hear something on his end of the phone slam down, and I know without even being in the same room with him that it's his fist hitting the top of his desk.

"Who are you with?"

"Sven…"

"Who the fuck are you with, Maggie?" he asks quietly, and I swallow.

"My sister."

"Jesus, what the fuck are you thinking?!" he roars, and I see my sister jump at the sound.

"Can I call you back when I leave here?"

"Call me when you get in your car then come straight here," he demands.

"I—"

"Call me when you get in your car then come straight here," he repeats, and I feel my spine stiffen at his tone, but I know now is not the time to get into it with him.

"Okay," I agree and his phone goes off, and I know he hung up without even a goodbye.

"Who was that?" Morgan asks as I drop my phone back into my purse.

"My boyfriend," I tell her while my insides twist into a knot, because that may not be the case for very long.

"He sounds like a dick," she states.

I glare at her then hiss, "He's worried."

"He still sounds like a dick, and why would he be worried?"

"I don't know Morgan, maybe because you have a tendency to bring trouble with you wherever you go," I bite out sarcastically.

"That's not fair," she whispers, and I run my palm across my forehead and notice my hands are shaking.

Trying to get my thoughts together, I close my eyes then open them back up to look at her. "You said you want to get help, so what is your plan?"

"I need to borrow some money so I can get it back to Carmine, and then I'll go into rehab."

"Morgan." I close my eyes again and feel myself deflate.

"Maggie," she calls, and I open my eyes once more to look at her. "I know you don't have much of a reason to believe me or trust me, but this time I really do want to get help."

Studying her, I see the truth in her gaze, or maybe I'm only seeing what I want to see. "How much?" I hear myself ask, and watch relief flood her features.

"Fourteen thousand."

"Fourteen thousand?" I choke.

"I know it's a lot of money, but once I finish rehab, I swear I'll pay you back, every penny."

"Morgan, I just…I just don't know. That's a lot of money to just give to you."

"I don't have anyone else to ask," she whispers, dropping her eyes to the coffee cup on the table which she's turning slowly around and around.

My heart twists in my chest as I watch her. If I don't help her she could really end up dead. If I do help her, she could run with the money and end up dead anyway. *This is a double-edged sword if there ever was one.*

"You're going to have to follow me to the bank. I don't have that kind of cash on me," I say, and the cup stops turning, her eyes meeting mine and are flooding with relief. "Morgan, this is it. This is the last time. I love you, but I can't keep doing the same dance with you. If you don't get help this time…" I shake my head, letting the unspoken words hang between us.

"I know," she whispers.

Letting out a long breath, I stand from the table. "How did you get here?"

"Amy dropped me," she mutters then continues when she reads the look of distaste on my face, "I've been staying with her the last few days."

"Morgan—"

"Don't say it, okay? I already know what you're going to say, but you don't need to."

"Fine, you can ride with me," I tell her, pulling my bag closer to my body. Once we're in my car and on our way to the bank, my phone rings again, but I ignore it knowing without looking that it's Sven. If I tell him what I'm doing now, not only will he be pissed, he will be *PISSED*, and I can't deal with that right now.

"Do you want me to come in with you?" Morgan asks as I park in front of the bank.

Looking at her, I turn off my car and shake my head. "I'll be back. I don't know how long this is going to take."

"I'll be here," she mumbles as I slam the door. It takes surprisingly less time than I thought it would to get the money. I don't know why I thought it would be a process, or that I would have to sit down with a banker, but all I had to do was go the teller and tell them how much I needed, show ID, and sign off on the amount.

When I walk back out to the car, I see Amy standing next to the passenger side door of my car, talking to Morgan through the open window. Ignoring her, I get back into the car, trying to keep myself in check.

"Hi, Maggie," Amy says, but all I can do is mutter a quiet acknowledgement back before asking, "Can you give me a minute to talk to Morgan?"

"Um, sure," she agrees, looking between the two of us before stepping back. Rolling up Morgan's window, I turn in my seat to face her fully.

"I asked her to come. She said she would give me a ride. I don't want you mixed up any more than you have been," she tells me before I can tell her how much her hanging with Amy will kill any chance of her getting better.

Pulling out the envelope from my bag, I hold it out to her but keep it in my grasp as I tell her quietly, "This is it, Morgan. I can't do this again. I *won't* do this again, so if you go back on your word this time, we're done."

"I know," she whispers, taking the envelope from me. "As soon as it's done, I'll call you and tell you where I am."

"Sure," I agree, not really believing her, but hoping she's being honest all the same.

"Promise." She holds her pinky out to me. Feeling tears fill my eyes, I place my pinky around hers and hold her eyes. Releasing me, she gets out of the car quickly without saying another word. I wait there for a few minutes until she and Amy are long gone then pull out of the parking spot and head toward downtown, praying Sven will understand why I had to help her.

"You didn't call," Sven informs me in a tone I've never heard from him before as I push through the threshold into his office.

I take him in as he sits at his desk with a pen in his hand and his head bent toward a paper before him, but his eyes don't lift to meet mine, not even as I close the door and mutter, "I know, I—"

"Did you know this morning you were going to go meet up with your sister?" he asks, cutting me off before I can finish my sentence.

"I did," I tell him truthfully, freezing in place when his eyes finally lift to meet mine.

"I'm so fucking mad at you right now," he whispers, and I sink into the chair in front of him, at a loss for words. I knew he would be mad, but this is more than mad, and more than pissed. The warmth he normally holds in his eyes for me is gone, and in its place is a completely blank look, one that scares me more than his anger.

"I know," I agree, feeling my lip tremble.

"My mom almost killed my dad, and then she tried to kill me," he says, stunning me. My body stills completely; everything in me stops. I swear even my blood ceases pumping through my veins. I have asked Sven more times than I can count about his parents and his family, but he has always changed the subject, never giving anything away. I thought that maybe he lost them and it was still too painful for him to talk about. I never, ever would have thought he went through something like that.

"I—"

"She was schizophrenic. I was a kid, so I didn't know, but my dad did. She was taking medication for it, to keep it in check, but then one day she quit taking her meds, started tossing them in the garbage, convinced that my dad was trying to kill her. She would show up at my school and flip out, or flip out at the house and call the police, tell them that my dad or I were trying to kill her. He knew she had a problem, but he was in denial about it. He convinced himself that she had it under control once and could get it back under control if he helped her.

"I would avoid being home with her. I couldn't even be in the same room with her without feeling like I was going to piss myself, because I was so afraid she would freak—something she did often."

"I'm so sorry, honey," I whisper, but I don't even think he hears me as he continues on, the blank, distant look in his eyes never changing.

"I didn't know until later, until it was too late, that a multitude of doctors told my dad that my mom needed to be placed somewhere she could get help. He didn't listen to them, thought that if he loved her enough he could love her through her issues, but that's the thing. You can't love someone through shit like that. Sometimes people are beyond help. My dad found out the hard way, when my mom stabbed him twelve times in the chest while he slept next to her."

Covering my mouth with my hand, I feel a sob crawl up the back of my throat and tears stream silently from my eyes.

"I woke up that night thinking someone was in the house. I didn't know the sounds I heard weren't someone breaking in, but my mom hacking away at my dad's chest. When I made it to their room, the door was cracked, and I saw my mom standing over my dad, covered in blood."

"Please stop," I whisper, feeling like he's punishing me with his words. The thought of Sven as a small boy witnessing something so gruesome kills me. I hate that for him. I hate he went through something like that. And I hate more that this is the time he's choosing to share this with me.

"How many times have you helped your sister, stood by her, bailed her out?" he asks, tilting his head to study me. Swallowing through the pain, I shake my head. Our stories are not the same, not even close. "How many?" he repeats on a rumble.

"It's not the same, honey," I whisper gently. I really want to go to him to wrap my arms around him, but his body is so solid I know he doesn't want that, not at all, not from me.

"You lied to me. Standing in my arms, you fucking lied to me."

Okay, that cut deep, not that it wasn't true. It was, *but…*

Dropping my eyes from his, I pull in a few deep gulps of air. I would do it again and again; I will always run to help my sister, because I remember there was a time she would have done the same for me I know that deep in my gut.

Hearing my phone ring in my bag, I cringe at the loud sound.

"Leave it," He snarls, and I bite back the tears I feel gathering in my eyes and pull my cell out of my bag.

Unknown Caller is on the screen, and I know, just *know* it's Morgan. Sliding my finger across the screen, I ignore Sven's curse and answer with a quiet, "Hello."

"It's done. Can you come get me? I need to get somewhere safe tonight."

"Where, when?" I rush out, standing.

"I'll meet you at the Galleria Mall. I'll have Amy drop me there— fifteen, twenty minutes tops."

"'Kay." I hang up, dropping my phone back in my bag, and look at Sven. The blank look is gone, replaced with rage.

"I need to pick Morgan up. She's going into rehab," I tell him, expecting him to look surprised or relieved, but his expression doesn't change.

"You do this…" He shakes his head and rips a hand through his hair. "That's it, Maggie."

I cringe at the sound of his tone and feel my heart split in two, not only from the look in his eyes, but the amount of finality in his words as he spits them at me. "I have to help her," I whisper through the pain the tears in my throat are causing as I swallow them down.

"She's going to end up getting you killed. Do you not see that?" he yells, standing, causing the chair he was sitting on to slide back and hit the wall behind him with so much force that the window rattles.

"Sven." I shake my head as my body begins to shake.

"No! Her or me, Maggie, you choose."

"You can't ask that of me," I tell him, lifting my hand toward him as I take a step in his direction around the desk. His eyes drop to my hand and he takes a step back.

"Make your choice."

"What?" I breathe as nausea and anxiety fill my stomach.

"Make your choice," he roars, and I stumble back a step while my heart shatters.

"That's not love, Sven. You asking that of me is not love," I tell him quietly. Then I turn on my heels, run from his office and down the stairs, passing Lane, who's eyes lift toward Sven's office, looking pissed as they come back to me. I'm not crying now, but I feel the tears building in my chest and I know...I know I don't have long before I break down.

"Maggie!" Eva yells, rushing toward me from behind the bar when she spots me.

"Sorry," I whisper, running past her.

"Slow down, girl," Teo says, stopping me with his large hand wrapped around my arm as soon as I pass through the outside door.

"I need to go," I cry, attempting to wrench my arm from his grasp.

"What's going on?" He frowns, studying my face.

"Let me go, Teo, please," I beg, feeling desperate. I want to cry. I want to scream, but more than anything, I want to get away.

"Let's go inside," he says gently.

"Let me go," I repeat, and his hand loosens and I'm able to get free. Running to my car, I get in then lock the doors. I don't think anyone is following me, but I can't risk anyone trying to stop me, not again. Putting my car in reverse, I hit the gas then slam on the brakes, causing the car to jerk and my body to slide forward in my seat. Putting the car in drive, I press the gas then swerve to miss Sven, who is standing at the entrance for the parking lot. I don't even look as I pull out onto the road. I just say a prayer there isn't a car coming and that I don't die.

When I reach the mall, Morgan is standing out front with a backpack on the ground at her feet. As she spots my car, she picks up the bag and rushes toward me.

"I didn't think you were coming," she whispers, getting in and buckling her belt, reminding me that I need to put mine on as well. I never go without a seatbelt, but I didn't even think to put it on. "Are you okay?" she asks, and I don't look at her. I can't. I just put the car in drive and take off toward the highway without answering.

PULLING INTO OUR parents' driveway, Morgan asks, "Seriously, Maggie?"

Once again, I ignore her, the same way I ignored her when she asked me where we were going when we got on the road. Then again, when I took the exit for Pullman, the community my parents live in, I honestly would never have planned on coming here, but the longer I drove, the more I thought about it, and the more I realized it's my mom and dad's turn to step the hell up.

I have been doing more than my fair share of taking care of people. It's time someone had my back. And that thought hurt, because Sven should have been the one to do just that. He should have put his personal feelings aside and had my back. Even pissed, he should be here for me, but he wasn't, proving to me that once again I picked the wrong man, but unlike all the others, he was able to hurt me.

Putting my car in park when I reach the end of the dirt road that stops near the front porch of my parents' home, I mutter, "You want help, Morgan, then you do things my way this time." I open the door, getting out without another word.

"MoonPie?" My mom calls in surprise, walking out onto the porch followed by my dad. They haven't changed much since the last time I saw them. My mom is beautiful for a woman her age, with long white-grey hair, big blue eyes, and a small frame. You can tell she takes care of herself, eats right, drinks water, and exercises—or in her case, does yoga regularly. My dad's age is starting to show, but he's still handsome. His hair is still thick, and is now greying around the edges, but blends in with the blond. His skin is dark from the Arizona sun, and his body is firm from working outside daily in his garden or on the house.

"Morgan," my dad whispers a second later with worry etched in his tone, and I look across the hood to see that Morgan has gotten out of the car and is staring up at the front porch at both of them.

"Oh my," my mom gasps, stepping down the stairs, only to pause on the last step and cover her mouth with her hand.

"Can we go inside?" I ask, slamming my door, probably a little harder than I need to, but I'm angry. I'm angry they didn't care when I told them that Morgan was missing. I'm angry they didn't send out the troops like most parents would and search for their troubled daughter. But I'm *pissed* they left all of this to fall on my shoulders while they pretended like everything was hunky-dory.

"Come on, we just sat down for dinner," my dad mutters, his eyes going hard in a way that's surprising. My parents are passive; they've always have been passive, never letting much of anything bother them, so seeing the look of anger and disappointment my dad is directing toward Morgan is more than a little startling. "Do you have any bags?" he asks, turning his eyes to me.

"No," I tell him, gaining a nod before he takes my mom's elbow and leads her inside. Following behind them, I take Morgan's hand and head in, letting her know silently that she's not alone.

My parents' house looks the same as it did when I was a kid. Three long steps lead to a large covered porch that has been white-washed every winter since I can remember. On one side of the porch is a hammock big enough to hold two people, a two-seated white wicker couch with brightly colored pillows, a wicker coffee table with a large metal plate full of different sized candles, and a bright red outdoor rug, where my mom always does her yoga.

Walking through the front door is more of the same vibe. The living room is small, but is done in bright floral colors with live plants on almost every flat surface. The kitchen is old but well kept, the wood topping the counters is the type you would find on a cutting board. Instead of cabinets, there are open white shelves holding dishes, and more plants, but these are herbs and things my mom cooks with. Stopping with my dad, I notice the round four-seated table is set for two, with a big covered pot in the middle. One of my mom's big things has always been family dinners around the table, and even with my sister and me long gone, she has still stuck to that tradition.

"Get two more plates, Maisy," my dad orders my mom, who hasn't looked at my sister or me again. Nodding, she goes to one of the shelves in the kitchen and grabs two more plates, along with silverware.

"I'm not hungry," Morgan tells Dad, and his head turns, his eyes pinning her in place then dropping, taking her in, and I know he sees what I see when I look at her.

When his eyes meet hers again, I can see his unchecked anger as he commands, "You're gonna eat."

"Okay," she whispers, shifting on her feet.

Dropping her hand, I take a seat. I know she's as surprised by Dad's behavior as I am, but I have to say I'm happy this is his reaction. When my mom comes back to the table a second time, she has two glasses full of water and sets them both down before taking a seat.

When my dad sits, Morgan does the same, and my mom opens the large pot in the middle of the table. Scooping out some kind of rice and vegetable mixture, she places some on each of our plates, the whole time avoiding looking at Morgan or me directly. I have no idea what that's about, but it's starting to annoy me.

No one says anything. I don't really eat; I push the rice mixture around on my dish, but am happy to see Morgan clean her plate and take seconds. My dad, who is across the table from me, is glaring at his food like it's the cause of all the problems in the world, and my mom is doing much like me, moving the food from one side of her plate to the other.

"Can I stay for a few days?" I ask. I don't know why that's my question, and not, 'What the heck are we going to do about Morgan?' but that's what comes out, and that's when everyone's eyes come to me.

"You know you can, MoonPie," Mom whispers, and my dad grunts something I can't decipher, with a nod.

"I thought you would be going home to your boyfriend," Morgan chimes in, but her words sound almost accusatory when she says them. Pain rushes through me at the thought of Sven, but I ignore it, because now isn't the time to have a breakdown, and I know once I really let myself think about him, that's exactly what's going to happen.

"You live with a man?" Dad asks, looking at me.

I really, really want to kick Morgan under the table for opening her big, fat mouth, but instead, I just mutter, "Something bad happened and—"

"What happened?" Dad asks, and I feel Morgan tense at my side, but I'm not going to lie for her. If one good thing came from Sven's story, it's that you can't protect the people you care about by covering for them, and I'm done covering for Morgan.

"Morgan stole some money from a guy. He came looking for her and found me. He roughed me up and—"

"What?" Dad hisses, turning to look at Morgan as Mom whispers, "Oh my," at the same time.

"Is this true?" Dad asks.

"I know it was wrong."

"You know it was wrong?" Mom repeats in disbelief.

"I…" She drops her voice. "I know I messed up. I—"

"I gave her the money to pay him back." I cut her off. "Hopefully it's done and we can move forward with getting her the help she needs,"

"I want help," Morgan says softly, and I find her hand under the table and give it a squeeze then drop it.

"What are you on?" Dad questions, and I freeze, because Morgan has never been honest about that. She's never told me straight out what kind of drugs she's taking and has always denied using, even when she's been picked up by the cops and taken in.

"Crack mostly, prescription drugs when I can't get enough money for a fix," she tells us, and my body sinks back into my chair.

"You're gonna go through withdraws. You ready for that?" Dad asks, and she wraps her arms around herself and nods, dropping her eyes to the table.

"Star," Mom calls, using Morgan's nickname, and my sister's eyes go to her, and this time they're wet. "We love you. I know we've mostly let you girls find your own way, but we love you and your sister."

"Why?" I ask, and Mom's eyes come to me.

"Why what MoonPie?"

"Why have you let us find our own way?" I ask as tears burn my eyes and my throat aches as I swallow the tears back.

"You girls have always been smart," Dad cuts in, and my eyes go to him and my brows draw downward.

"No, I was a kid. Morgan was a kid when we left home. Yes, we were both eighteen, but we didn't know much about the world outside of this place, only what friends told us and what we saw when we were at school. Neither of us were at all prepared for the real world, and you both just left us to find our way."

"You did okay for yourself," Mom argues, and I close my eyes and let out a frustrated breath.

"I didn't, not at first anyway. I was free to make choices, and a lot of them were bad ones."

"You never said anything," Dad defends, and I shake my head.

"Even if I wanted to ask you guys for advice, it would take days to get word to you."

"We didn't know," Mom murmurs, and I look at her.

"That's my point. You guys as parents should have wanted to know what was going on, how we were doing. Not, 'They will find their own way.' Even when I sent you letters explaining things that were going on, you weren't there. You two just live here in your little bubble, where nothing ever penetrates. It's not fair to me, and it it's not fair to Morgan."

Turning when I hear Morgan's whimper, I watch tears fall from her eyes and her body shake.

"We're sorry you felt like that way," Dad says gruffly, and I hear a sound of distress come from my mom as she gets up and moves to Morgan, wrapping her in a hug.

"I can't do this alone, Dad. I've been doing it alone for too long, and I can't do it anymore," I whisper, and his hand comes across the table and I place my hand in his.

I don't know if things are going to change, but I really hope they do.

Chapter 8

Sven

Second chances

"**I** FUCKED UP," I mutter as soon as Asher answers the phone. Asher has been my best friend since I was ten. I would hide out at his house every chance I got. He knew what was going on with my mom, was there when shit went down, and his parents took me in while my dad recovered in the hospital. He's the best man I know, a man I respect and a man who laughed his ass off when I told him months ago that Maggie was driving me to the brink of insanity.

"Give me a sec," he mumbles, and I hear him moving around. I'm sure he's in bed with his wife, November, or has one of his girls close and is trying to get away so he can talk. Hearing a door open on his end, I wander into the den and take a seat in the dark, feeling my nostrils flare when I sit on something hard and know it's one of Maggie's books.

When Justin called and told me that Maggie was with her sister, I didn't even think, or I did, but none of it was good. All I kept seeing was my dad, his constant excuses for my mom's behavior, what that led to. It's not an excuse for my behavior, but it's the truth. By the time I realized what the fuck I did, what I asked Maggie to do, it was too late.

"What happened?" Asher asks, and I press my fingers to the bridge of my nose, trying to get my thoughts in order over the pain in my chest.

"Maggie and I got together a few weeks ago." I tell him, realizing how long it's been since we last spoke.

"We both knew that was coming," he mutters, not sounding at all surprised. "That doesn't explain a middle of the night phone call, unless you're calling so I can congratulate you on finally pulling the stick out of your ass."

"Fuck," I curse under my breath, feeling pain slice through my chest, the same pain I felt when I saw tears in Maggie's eyes and heard her soft words.

That's not love, Sven. You asking that of me is not love.

She was right; me asking that of her had nothing to do with love.

"What did you do?"

"Told her to choose between me and her sister."

"What the fuck, man?" he rumbles, sounding pissed.

"Yeah." I agree.

"Jesus, you seriously fucked up."

"I already know that. Now I need to know what the fuck to do to get out of this mess."

"Where is she now?" he asks, blowing out a breath, and I know he thinks I'm as fucked as I think I am.

"At her parents'." When she left, I had Justin follow her to make sure she was, and still is, safe. I wanted to go after her, but after what happened, I didn't want her to spot my car, get pissed, and get hurt while trying to get away from me.

"Can you go there?" he asks quietly.

"Not sure how that's gonna go over, and not sure I want the first time I meet her parents to be the same time I'm dragging her kicking and screaming from their house."

"Kicking and screaming?" He chuckles, but I'm not joking. If I got there and she refused to come home with me, I'd bring her back with me no matter how that came about. "You're not joking." His laughter dies and I shake my head, even though he can't see me do it. "You call her?"

"Yeah, voicemail."

"Christ, man."

"What the fuck do I do?" I growl, standing from the couch.

"Go get her," he states softly. "If it was November, I'd go get her ass and bring her home. No way I'd let her stew on that shit."

"You think that's the right move?" I ask, already heading for the door.

"You love her?"

His question has my hand pausing on the handle, and I drop my head forward and close my eyes. "Yeah, man," I mutter, feeling a pain in my chest at the thought of her not being mine, of losing her.

"Go get her, plead your case, and bring her home."

"Thanks, man."

"Anytime, you know that."

"Yeah, man," I agree, hanging up the phone. Getting in the car, I have no idea what the fuck I'm gonna say when I see her. I just hope that whatever I come up with is enough to convince her to give me a second chance.

PULLING ONTO THE side of the road, I watch Justin get off a Harley and do a double take. The kid who once looked like a high wind would blow him over, now looks like he could take Teo on in a fight and would come out on top.

I roll down my window when he gets close, and he grins as I ask, "You start doing steroids?"

"Seven-Eleven," he replies, ignoring my comment. "Good to see you, man." He places his hand out toward mine and I shake it once.

"She still at her mom and dad's?" I ask, and his face changes.

"Yeah, she's still there. All's quiet."

"Thanks for looking out, man."

"You know I got your back, just glad I was in town and could help."

"You didn't tell me we're still searching for her sister." The call from Justin telling me Maggie was with her sister was unexpected. I didn't even know he was in town, let alone following Morgan.

"I was working a separate case and spotted her, followed her then saw she was with Maggie and called you."

"What case?" I ask studying him and seeing something's off.

"Talked to Kenton and Kai. Shit's going down with Paulie," he says effectively changing the subject.

"Fuck," I rumble, squeezing the steering wheel.

"Go get your girl. The guys will be in town in a few days. We'll figure everything out then."

"Not looking forward to that," I tell him something he already knows as I look out at the empty desert beyond my windshield.

"We'll probably set up shop at Kai's place. He's got the best location and the best security. The women can all stay there while we figure out our next step."

Rubbing my forehead, I wonder how the fuck this is gonna go down. We all knew things would come to an end with Paulie, but none of us thought it would be happening this quickly. "Just go get your woman, and the rest can wait."

"You going back to the city?"

"Yeah, I have a few things to take care of before everyone gets to town."

"Don't go off half cocked, Justin. Wait for us to meet."

"What do you take me for?" he asks, taking a step back, holding his arms out at his sides.

"What the hell happened to you?"

His eyes go darker, a darkness that comes from seeing too much, doing too much. I don't know what the fuck happened to him, but something flipped in him. But right now, I don't have time to talk to him about it.

"Go get your girl," he rumbles as he hits the hood of my SUV once then walks back to his bike and throws one leg over it. He starts it up, the loud rumble sounding through the quiet desert as he takes off.

Turning down the dirt drive toward Maggie's parents', I see houses scattered here and there, and lots of green houses between them, along with pens holding goats, chickens, cows, and such. I know from rumors that this community sticks to itself, most people living off the land or using the barter system to live among each other. They make their own rules and don't accept outsiders often. When I turn down another dirt road, a two-story house appears in the distance. The bright blue color stands out, even in the dark.

Pulling in a deep breath, I let it out and stop in front of the house. The moment I park, the front door opens. As I hop down from the cab, a woman who looks like an older version of Maggie steps out onto the front porch.

"Are you here for my daughter?" she asks in a soft voice that reminds me of the way my mom used to sound when I was a kid before she stopped taking her medication.

"Yes, ma'am."

"She cried herself to sleep. Didn't think we could hear her, but the house is old and I heard," she says as I step onto the bottom step.

Rubbing my chest over my heart, I'm at a loss for words.

"My MoonPie is tough, always has been," she says quietly, looking over my shoulder. "I don't know what happened between you two. She didn't tell us anything, but I know she must love you," she whispers studying me.

"Maisy," a man calls, stepping out on the porch, stopping when he spots me. Just from looking at him, I know he's Maggie's dad. They have the same eyes, and the same expression when they're pissed, which he obviously is.

"Who are you?" he demands, letting the door slam close behind him.

"Sven, sir." I take the last two steps up the porch and stick out my hand. His eyes drop to it then lift to look at his wife.

"Go inside, Maisy."

"Monroe."

"Go inside, check on Morgan, and make sure she's okay," he tells her, and she looks at me then at her husband before nodding and heading toward the door, stopping when she has it open an inch.

"I hope to see a lot more of you, Sven," she says quietly before disappearing inside.

Monroe's eyes go from the closed door to me and he nods toward the desert as he takes the steps down the porch. Maggie told me her parents were hippies, but I'm not getting the peace, love, and happiness vibe from her father. In fact, he looks ready to commit murder.

I follow him into the sand and dirt off the side of the house, where he stops and places his fists on his hips. "What are you doing here?"

"I came to bring Maggie home," I tell him honestly. There is no sense in lying about what's gonna happen, and whether he likes it or not, his daughter is going home with me.

"You know about what's happening with her sister?" he asks, and guilt assaults me when I answer.

"Yes, sir."

"You're the man my baby girl's been living with?" he asks, locking his eyes on me.

"Yes." I nod, shoving my hands in the pockets of my slacks.

"Figured," he mutters, looking me over, and for once in my life, I feel unsure and on edge. I've never sought approval from anyone, never given a fuck what anyone thought of me, but standing outside of Maggie's parents' house with her father's eyes on me, I hope he sees something worthy of his girl. "She's upstairs. Tomorrow, her sister's going into rehab, so I ask that you both stay here until she's there."

"I'll do that," I agree, and his eyes move over me again.

"Are you a model like my girl?" he asks, and I smile for the first time in hours.

"No, sir, I own a club and have a few other businesses around Vegas."

"Good," he murmurs then walks off, leaving me standing while he heads toward the house. "You coming, or you gonna stand out here all night?" Without a word, I follow him into the house. "She's upstairs, second door on the left." He dips his head toward the stairs.

"Thanks," I tell him, seeing his wife come to his side, wrapping her arm around his waist.

Heading up the stairs, I stop outside the door then push my way through. The room is dark, but I can still make out Maggie's outline on the bed. Taking off my suit jacket, I place it on the chair then kick off my shoes and socks, strip off my shirt and pants, and then go to the bed. I pull back the blanket and settle myself in, pulling her against me and feeling her wet cheek hit my chest.

"Wha—" she whispers sleepily.

Rolling her to her back, I cover her mouth with mine and her arms wrap tightly around me for a moment before moving to push me off. Pulling her arms above her head, I hold them there and whisper, "I'm so fucking sorry, baby," against her lips. "I was a fucking dick, and you didn't deserve that."

Turning her face from me, she sobs, and that sound cuts me. Placing my mouth near her ear, I tell her softly, "I love you, Maggie, so fucking much. The idea of something happening to you kills me. I'm a selfish fucking bastard when it comes to you, baby."

"Shut up," she whispers through her tears.

"So fucking sorry," I repeat, dropping my forehead to the side of her head.

"You—"

"I know," I agree without knowing what she's going to say. Crying harder, her fingers wrap around mine and I kiss her forehead, cheek, and neck then let her hands go and roll to my back, pulling her up my body. Her face presses into my neck and tears wet my skin as she cries.

"You let me down when I needed you," she breathes when her body has stopped shaking and the tears have died down.

Fuck.

"I know," I agree, and her arm moves from where it was tucked between us to slide over my waist. Feeling her settle into me, my body relaxes. We lay there for a long time in silence before I finally ask, "Why'd you lie?" Her body tightens, and she goes to pull her arm back, but I grab her wrist and hold it in place against my abs. "I won't be pissed. I just need to know so it doesn't happen again," I tell her gently, using my free hand to run my fingers through her hair.

"You hate my sister," she whispers, and my muscles lock.

"I don't hate—"

"Every time I mention her, you get a look on your face." Her cheek moves against my chest and her hair slides over my skin. "It's not a nice look."

"I don't hate her, Mags. I worry about you and what will happen if you let her in again. There is a difference."

Her head lifts and she looks down at me. "Because of your mom?"

"Yeah." I nod, wrapping my hand around the back of her neck under her hair.

"Our stories are not the same, honey," she whispers with concern in her tone. Lifting her hand, she places it against my jaw, and her fingers trail toward my chin. "I hate what happened to you. I hate it and I'm so sorry."

Closing my eyes, I let her words settle through me and her touch heal a wound I didn't even know was still wide open. Only she could do that; only she could heal me with a touch and a few soft words.

"I love you, Sven. I know I shouldn't have lied about meeting up with Morgan. I don't know that she'll get better, but I know I love her enough to want her to have the chance to get help."

"Family," I whisper, and her face goes soft. She's right; family does that kind of shit and our stories aren't the same. My dad fucked up, even after he was released from the hospital. He tried to plea for my mom's return home. Thankfully, the judge sent her away to a place where she wouldn't be able to hurt anyone else. On weekends, my dad would go stay near the facility to spend time with her, and when I graduated high school, he moved to be closer to her. Every time my father left me to be with her, my resentment grew a little more.

If I was honest, I felt abandoned. To this day, we talk rarely. He checks in sporadically, and I do the same. Our phone conversations are never long, neither of us willing to talk about the shit that's bothering us.

If it weren't for Asher's family, I wouldn't understand the way family worked. I wouldn't know that parents, real ones, never turned their backs on you. They didn't push you aside to get what they wanted or needed. I wouldn't know that family stuck by you. No matter what, they didn't abandon you; then again, I knew how badly I fucked up with Maggie when I asked her to choose me, testing her loyalty instead of doing what she needed me to do.

"I should never have asked you to choose."

"You shouldn't have. I understand why you did, and that killed me, but even knowing it's just a hope that Morgan will get help, that hope is enough for me to want to help her."

"You should feel that way. She's your sister," I tell her, and she presses a kiss to my chest then lays her head back down.

"How did you know I was here?" she asks after a long moment.

"A friend of mine followed you."

"Seriously?" she asks, lifting her head once more.

"Yeah, I was gonna, but didn't want you to spot me and do something stupid that would cause you to end up getting in a wreck in that death trap."

"I'm a good driver."

"Baby, you almost ran me over then pulled out on the road without even touching the brakes."

"I was upset."

"Yeah, I know. That's why I didn't follow you," I remind her.

"How did you get in the house?"

"Your dad and I talked. He told me what room you were in and sent me up."

"What?" she whispers.

"Though I gotta say, baby. I thought you said your dad was a hippy. He sure as hell doesn't strike me as one."

"I don't know what's going on with my dad," she mutters.

"He's probably seeing that his brand of parenting hasn't been working."

"I don't know. I've never seen my dad look disappointed or angry, and he was both tonight. It was freaky."

"Freaky," I repeat with a smile that she must hear, cause her hand smacks against my chest.

"Freaky, and it's not funny; it's weird."

"I think it's a good thing. He cares, baby, and he's showing it."

"I guess you're right," she mumbles, and I run my hand down her back and pull up her shirt so I can run my fingers over her skin, and realize her ass is bare. "Sven," she whispers as I tug her up to straddle me.

"Gotta be quiet, baby. Your mom said she heard you cryin' through the walls, which means she'll hear if you're too loud." I shift and pull down my boxers, feeling her wet heat against my abs as I do, and then whip her shirt off over her head.

"I don't know if I can be quiet," she whimpers the truth as I adjust her again and fill her with one stroke. Wrapping my arms around her waist, I hold her in place, drop my forehead to her chest, and grit my teeth to keep from coming. No matter how many fucking times I get inside her, nothing can prepare me for it.

Her hands move to my shoulders and her hips rock forward ever so slightly.

"Fuck," I hiss as I tilt my head back, smooth my hand up her back and into her hair, and pull her mouth down to mine. I then use my grip on her waist to rock her against me as I swallow down her moans. Her hands wrap tighter around my shoulders and her nails dig into my skin as her rhythm picks up. Lifting her, I get to my knees then put her on her back. "I want to fuck you," I whisper against her mouth, keeping my pace slow, knowing I can't do what I want to do. Maggie's parents are somewhere in the house along with her sister, and Maggie doesn't know how to be quiet.

"Sven," she whispers back as her walls contract. Covering her mouth with my hand, I dip my head and tug her nipple. Her walls contract again, this time pulling me deeper. Kissing the tip of her nipple one last time, I move to her other breast. As she moans against my palm, her legs lock around my waist and her hips buck as she comes. Lifting up, I cover her mouth once more with mine and groan down her throat as I come hard, planting myself deep, and pull my mouth from hers.

"I love you," she says, sliding a hand up my back.

"Love you too, baby." I kiss her softly then roll us and settle her against my side.

"We're upside down," she whispers then giggles, burying her face against my chest to cover her laughter. Smiling, I fix us both in the bed, settle her at my side, and drag the covers up over us.

"Tired?" I ask, feeling her smile against my chest before she answers softly.

"It's been a long day."

"We need to talk about one more thing before you go to sleep," I tell her quietly, running my hand up her back again, wrapping my fingers around the back of her neck.

"That doesn't sound good."

"It's not," I agree, and her body tenses.

I smooth my hand down her back again. "Some shit's been going down for awhile, shit that you don't need to know the details of, but shit that has put me in the position of telling you about it, regardless."

"Okay, now I'm freaked," she mutters, pressing closer.

"Don't freak, baby. Just listen and know that no matter what happens this shit won't touch you," I say softly then tell her the rest, filling her in on Kenton and what happened with him and his wife, Autumn, about Kai and his wife, Myla, and then I fill her in on Paulie and his now dead son, and what that means for me and her.

"Holy cow," she whispers when I finish, and I fight it, but I can't help it; I feel myself smile. I just told her that we are planning on taking out one of the biggest crime bosses in Vegas, and her response is 'Holy cow.'

"You okay?"

"I don't know that I would say. I'm okay, but I will say that no matter what happens, I'll have your back."

Shaking my head, I roll her to her back and loom over her. "You're not going to be involved in this, Maggie. When the time comes, we'll stay at Kai's place. Myla and Autumn will be there as well. You girls will stay put and under radar, where you will be safe."

"So I'm supposed to just let you do whatever it is you're doing, while I sit at home."

"Yep," I agree, and even in the dark, I see her eyes narrow.

"Don't get pissed, baby."

"Too late," she replies, and I laugh. "You're not the boss—"

Covering her mouth with mine, I spread her legs with my knees and sink into her so hard that her breath leaves in a whoosh, and then I spend my time keeping her quiet.

"HOLY CRAP." OPENING one eye then the other, my gaze focuses on a woman, and it takes a moment for me to realize where I am. Moving my eyes from the woman I know to be Maggie's sister, Morgan, to Maggie, who is holding a cup of coffee in her hand close to her mouth, hiding the smile I can still see in her eyes, I blink.

"Hungry?" Maggie asks, and my eyes move over her and they heat.

"Okay, I'll see you guys downstairs," Morgan mutters, leaving the room quickly, and I sit up then lean back against the headboard.

"Come here." I hold out my hand to Maggie, and she gets into the bed on her knees then scoots toward me. Taking the cup from her, I drop it on the side table then tug her forward. "Morning, baby."

"Morning," she whispers, studying my face for a moment, and then her cheeks go dark and her eyes drop to my mouth.

"What time did you wake up?" I question, noticing her hair is damp but not wet, so I know she showered a while ago.

"An hour ago."

Running my hand up into the back of her hair, I tilt her head toward me then whisper, "You should've woke me."

"You needed to sleep."

"You still should've woke me up, rather than bringing your sister in here to stare at me."

Pressing her lips together, I can tell she's trying not to laugh, and her eyes move over my shoulder before she mumbles, "Mom was talking to her about you before I got downstairs and told her you look like a movie star, and Morgan wanted to see for herself and wouldn't take no for an answer when I told her she couldn't come into the room because you were sleeping."

"She was in the room when I woke up," I point out the obvious.

"Yeah, she made me mad, so I let her in to prove a point."

"To prove a point," I repeat, feeling my brows draw together.

"It's not important," she mumbles, trying to pull away, but I hold her in place.

"Kiss me then show me where the bathroom is."

"Or what?" she asks, and I smirk at that, and her eyes drop to my mouth again before flaring. "Fine, but only because I want to," she grumbles, kissing me briefly then pulling away.

Letting her go, I can see the confusion in her eyes, but I ignore it and move to sit on the side of the bed then stand, letting the sheet drop from my waist. Hiding my smile, I tilt my head to the side and prompt, "You see my boxers, baby?"

"Boxers?" she asks, licking her lips.

"My eyes are up here, Mags."

"Your eyes," she murmurs, and I laugh, wrapping my hand around the back of her neck, pulling her stumbling into me.

"House is awake, baby. Everyone's up. I'm sure they're waiting for you and me to get downstairs, so as much as I'd like to bend you over the bed and fuck you, I can't—not right now anyway. When we get back home, that's a different story."

"Right," she whispers, dropping her forehead to my chest. "Dad and Mom want to go with me to drop off Morgan."

"Good, I'll drive," I tell her on a squeeze.

"I'll drive," she mutters into my skin.

"Only two people can fit in your car, baby. We'll leave your car here and pick it up when we drop your parents home."

"Fine."

"Fine." I smile then kiss the top of her head. "How are you feeling this morning?"

"Okay," She shrugs then rubs her hands down her face. "I just want this part over with."

"You're doing everything you can, but in the end, it's gonna be her choice if she gets better or not, and nothing you do will change that."

"I know you're right," she whispers dropping her eyes from mine.

Using my fingers under her chin, I pull up. "You gonna be okay?"

"Yeah."

"Yeah," I agree, knowing she will be. "Show me the shower and I'll meet you downstairs when I'm done."

"Okay," she agrees, leaning up on her tiptoes and kissing my jaw before walking to the bed, nabbing my boxers from the mass of blankets, and tossing them at me. Grabbing her coffee from the side table, she opens the door to the room once I have my boxers on then heads down the hall and pushes open the door for the bathroom. Following her inside, I watch her grab a towel from the closet then a bar of some kind of soap from one of the shelves. "I'll be downstairs."

"I'll be there shortly."

Nodding, she runs her hand across my abs then disappears, closing the door behind her.

Once I'm showered, I head back to the room and open the door, surprised when I find Morgan sitting on the bed with her hands in her lap and her head bowed toward them.

"Morgan?" I question, and she jumps briefly then her eyes run up my chest and lock on mine. "Why are you in here?" I ask, trying to keep the annoyance I'm feeling out of my tone, and her eyes drop to her lap again as she speaks.

"I...I wanted to talk to you about Maggie." Leaving the door open, I go to my pants and step into them then shrug on my shirt, waiting for her to say whatever the fuck it is she came to say.

"Talk," I bark, and she jumps. "You were waiting in this room when

I got out of the shower, Morgan, while your sister's downstairs. I gotta say I'm a little pissed."

"A *little* pissed?" she mutters like '*Yeah, right.*'

"Morgan," I say, losing patience.

"Why are you with my sister?" she asks, looking up at me.

My fingers still on the buttons of my shirt and my eyes narrow. "Pardon?"

"It took me awhile to figure it out, but I know you," she whispers the last part, and my nostrils flare. "Maggie wouldn't know you, because she doesn't go out much anymore, but I know you. Women talk, and they talk about you a lot." She drags out the last word, taking me from pissed to furious. It also has nausea turning in my stomach, because she's right.

"Not that I need to justify my relationship with Maggie to you, but I'm in love with her, have been for a long fucking time, and there hasn't been anyone since the moment I met her," I growl.

"Morgan?" Maggie calls, stepping into the room. "What are you doing in here?" she questions, looking between her sister and me.

"Just talking to Sven," she answers while standing up from the bed and running her hands down the front of her shorts.

"I heard you," Maggie tells her quietly, and Morgan looks at me before looking at her sister again, shaking her head.

"He's a… You have no idea the kinds of stories I've heard about him," Morgan tells her, and I feel myself still.

"You're a druggie, Morgan," Maggie whispers, and Morgan pales then whispers back, "That's not fair."

"It's not? And why's that?" Maggie asks, taking a step toward me, reaching back and placing her hand in mine.

"I'm going to get help," she says, dropping her hands to her sides, standing taller as her hands form fist.

"So you're going to change?" Maggie asks, studying her.

"Yes," she states vehemently, and I see it then in her eyes, the will to get clean, the reason Maggie's put herself on the line time and time again to help her.

"That's good, Morgan." Maggie nods taking another step back toward me. "But I hope you remember this moment. I hope that one day, when someone is judging your character by your past, you remember this moment," she whispers, turning to face me, missing Morgan's flinch as she does.

Placing her hands against my abs, her head tilts back, and I rest my hand around the side of her neck and dip my face closer to her. "Mom made breakfast, and she made a lot of it. Come eat."

"Is it tofu?" I ask with a fake grimace.

Smiling, her hands move up my chest and she answers with a quiet, "Yep."

"Great," I lie, leaning in, placing a kiss on her forehead, and then standing, and my eyes meet Morgan's, who is looking between the two of us with an almost startled look on her face before ducking out of the room without another word.

"I'm sorry about that," Maggie says, bringing my attention back to her.

"Don't be. She was coming from a place of concern for you."

"Yeah, well, I'm still peeved at her for doing that," she grumbles.

"Peeved, huh?" I ask with a smile, and she smacks my chest, rolling her eyes. Kissing her forehead once more, I grab my shoes and take a seat on the side of the bed, putting both on before letting her lead me downstairs to the kitchen, where her mom has made a breakfast for fifty instead of five, and it's all piled in the middle of a small round table. Taking a seat next to Maggie, I lean over and whisper, "Where's the tofu?" making her laugh and lean into my side.

"What's funny?" her dad asks, placing a stack of what looks like whole wheat pancakes on his plate.

"Sven isn't a fan of tofu," Maggie tells him, smiling.

"Really?" he asks, looking at me.

"It's not one of my favorite things to eat," I tell him, giving Maggie's inner thigh a squeeze, and her legs trap my hand.

"I miss bacon," he admits, and Maggie's mom glares at him. "What? It's true," he grumbles.

"I didn't even know you've tried bacon," Maggie says quietly, looking at him like she's never seen him before.

"I wasn't always a vegetarian. Neither was your mom."

"Really?" Morgan asks as she takes a seat between her parents on a chair that doesn't match the rest around the table.

"Really," their mom answers, kissing Morgan's cheek.

"Did you sleep okay, Sven?" Maisy asks as Maggie piles pancakes and fruit on my plate.

"Slept great. It's so quiet here."

"Yeah, one of my favorite things about living out here is the silence," Monroe says, and then his eyes move between his girls at the table. "But I do miss the house being noisy, like when you girls were home."

Looking across the table, I see Maisy's eyes fill with tears then look at Morgan, and notice hers are the same. I feel Maggie's hand move to mine on her lap and squeeze.

"I miss you, too, Dad. I miss you and Mom both," Maggie whispers, and her dad reaches over, giving her shoulder a soft squeeze, then his eyes move to me.

"Promise you'll bring my girl around more?"

"I'll do that," I agree softly, and Maggie's hand spasms in mine. I'm not sure what happened with them, but I can see they all want to be a family; they just got off track at some point.

"Next time you come, I'll teach you guys some of the Kama Sutra," Maisy says happily, and my head swings her way. I'm not someone who gets surprised easily, but that comment definitely threw me.

"Mom!" Maggie cries turning red.

"What, MoonPie? A healthy sexual relationship is good for the soul," Maisy says seriously, and Maggie's face turns a darker shade of crimson before she covers it with her hands.

Hearing Monroe laugh, I look at him as he mutters, "Welcome to the family,"

Jesus.

Thankfully, the rest of breakfast is somewhat normal, with Maggie and Morgan catching up with their parents. When we're finished eating, we have a little over two hours to get Morgan to the facility for check-in at twelve, leaving us just enough time to stop on the way there to pick her up some clothes and necessities before getting back on the road.

When we arrive at Guiding Light, the rehab facility, I'm surprised to find a beautiful three-story, adobe-style home, instead of a stale hospital. The house is set on the side of a rocky cliff, with open balconies off all three floors in the back of the house. The landscape is open and done in a way that reminds me of a spa or retreat.

Looking around, I don't doubt this place costs some serious dough, and I know there is no way in hell Morgan can afford something like this, and I don't think Maggie's parents can either, meaning this is all coming out of Maggie's pocket, showing just how much faith she has in her sister's recovery.

"I'm gonna help Morgan get checked in. Do you want to come?" Maggie asks softly from my side as I put the SUV in park. Turning, I look over at her and shake my head. Morgan doesn't need me in there; she needs her family.

"No, baby, I've got my cell on me. Call if you need me," I tell her gently, giving her hand a squeeze.

"I won't be long." She leans over, kissing my cheek, then opens her door and gets out, followed by her mom, dad, and Morgan from the backseat.

"Morgan," I call before she shuts the door. Her eyes come to me, but I can tell she's still got her guard up.

"You got this," I tell her, and her eyes go soft and she chews on the inside of her cheek before nodding and slamming the door closed.

AN HOUR LATER, I spot Maggie and her parents pushing through the door, and I get out of the SUV and lean back against it, noticing each of them have varying looks of sadness and hope etched into their features. I know this isn't going to be easy for Morgan, but this is also going to take a toll on their family. Watching Maggie, she takes her mom's hand and says something to her dad, who nods before Maggie leads her mom to one of the benches along the path that leads to the front door.

"Everything okay?" I ask Monroe when he's within earshot.

"It will be. The place is nice, and the doctors inside seem to know what they're talking about."

"That's good," I say quietly then look back toward Maggie and her mom, who are now hugging.

"She loves you." Titling my head toward him, I feel my throat get tight. No matter how many times Maggie says those words to me, I don't feel worthy of them, and don't know if I ever will.

"I know," I agree after a moment.

"Are you gonna marry her?"

"Definitely."

"I want to walk her down the aisle, so don't go dragging her to some chapel on the strip."

"I'll try not to, but I'm not making any promises," I mutter honestly, and his eyes crinkle.

"I just gave you an idea, didn't I?" he asks, and I laugh, 'cause fuck yes, he did.

"Never thought I'd be happy seeing one of my girls with a man like you, but I have to say I'm pretty darn thrilled."

Staring at him, I do it for a long time. I never believed myself to be a good man, or even a good person, but having Maggie's father's approval means something more than he will ever know. "Thanks," I mutter and he shakes his head, crossing his arms over his chest.

"Is everything okay?" Maggie asks, walking up to us, hand-in-hand with her mom.

"Everything's fine. You okay, Maisy?" Monroe asks his wife, wrapping his arm around her shoulders.

"It will be," she whispers, repeating his earlier statement while leaning into his side.

Looking down at Maggie, I place my hand against the side of her neck, pulling her closer to me, and ask, "Are you ready to go home?"

Her face goes soft and she nods then looks at her parents. "Thank you for coming with me today," she tells her mom and dad, wrapping her arm around the back of my waist, dropping her temple to my chest.

"We love you and your sister, MoonPie," Maisy says softly, taking Maggie's hand in hers, giving it a squeeze. "We're just sorry we weren't here for you two before now," she says and I can see the regret in her eyes.

"We'll be here from now on," Monroe, states pulling in a deep breath. Watching him with his eyes soft on Maggie I vow to hold him to that declaration.

Chapter 9

Maggie

Bullets don't stop bossy

S HOUTING, "ARE YOU almost ready?" toward the bathroom, I walk across the bedroom to the closet while zipping up the back of my tight black pencil skirt.

"I still think you should stay home."

My hand pauses on my top hanging on a hook near the closet, and I look over my shoulder at Sven, who is leaning against the doorjamb with his arms crossed over his bare chest.

"I'm not staying home. I've been gone for two days, and yesterday we took care of my family stuff, which means for two days, I haven't been to the club. And although you keep things organized, you don't always make sure everything that needs to be ordered is ordered," I tell him, watching his eyes narrow in a way that proves I'm right, even if he'll never admit it.

"Would you ever consider moving?"

Caught off-guard by his question, I ask, "What?" while taking my sheer, dark pink blouse off the hanger and slipping it on over my thin cami.

"Would you ever consider moving somewhere else?" he asks when I turn to face him, buttoning the buttons of my shirt.

"Somewhere else, like where?" I ask, studying him and wondering where this is coming from.

"Tennessee?"

"Where you grew up?" I prompt. He's talked about his hometown a lot, and about the family he grew up with, and I know he misses them, even if he doesn't say it.

"Yeah." He nods, uncrossing his arms and pushing away from the door.

"Do you want to move?" I question as he gets closer, and then start backing up when his eyes drop to my fingers working the buttons over my breasts then darken. "Stay back. I need to get ready." I hold out a hand, hoping to keep him at bay.

"I think I should just keep you tied to the bed," he mutters, trapping my hand between us as my back hits the wall, and his hands wrap around my waist and slide back over my ass, pulling my hips into his.

Whispering, "That's not going to happen," I bite my lip as his mouth travels down my throat. Resting my hands on his shoulders, I push. "Sven."

"I'm right here, baby."

"We have to leave for work," I moan as his hand slides down my hip, up my thigh, and under my skirt, and as he pushes the lace of my panties to the side, his fingers zero in on my clit with such accuracy that my hips buck.

"You may have forgotten, but I'm the boss." He nips my ear. "Promise if you're a good girl, I'll let you keep your job." His lips travel down my neck and my eyes slide closed.

Running my hands up his neck into his hair, my fingers tangle with the strands and I pull back until his eyes meet mine.

"We really need to—" Words lodge in my throat as two thick fingers enter me and his mouth crashes down on mine. Thrusting his tongue into my mouth, his thumb circles my clit and his fingers work faster until I'm riding his hand.

"Give it to me," he demands against my mouth, and I do.

My core convulses, sucking his fingers deeper as I orgasm hard, my eyes slide closed, my head falls back against the wall, and my body turns liquid.

"One taste," he whispers, pulling back, and his hands bunch my skirt up over my hips and he drops to his knees in front of me. Looking down the length of my body, I watch him press his nose into the juncture between my thighs then he rips my panties to the side and his tongue comes out, lapping at my folds. Watching his eyes close, my head falls back against the wall once more. There is nothing better than him touching me, nothing better than seeing him enjoy my body.

"Sven," I whisper, grabbing onto the top of his head so I don't fall over when his tongue moves rapidly against my clit and his thumbs spread me open. I'm close, so close. Rising up on my tiptoes, the feeling of his mouth on me starts to overwhelm me. Hearing a loud smack sound in the quiet room, my eyes fly open and my core convulses as the sting of his hand settles into the skin of my thigh. Tilting my head back down toward him, our eyes lock and he smacks me once more, this time harder, the sting and the look in his eyes sending me into an orgasm that has my body lighting up from the inside out, every cell detonating at the same time, sending me into the stratosphere. I don't even realize it's me making the whimpering noises I hear until I recognize that Sven is shushing me as he holds me in his lap on the floor. Opening my eyes, I try to catch my breath then bury my face against his neck as tears fill my eyes.

"Don't cry," he whispers into my ear as his hand moves over my back in a soothing motion.

"I don't know why I'm crying." I sniff, wiping my face with the back of my hand as I cling to him with the other.

"You've had a lot happen in the last few days." He kisses the top of my head once more then pulls my forehead out of his neck and his eyes scan my face.

"I'm okay," I whisper, and his head tilts slightly, like he's saying 'Yeah right.' "I promise. It was just a really good orgasm," I tell him, and he smiles his beautiful smile then rests his lips against my forehead.

"All you have to do is tell me and we'll leave work early," he says gently against the skin above my brow.

"I'll be fine."

"I know, but I want you to be more than fine, and if I have to hold you hostage in bed for another day to make sure that's so, then that's what I'll do."

"Sven," I sigh, closing my eyes.

His hand in my hair at the back of my head tugs gently, and my eyes open back up to meet his concerned ones. "You need rest. The club'll be fine."

"You just don't want me to be there," I mutter, and he shakes his head.

"I don't want you there after what happened, but I know that's not realistic."

"I—"

"I don't want you sick," he cuts me off before I can get any words out. "You can fight me on this all you want, but you need rest."

"What's really going on?" I ask, running my fingers down his jaw. "Why the question about moving?"

He moves to help me stand then stands with me and leads me to the bed.

"I've been thinking about us," he tells me as he settles me against him on the bed, my body tucked alongside the length of his.

"Like what?"

"The club was good when I didn't have any responsibilities outside of myself, but with you, and hopefully—one day—kids, I don't think that's true anymore," he states, and my body goes solid against his.

"I thought you loved your club."

"I do, or I *did*," he mutters, looking across the room.

"Sven," I call, bringing his gaze back to mine, and then rest my hand against his chest over his heart. "You don't have to change—"

"I know," he interrupts, running his fingers softly down my cheek. "I just want more. I don't know what the next few years will bring, but I know that with you in my life, I don't want to be working the club 'til all hours off the night."

"I'm there with you," I remind him, and his eyes go soft...softer than I have ever seen them.

"If we have a child, you won't be, and I don't want to be a part-time parent like my father was."

"I can understand that, but you love Vegas."

"I don't love Vegas. I love you. Vegas is just the place I moved to because it fit the life I was living. Now it doesn't fit anymore."

"And Tennessee fits?" I ask, running my hand up the side of his neck, curving my fingers there.

"It's a good place to raise a family, the people are nice, and the town I grew up in is somewhere I can see my kids growing up. I want that for them. I want them to grow up in a town where people know who you are and care about you. You're not just one more person to them."

"You've thrown around the family word a lot in the last few minutes," I tell him.

His brows pull together then he asks, "What?"

"You keep talking about your kids. Are you pregnant?" I ask, and his lips twitch.

"No, but you could be."

"I'm not." I shake my head in denial. "You know I had my period."

"That was last month," he mutters.

"Okay, there is a slim chance monthly that I could become pregnant, but if you're doing all of this on the thought of me being pregnant right now, please don't. Take your time and think about this, and if in the end you want to move, I'll go with you."

"This isn't something I just came up with. It's something I've been thinking about for a few months now."

"We weren't even together a few months ago."

"You weren't in my bed, but there wasn't a time I didn't think of you as mine. I was just waiting for you to catch up."

Feeling my heart grow warm, I lean forward and rest my mouth against his then whisper, "What am I going to do with you?" as tears fill my eyes.

"We'll have a whole lifetime to figure it out." He kisses me softly then tucks my face into his neck. I couldn't fathom this moment a few months ago. I had no idea this kind of relationship, this kind of love, was even possible, but having it now, I know I will do everything within my power to make sure I always have it.

"How do you feel about staying in bed and watching movies today?" I ask quietly, and his body relaxes under mine.

"Is that what you want?" he questions as his hand pauses on my back where it had been moving in soothing strokes.

"Yeah," I lie. I know he needs a break from everything, and if me staying home so he will stay home gives that break to him, then that's what I'm going to do.

"Go change and I'll meet you back here."

"Okay." I nod then lean up, pressing my mouth to his jaw before sliding out of bed and going to the closet. When I come back from hanging up the clothes I had on and have changed into one of my old tanks and a pair of baggy pajama bottoms, I find Sven in a pair of basketball shorts with a stack of movies in his hands, heading across the room to the TV. "Do you want anything from the kitchen?"

"A beer."

Nodding, I head downstairs, grabbing a beer for him and glass of lemonade for myself, along with a bag of Pirate's Booty to munch on. When I get back up to the bedroom, the curtains are drawn and the room is mostly dark except for the light coming from the TV. Sven is in the bed with his back to the headboard, his chest bare and his ankles crossed, with the remote resting on his abs.

"I called the club. Everything's okay," he tells me as his eyes meet mine.

"Did everyone show up tonight?"

"Everyone except you and me."

"That's good. You should probably give Zack a bonus for all the extra work he's been doing," I tell him as I put my knees in the bed.

"He gets compensated," he mutters then asks, "Have you seen *The Walking Dead?*" as I hand him his beer and crawl toward him on my knees, settling myself close to his side.

"No, what is it?"

"A show on TV. I got the DVDs a few months back but haven't had time to watch them. I figured we could start now."

"Sure." I shrug as he wraps his arm around my shoulders and tucks me closer to him.

Five hours later, my eyes are glued to the TV and my brain is in some kind of trance as the episode we were just watching comes to an end.

"Jesus," Sven mutters, and I turn to look at him.

"I know," I whisper, even though I'm not sure if that's a good 'Jesus' or a bad one. "This show is awesome. I mean, I feel bad for Rick, obviously, but wow. He's a total badass."

"Badass?" he asks with a smirk. "Isn't that a bad word?"

"No." I scrunch up my face and roll my eyes.

"God, you're cute," he mutters, searching my face, then asks, "You ready for the next episode?"

Looking at the TV then back to him, I inquire, "How many episodes are there?"

"Not sure. I think I have about four DVDs, and each has about 8 episodes.

"You know, you may get your wish."

"What?" He chuckles, tucking a piece of hair behind my ear.

"I won't be able to do anything until I've seen every episode—no work, no eating, no shower...nothing. This show is rendering me useless."

"I'm sure I can find a way to take your mind off of it." He smiles.

"I don't know. Rick is growing on me."

His eyes go funny, and next thing I know, my back is to the bed and he's looming over me, and then his mouth is on mine.

Then his mouth is on another—better—place, proving he can definitely take my mind off the show.

Looking over at Sven and seeing he's asleep, I reach over him, grab the remote for the TV, push pause, and then roll quietly out of bed and head downstairs. We haven't eaten anything since breakfast, and I don't think Pirate Booty or each other can be considered a meal. I'm hungry, and I know Sven will be too when he wakes up.

Heading into the kitchen, I open the fridge and scan the contents. There are two large steaks on one of the shelves, along with two giant mushrooms on another. I have never cooked a steak before, but for Sven, I'll at least try. Going out the back door off the kitchen, I attempt to light the barbeque. After three failed attempts, I try once more then do a little clap when I see the bars along the bottom light up.

Going back inside, I find a pair of new yellow gloves under the sink, the kind of gloves you use to wash dishes in, so I put them on, go back to the fridge, grab the steaks, and cut them out of the plastic wrapper, setting them on a plate. I take off the gloves, search through the cupboard, and find a few seasonings, sprinkling them on the meat. Heading back to the fridge, I grab the two mushrooms, wash them both off along with a few bell peppers, and cut them in half, placing them on a separate plate from the steaks. Done with all my prep work, I take both plates outside, along with the gloves.

"What the hell are you doing?" Looking to my right, I hold the steak in my hand up higher so Sven, who is standing just outside the sliding glass door that leads to the deck off the kitchen, can see, and then lay it on the grill before doing the same with the second one. "The neighbors are going to think you're nuts," he mutters as I shut the lid on the barbecue.

"Oh well," I tell him, pulling off the gloves. "They've probably already seen me naked. Me wearing yellow gloves is better than that."

"Nothing better then you naked, baby." He smiles, and then his eyes drop to my hands. "Are these really necessary?" He chuckles as he takes the gloves from me.

"I didn't want to get blood on my hands."

"If you would have woken me up, I would have done it."

"You needed to sleep."

"I didn't need to sleep. I fell asleep."

"Because you were tired," I point out, walking back into the kitchen, where I take out two baked potatoes from the microwave and cut them out of the plastic surrounding them.

"How long have you been down here?" he asks, leaning back against the counter watching me.

"Not long," I mutter as I move around him to the fridge and grab the butter, stopping when he grabs me around my waist.

"I could have eaten you for dinner," he says against my neck as his arms wrap around me.

"Oh," I moan as his tongue licks up my neck, and then squeak as he lifts me up to the counter. "Dinner is going to burn," I groan into his mouth as his hands move up my sides under my shirt.

"Let it burn." He grinds against me, then mutters, "Fuck," when his phone rings. Stepping back an inch, he pulls his phone out of the pocket of his shorts and looks at the number. "Give me a second," he mumbles, kissing my forehead and putting his phone to his ear, walking away.

Letting out a breath, I hop off the counter then go to the fridge. I grab a bowl of salad and freeze when I hear Sven in the next room snarl, "You have got to be shitting me."

Dropping the bowl to the counter, I walk toward the living room, where I hear him tell whoever is on the phone, "I'll be there in fifteen." Then he hangs up and looks at me.

"Is everything okay?" I ask, studying the pissed-off look on his face.

"A fire broke out at the club in one of the bathrooms. I gotta head out. The cops and the fire department are there."

"What?" I gasp.

"I'll call and explain everything, but I gotta go, baby."

"I'm coming with you," I tell him, but he shakes his head.

"Yes, I'm going with you." Without giving him the chance to argue with me, I run through the house, out the backdoor of the kitchen, turn off the grill, and then run back through to head up the stairs, finding Sven in the bedroom. He's already dressed in a pair of dark jeans and a grey V-neck tee. Running past him, I go to the closet, grab a pair of jeans, slip off my sweats, and put on the pants while hopping around before slipping my feet into a pair of sandals.

"You're not coming," he says blocking the closet door with his arms across his chest and his feet planted apart.

"I am." I put my hands on my hips and glare at him.

"No, you're gonna stay here. I don't know what the fuck happened tonight, but I don't want you there."

"Sven—"

"Maggie, I'm not fucking around. You are not coming. As soon as I'm gone, I want you to set the alarm, keep your phone on you, and stay put."

"I'm coming, Sven, and if you think I'm not, you need to think again, because the minute you leave, I'm in my car following behind you, so you can either suck it up and let me ride with, or—"

"Fuck!" He tilts his head back and looks at the ceiling then his eyes drop to meet mine. "Why the hell couldn't I fall for a chick who does what the fuck I tell her to do?" he asks, and I feel my eyes go squinty.

"You would have been bored out of your gourd with a woman like that." I tell him the truth; he would ruin a woman who didn't stand up to him.

"You stay at my side. You are not out of my sight, not even for a second," he barks, and I fight my smile, 'cause I know he won't appreciate me gloating right now.

"I'll stick to you like glue," I agree.

"Don't make me regret taking you."

"You won't." I smile, then walk past him out of the closet and then rush down to his Suburban before he can change his mind.

Driving past the club into the back parking lot, my head turns as we drive past the chaos. There are hundreds of people gathered on the sidewalks out front, along with police cruisers and fire trucks blocking the road.

"I thought it was a small fire in one of the bathrooms," I mutter to

Sven as I swing my head back around to face the windshield when I can no longer see the front of the club.

"When you're dealing with any kind of fire in a club like this, they evacuate everyone and every cop and fire department in the city shows up," he says, pulling into the parking space reserved for him.

"I hope no one was hurt."

"The alarm sounded, they followed procedure, and they got everyone out. No one got hurt."

"It's kinda weird that the fire was in the bathroom."

"People rarely follow the rules. My guess is some kid was smoking in one of the bathroom stalls and either tossed a joint or a cigarette into the trash. It's not the first time something like this has happened," he says, shutting down the Suburban, unbuckling his belt, and hopping out. Unhooking my belt, I open the door then take his hand when he helps me down.

Wrapping his arm around my shoulders, he leads me to the road then moves us toward two police officers who are trying to disburse the crowd.

"I own this—" Stopping midsentence, Sven turns and shoves me to the ground. My hands hit the concrete right before my knees do. Starting to push myself up, his body covers mine and his arms wrap around my head. People around us scream and the sound of gunfire registers.

"Stay down!" someone yells as the windows explode, causing glass to rain down on us.

"Sven!" I scream when his big body jolts on top of mine.

"Shhhhh." His hands wrap tighter around me, and I feel the top half of his body lift an inch and I cry out.

"Don't leave." Wrapping my hands around his arms at my head, I hold on tight.

"I'm not going anywhere," he whispers gently, and tears fill my eyes.

"They're gone!" someone close by yells, but Sven doesn't let me up. He stays on top of me, and I notice his breath is shallow and his weight has gotten even heavier.

"They're gone," I whisper, digging my fingers into the skin of his arms. Rolling him to his back, I scramble to my knees, pressing them to his side as I lean over him. Running my eyes over his torso, I see his grey shirt is turning red near his ribcage.

"Help!" I shriek, pressing my hands over the wound at his side.

"Are you okay, baby?" he asks, sounding short of breath, and my eyes swing up from my hands to his face, noticing his eyes look glossy and his face is pinched in pain.

"Stay still. Don't talk," I whimper, resting my forehead against his.

"Tell me you're okay."

"I'm okay, and so are you." I kiss him then lift my head when a shadow falls over us. "Please," I breathe, looking into the eyes of the firefighter across from me. Jerking his head once, his hands move over mine and he pulls them away, and then he yells at someone behind me.

"Miss, I need you to stand back," an officer says, wrapping his hand around my bicep. Tilting my head back to look up at him, I feel tears fall from my eyes and down my cheeks.

"I need to stay with him," I whisper, and his eyes fill with concern.

"I promise you won't be far, but the paramedics need room to work."

Biting my lip, I look from him down to Sven, drop my body forward, and press my mouth to his ear.

"I'm not going anywhere, but they need to look after you, honey." He doesn't reply or even move, but when I lift my head above his, his eyes lock on mine. "Promise I'm not going anywhere." I lean in and press my mouth to his, holding it there as I try to control my tears.

"We'll stay close," the officer says as he places his hand on my back. It takes everything in me to go with him, moving away from Sven. All I want to do is lie down next to him, to absorb his pain, to make him better. Reaching down, I grab his hand, squeezing gently, feeling his fingers tighten on mine before releasing. Moving back with the cop, I watch the paramedics and firefighters swarm, blocking him from view.

"Let's get him in the ambulance," I hear an EMT say, and I feel my world falling out from under my feet.

"Can I go with him in the ambulance?" I ask the officer at my side as my arms wrap tighter around my waist, trying to hold myself together.

"I'll find out for you. If not, I'll take you."

"Thank you," I whisper shakily then look toward the front door of the club. My skin prickles as I watch Zack, Teo, and Lane make their way toward me. Each looking worried and seriously pissed off.

"Maggie," Zack says, and a fresh wave of tears fills my eyes and I move quickly in his direction.

"Sven," I choke out on a sob, and his arms wrap around me.

"I'm so fucking sorry. We were talking to the cops inside when we heard the shots start. They wouldn't let us out 'til now."

"He got shot," I tell him, pulling away and moving my hands over my cheeks in a jerky movement. "Who would do that? Who would shoot at us?" I ask, panting, and his eyes move over my face.

"Can you ride with Sven in the ambulance, or do you need a ride to the hospital?" Lane asks, cutting in, and my eyes turn to meet his.

"I...I don't know. A...an officer was going to find out," I stutter out, noticing my body has started to tremble.

"Miss, I'm going to take you to the hospital. There's no room in the ambulance."

"I'll take her," Zack says, and I look at him then to the cop, and I know I have a much better chance of getting to the hospital quickly if I'm in a cop car.

"I'm go...going t-to—" Placing my hand to my stomach when a sharp pain hits me, my eyes try to focus, but blackness seeps in around the edge of my vision until I see nothing.

Hearing low murmurs, I wonder who Sven's talking to as I fight to the surface of consciousness. Blinking my eyes open, I know I'm missing something; something's not right. Then everything comes back to me, every detail.

"Sven," I breathe, tossing the cover over me back as I groggily attempt to sit up.

"MoonPie!" my mom cries, rushing to my side and holding me down.

"Where's Sven?" I ask frantically, and my dad moves to my other side and places his hand against my chest.

"Stay down. Sven's okay," Dad says, and I look at him and search his face, seeing a deep sadness in his eyes.

"I need to see him. I need to know he's okay." I lift my hand and notice an IV line then look down and see I'm in a hospital gown.

"You'll see him. The doctor should be back in soon. Until then, you're going to lay down."

Feeling confused and lightheaded, I ask softly, "Why would I need a doctor?"

"Oh, MoonPie," Mom whimpers, and my eyes fly to hers.

"What's going on?" I question, seeing tears in her eyes.

"You were pregnant," Dad says, and my head swings in his direction.

"What?" I whisper as my hands move to rest over my abdomen, and now that it's been brought to my attention, I notice a slight pain there and can feel some kind of gauze or something under my gown.

"Mom," I whisper as she settles herself at my side near my hip and runs her hands down my hair like she used to do when I was little.

"It was a ectopic pregnancy. Your tube ruptured and they had to rush you into surgery. We got a call from a guy named Zack, and he told us Sven was in surgery as well and that we needed to get here." She presses her lips together and more tears gather in her eyes. "I'm so sorry."

Closing my eyes, I lean my head back against the pillow as a feeling of loss washes over me. I didn't even know I was pregnant, didn't even have any inkling, but knowing I was and knowing I'm not anymore, my heart hurts.

"I need Sven," I whisper, hearing my mom sob.

"You'll be able to see him soon enough. He's being taken off the ICU floor as we speak and should be here with you soon."

"Promise me he's okay." I open my eyes, pinning my dad in place.

"Promise. He's tough. He's more worried about you than he is about himself."

He would be; he was probably worried out of his mind. "Does he know about the baby?" I ask, and for the first time in my life, I watch my dad's eyes glitter with tears.

"I had to tell him. He was causing a scene, thought they were just keeping you from him. No one would give him any answers."

Closing my eyes, pain cuts through me, and I pull in a ragged breath, feeling my bottom lip wobble.

"He told them that he wants to be moved in here with you, tossed around a few names, names of men I only know because everyone knows them, and they agreed to it," he says, and a silent tear slides down my cheek.

"HAS SHE WOKEN?" I hear Sven ask, and my eyes fly open seeing Sven in a bed next to mine. As I try to sit up, my dad puts his hand against my chest as my eyes lock on Sven's.

"Easy," Dad says gently.

"The doctor said I can get up," I remind him softly, looking up at him.

When the doctor came in to talk to me, he told me it was okay for me to move around as long as I didn't do anything strenuous. I had gotten up and gone to the bathroom on my own with only minor pain in my abdomen. But that didn't mean I wasn't in pain. My heart hurt badly. The doctor explained I was approximately six weeks pregnant and that the baby was growing inside of my left fallopian tube, which ruptured. The surgery they performed—removing my left tube completely—left me with only one, which he explained would make conceiving in the future a little more difficult, but not impossible.

"Baby."

That one word has me coming out of my thoughts and my dad's

hand moving to my elbow to help me up. Gaining my feet, I walk slowly across the space separating me from Sven, our eyes never leaving the other. "Fuck, baby." He reaches out to me with his left hand when I'm close.

"Please, be careful." I take his hand in mine and pull it up to rest against my chest.

"Come here," he demands softly, sliding his hand around my back, pulling me closer, proving that not even a bullet wound will stop his bossy ways.

"We're gonna step out for awhile," my dad says from behind me, but I don't turn to look at him or my mom as I hear them moving around or when the door closes a few seconds later.

"I was so scared," I whisper after a long moment of my eyes taking him in and the various machines he's hooked up to.

"I need to hold you. Climb up here with me." He scoots over, and I know I should protest, but I need his touch right now. I need to be in his arms, where I feel safe, where the world outside of us doesn't exist. Being cautious of the IV in his hand, I get onto the bed with him and tuck myself into his side. "Please don't cry," he whispers, and I move my hands over my face, feeling wet on my fingers when I do. "I'm so sorry baby, so fucking sorry," he says, and I know he's not talking about getting shot, but about the baby.

"Me too." I move closer to him, pressing my face against his neck.

"I'm sorry I wasn't here for you."

"You were kind of busy not dying." I swallow down a new wave of tears, bringing my head out of his neck to look at him, noticing his face is pinched in pain. "How much are you hurting? Do you need the doctor?" I ask softly trying to move off the bed.

"Stay." He pulls me back to him, wincing when he does. "I'm worried about you. It kills me that you woke up and I wasn't here."

"Are you sure you're okay?"

"I'm fine baby. I'm down for about three weeks, but I'm fine. The doctor even said I was lucky."

"I thought you…"

"Shhhh, I'm okay. A week, and then we go home."

Fighting myself to keep quiet, to not bring it up—not yet—I still ask, "Who shot at us?" Yes, there were other people outside the club, but those bullets were all aimed in our direction. No one was hurt besides Sven, not one person.

"You don't worry about that right now. The club's closed down for now. Zack, Lane, and Teo are going to be doing security for us while we're home."

"They're bouncers. No offense, but what do—"

"They we're special ops. I trust them," he cuts me off. "I know them. I know they care about you, and they're the only people here right now that I know would lay down their lives for you."

"Don't say that." I squeeze my eyes closed. I don't want to see anyone else I care about hurt. "You were on top of me when you were shot. I know that bullet could have hit me, and knowing that doesn't make me feel any better. I don't want any of them hurt."

"Baby." He pulls me gently until I'm pressed tighter against him. "Don't think about that right now. You need to rest."

"You need rest," I mutter, and I hear a smile in his voice when he mutters back, "Let's both rest."

"You're still very bossy."

"Rest, Mags."

"Fine." I let out a breath, carefully resting my hand over his abs, thinking I would get bored if he wasn't exactly who he is. And with that, I fall asleep in his arms, which I know now more then ever will always keep me safe.

Chapter 10

Sven

Missing pieces

FEELING MAGGIE BEHIND me, her tits are pressed tightly to my back. Her arm is over my abs, and her leg is shoved between mine. I roll to face her, noticing the dark circles under her eyes are slowly disappearing. When I was in the hospital, she stayed with me every night, even after I told her she needed to go home and get some rest—the kind of rest you can't get in a hospital because there is someone coming into the room every fucking hour, disturbing you. She didn't agree to this and insisted she stay with me.

Knowing I wasn't going to win the battle, I had the nurses push her bed close to mine so she could sleep close by but not be disturbed. Yet she always woke anytime someone even opened the door, and she didn't sleep again until after they finished checking me over and told her I was okay. Even now, two weeks after they released me to come home, she was still waking up almost as often as when the nurses had come in to check on me. Every night I wake to find her with her hand on my chest or her fingers at my wrist, taking my pulse—literally. I knew she would be shook up for a while over what went down, but I didn't want her to dwell on it, especially when she had lost our baby the same night and hadn't really had a chance to process that.

I hadn't even had a real moment to process it either. I just know there is now a pain in my chest that wasn't there before, a pain I knew I would have for the rest of my life, because whether or not Maggie and I knew about the baby, he or she was still ours, still something we had created together, a part of us that was now lost.

Wrapping my hand over the curve of her waist, I carefully pull her closer so I don't wake her then rest my chin on the top of her head and close my eyes. Kenton and Kai are hitting town tomorrow night, and then we're moving to Kai's place until shit gets sorted and we figure out exactly what our next move needs to be. They were going to show up after I got shot, but I told them to stay put. I didn't want to send Paulie the signal and knew I needed time to recover.

I know Paulie put a hit out on me, because I got the message from Justin after I got out of surgery and got my phone back. Only I got that message way too fucking late, and by the time I got it, I had already been shot and had a six-hour surgery to repair my lung and make sure there was no other internal damage.

I didn't give a fuck about me getting shot. Yes, that shit hurt more than any pain I've experienced in my life, but nothing compared to the fear I felt knowing it could have been Maggie. That bullet could have hit her, and the way I was laying on top of her, I'm still surprised it didn't. The bullet hit under my armpit, inches away from her, so fucking close that had she moved, had I not wrapped my arms up and over her, it would have.

I'm done with this shit with Paulie. His rein of terror is coming to an end, and I don't give a fuck if I'm the one who has to put a bullet in his head to do it. Over the years, he and his son have fucked me over on a variety of occasions, but this time, he went too far. This wasn't drugs in my club or dead bodies at the door; this was him taking a shot at me and my woman. A woman who was carrying my child when he had his men do it. Yes, this shit is coming to an end, and then I'm moving Maggie to Tennessee to start over. I can't say I haven't enjoyed Vegas, but the life I was leading was a life I was never really living at all. I moved through the motions, not really connecting with anyone. I have no roots here, no family, and only a handful of people I would consider friends. I want more than that for Maggie and me. I want her to have people, family around, bonfires, dinner with friends, and a house eventually full of kids. Vegas isn't the place I see myself building that dream for us.

I wasn't lying when I told Maggie I've been thinking about moving for a while. The day I took Mags skydiving, I set up that meeting with Ace, needing to get a feel from him about his interest in buying me out of the club. He mentioned wanting to be partners in the past, but if I left town, I was going to be out completely. There would be no looking back.

"I know you're awake," I whisper, running my hand down her back when I hear her breathing change.

"Do we really have to leave?" Her head comes out from under my chin and my eyes dip forward to meet hers. I told her last night about moving to Kai's place out in the desert. She doesn't want to go. I know this, but I also know it's the safest place for her to be while Kai, Kenton, Justin and I take care of what needs to be taken care of.

"It won't be but a few days, baby, then this shit will be done and we can move on with our lives," I tell her, pressing a soft kiss to her lips.

"I'll follow you anywhere," she whispers after a long moment, and I hear the truth in her tone. I never knew love could be like this, never understood the depth of my dad's devotion to my mother, but having Maggie, I now understand why he stood by my mother for years, even after she tried to take his life.

"HONEY, DO YOU really think you should you be doing that?" Maggie asks softly as she steps through the door of the spare bedroom, where I keep my workout equipment, and eyes the dumbbell in my hand as I curl it upward once more.

"You heard my physical therapist, Mags." I set the weight on the rack with the rest of the weights then go to her, taking her face gently in my hands. "I know you're worried, but you need to understand I have to get back into the swing of things, and that includes working out," I tell her softly, and her eyes move to the weights behind me before coming back to meet mine with a look of worry and anxiousness in their golden depths.

"He also said to take it easy," she whispers, resting her hands against my tee over my wound.

"I'm taking it easy." I press a kiss to her forehead muttering, "Promise," there before leaning back to catch her eyes. "How are you feeling?" Her eyes move away from mine. Using my fingers at her jaw, I nudge her cheek gently, gaining eyes once more.

"I'm okay," she lies. I see it in her gaze, and know she's trying to be okay, but she's not. I know that the loss is still hurting her even if she hasn't brought it up.

"We'll try again, baby." I run my thumb over her cheek. "And if it doesn't happen, we'll work at it until it does or we'll adopt."

"I feel like a piece of me is missing," she murmurs, closing her eyes. "I had no clue I was pregnant, but still feel like a piece of me is gone."

"Mags."

She opens her eyes and my heart stutters when I see the pain she's been hiding from me there, shining so bright that it takes everything in me not to pull my eyes from hers.

"How do I get it back?" she asks as her hands clutch the fabric of my shirt.

"You find out, you tell me," I say, dropping my voice, watching her eyes search mine as I dip my face closer to hers. "I don't know how you feel, but since the moment I found out, I know there's a hole in my heart from the loss," I tell her softly, honestly. "I'm not sure that hole will ever be filled, but I know when it does happen for us, Maggie, and it will happen for us; time will go a long way in healing that pain."

Her eyes fill with tears and she leans in, whispering, "You...you never said anything," as her bottom lip wobbles.

"I've been waiting for you to come to me. I don't want to push you into talking about it. But I'm here baby—anytime you want to talk about it or cry about it, I'm here."

Nodding, her forehead drops forward and lands against my chest as her arms wrap around my back, and mine do the same, wrapping around her, holding her close.

"What time are we leaving?" she asks against my shirt after a few minutes.

Looking at the clock over her head, I see it's already after four. "We'll leave in three hours. Are Zack and Lane still downstairs?" I ask, and her head moves against my chest before she mutters quietly, "Yeah, and Teo was coming in when I came up to check on you."

Pulling her away from my chest, I run my eyes over her face. The tears are gone; the sadness is not, but that's going to take time. "You wanna tell them what time we're heading out while I finish working out?"

"They're coming with?" she asks, looking slightly surprised by this news.

"They will help watch over you, Autumn, and Myla while me and the guys get stuff sorted."

"Then who will be watching over you?" she asks quietly, and I smile.

"Kenton's man, Justin, will be with us, along with one of Kai's men."

"The guy I met, what was his name? Frank?" she asks, looking more concerned at the idea of Frank taking our backs.

"No, Frank will be at the house with you and will probably think he's got guard duty, but don't worry. He absolutely does not."

"Thank God," she breathes, and I chuckle, running the back of my hand down her jaw.

"This will be over soon."

"I believe you."

"Good, now go tell the guys what's going on then come back up and shower with me," I tell her, watching her eyes heat before dropping to my side where I was shot.

"I think I'll make lunch," she mutters, sounding disappointed.

"Maggie—"

"Do you want me to make you a turkey and Swiss?" she asks, and I fight back the smile I feel, thinking about her wearing her meat-gloves and making me a sandwich.

"I want you sitting on my face. That's what I want."

"Sven," she breathes, swaying toward me.

"Go tell the guys what I said then come back up here."

"I don't think—"

Bending my face closer to her, I repeat, "Go tell the guys what I said, and if you don't come back to me and I have to come hunting for you, I will fuck you wherever I find you. So unless you want to piss me off, come back to me quickly."

"Sven," she repeats, breathlessly, leaning up on her toes touching her mouth to mine, then turns and walks out of the room.

I haven't had her in weeks. I wanted her to heal and knew I needed to do the same, but I got the go-ahead from the doctor a few days ago. She heard him tell me it was all good, and still she was keeping herself from me, but that was going to end. No way did I want to fuck her in Kai's house with everyone there to hear her moan. Finishing my workout, I head for the bedroom and notice she still hasn't made her way back upstairs. Giving her the benefit of the doubt, I head for the shower, turn it on, and let the water heat up while I take off my shirt. The scars on my chest are small from the surgery, but the skin is still red around the bullet wound. The doctor's biggest concern is that since my lung has been collapsed, that could reoccur once more. He has no other worries and wasn't surprised by how quickly I was healing. Hearing the bathroom door open, I watch Maggie stick her head in with her eyes glued to the shower stall.

"You didn't miss anything," I tell her, watching her jump when her eyes swing to me.

"I...I've been thinking about this, and I don't think we should do it," she mumbles, still standing outside the door with just her head inside.

"We've done this more times than I can count, and I know we

should do it, because if we don't, when I take you at Kai's house, you're going to wake up everyone in the fucking place. I know you, baby, so I know you're not going to want to be embarrassed when they hear you coming."

"I'm not loud," she hisses, and I move toward her, pull the door from her grasp, take her hand, and pull her inside.

Pushing the door closed, I mutter, "You are," while covering her mouth with mine and moving with her as she tries to back up, only to hit the door, leaving her with nowhere to go. Her hands move to my chest to push me off, but the moment my hand moves up over her breast, her mouth opens for me, my tongue slides in, and she moans.

"Sven," she breathes as my mouth leaves hers and travels down her neck while my hands skim her shirt up and over her head, noticing she doesn't have on a bra. Sliding one hand into her shorts, I roll my fingers over her clit and dip my head, pulling her nipple into my mouth and biting down on the tip as my fingers work faster.

I pull back and catch her eyes. "Unless it's just me and you, you wear a bra when there are men in the house."

"I—" Her chest heaves and her pussy convulses.

"That wasn't an intro to a conversation, baby. It's just me telling you straight-up I will be pissed if you don't do what I say, now lose the shorts." Her hands drop from my shoulders and move to her waist. I bite back my smile as she quickly unhooks her button, pushes her shorts to the floor, and kicks them away. I slide my hand deeper between her legs. "Wet," I groan, slipping one then two fingers inside of her.

Her hips start to move in sync with my fingers and her hands move, one wrapping around my hip, the other moving to hold onto my hair as my mouth covers her breast, and I pull her nipple in, sucking hard. "Counter. Bend over it now," I order, taking a step back and feeling my chest heave. Her eyes scan my face for only a moment before she moves to the counter and tentatively bends over it. Moving behind her, I catch her eyes in the mirror, lean forward, and kiss her back while my foot kicks her feet farther apart.

"Honey," she whispers, her back arching and her ass tipping. Moving my hands up the curve of her ass, I hold her open and watch as the tip of my cock pushes inside of her slowly, inch-by-inch. Pulling my eyes from us, I look at her and watch her head fly back, her mass of hair flying through the air, her eyes closing, and her lips parting on a gasp.

"Look at me." I plant myself inside her, feeling her walls contract. Her head dips forward, and her eyes slowly open and lock on mine. "Never keep yourself from me," I grunt, pulling out slow, moving back in even slower. "Never, baby."

"Never," she whispers, tilting her ass higher and sending me sinking deeper.

Wrapping one hand around her hip, I slide the other forward and roll it over her clit, watching her eyes go half-mast.

"Please, harder," she whimpers, but I don't change my pace. I keep at her slowly while my fingers roll. When I feel her walls start to clamp down around me, I skim my hand that was around her hip up under her breast and pull her back.

Her head turns toward me and I cover her mouth with my own as I pinch her clit, sending her over the edge. Her loud moan vibrates down my throat as I shift my hips forward once more, planting myself there as I come hard, groaning down her throat when I do it. Breathing heavily, I pull my mouth from hers and rest my forehead against the crook of her neck, placing a kiss there.

"I missed you," she whispers, and I lift my head to catch her eyes in the mirror. "I missed this." Smiling at her, I watch her pull in a breath then let it out slowly. She doesn't smile; her face goes soft, but her voice drops. "Don't do anything that will take this away from me." Tears fill her eyes right before she drops them to the countertop in front of us. "Please don't do anything to risk this." Losing our connection, I turn her in my arms, take her face in my hands, swipe the tears from her cheeks, and wait until I have her attention before speaking.

"You don't have to worry. Promise. Nothing is going to happen."

"You can't know that. You were just shot."

"I know, but I need to know you trust me to get this done so you and I can move on. I want to start our future, and until this is behind me, behind us, our future is at a standstill. Trust me to do right by us."

"I do, but if something happens to you, I'm going to be so mad at you," she mutters, and I burst out laughing. As I tug her into me, she glares. "That's not funny."

"It's a little funny." I chuckle, kissing her forehead.

"You're so strange," she murmurs, wrapping her arms around my back, resting her cheek against my chest.

"I love you, Maggie," I whisper, kissing the top of her head and feeling her arms convulse. "So fucking much."

"I love you, too," she whispers back.

We stand holding each other for a long time, long enough for Lane to come up and pound on the door, making sure we're good and causing Maggie to turn a shade of red that I've never seen her turn before— worse than when her mom asked if she could teach us the Karma Sutra.

After that, we showered and dressed, and then got us and our shit in the car and headed out, with Zack, Lane, and Teo following behind us.

When we arrive at Kai's, I know bringing Maggie here was the right decision. The house, surrounded by a seven-foot fence, lit up like Christmas, would be a deterrent for most. But if someone was stupid enough to fuck with us here, there was no fucking way they would be able to sneak up on the house without someone seeing them coming. Kai put in the best security money could buy, and I have no doubt that even if someone was walking through the desert, we would know they were out there before they even got close.

As the gate for the driveway opens, I look over at Maggie and see she's still asleep. She passed out not long after we hit the road and would probably sleep the rest of the night if I didn't wake her. I don't want to wake her; she needs rest, and even if she was upset about leaving the house we made our home, I know she was on edge there.

Getting out from behind the wheel, I quietly shut the door and walk around to meet Pika and Aye, Kai's two bodyguards standing at the end of the sidewalk, then wait for my men to join me.

"Good to see you, man," Pika greets, and Aye lifts his chin.

I lift mine back then mutter, "Not sure you know Zack, Lane, or Teo, but they'll be with Maggie when I'm not."

"What's up? I'm Aye, and he's Pika," Aye returns, dipping his head toward the other bodyguard.

"Zack?" Pika's eyes squint, looking at Zack, then he smiles. "Shit, man, how the fuck are you?"

"Didn't think you recognized me." Zack smiles, putting out his fist toward Pika who bumps his against it.

"You're uglier now, so it took me a minute," Pika replies, and Zack chuckles then looks at me and mutters, "Pika used to take over the VIP in Bistros every time he was in town. He had bitches ten-deep every night, all of them cool with sharing his affections."

"I miss Vegas." Pika smiles then looks at Aye. "We get some time before we have to head back to the island, we're going out."

"Sounds good to me." Aye grins, and I look between him and Pika, knowing that at one time, I would have been right there with them, but not anymore. Now the idea of random women isn't even a little bit appealing.

"You wanna show me where we're staying? Maggie's asleep. I want to get her settled then we'll talk," I say, and Aye looks at the car behind me.

"Heard about her. Uncle Frank wouldn't shut up about her," Aye mumbles, bringing his eyes to me. "Sorry about what happened. It's fucked up, but in the end, you'll get yours," he assures, and I know he means that in more than one way.

"Yeah."

"I can take Maggie in while you guys get shit sorted," Lane puts in, and I look at him, but his eyes are on the Suburban where Maggie's sleeping.

"I got her," I tell him, and as his gaze comes to me, I see something there that sets my teeth on edge when he nods. Looking from him to

Zack, I see his eyes on Lane, watching him in a way that has me wondering what the fuck I'm missing. I know Maggie and the guys are cool; they've been cool since the first night she showed at the club, but now I'm wondering if I missed something in all the shit that's gone down.

"I'll show you."

Pika claps my shoulder, and I pull my eyes from Zack to look at him and mutter, "Thanks."

Once I get Maggie settled in bed, I find the guys sitting in the dinning room at the table talking. Pika and Aye are filling Zack, Lane, and Teo in on the house and the parameter, including the sensors in the desert.

"Zack," I call, and his eyes move from Pika at the head of the table to me, and I nod toward the front door.

Mumbling, "Be back," he scoots away from the table and follows me out of the house.

"What the fuck was that?" I question, and he doesn't even hesitate before he speaks.

"Not sure, yet."

"What the fuck does that mean?" I run a hand through my hair. "If he—" I pause, clipping, "Fuck," and dragging my hand through my hair again. "This shit is not okay, not with all the other shit going down."

"I've got nothing to go on but my gut right now," he rumbles, looking toward the house. "Teo sees it. He knows something's off too."

"Why the fuck didn't you bring this to my attention before I had him in our house?"

"How could I watch him if he wasn't with me?" he asks back, and—*fuck*—I know he's right, but this shit isn't sitting well with me right now.

"Flipped, man," he whispers, looking back at the house.

"What?"

"When he knew Maggie was with you upstairs today, he flipped."

"Jesus," I whisper, wondering how fucking blind I've been. "He is not to be alone with her under any circumstances."

"You don't even have to tell me that shit. He hasn't been alone with her, and won't be. Teo and I are watching, waiting for his move."

"He touches her, I'll kill him. I know you guys are tight, but I'll kill him."

"If it comes down to that, I'll do it for you," he mutters, and I watch his eyes change in a way that shows how serious his statement is.

"He drugged her," I whisper to myself, knowing down to my gut I'm right. "The only one who got close to her. She fucking trusted him."

"Fuck," Zack hisses, and I know he sees it now too. Eva wouldn't do that shit. She wouldn't. I saw the worry in her eyes when she found out what happened. Justin ran her check and it came back clean, no red flags. Lane has been playing the good guy, playing me, and playing her. I close my eyes, hating that I need to fucking tell Maggie about this shit. She's already on edge; this shit will likely push her over.

"I can't be here with her. With him here, I can't risk something going down, not right now."

Stepping closer, he drops his voice. "This is the safest place for her."

"He's sleeping down the hall," I remind him, narrowing my eyes. "Right down the fucking hall."

"Right next to me," he says calmly, and I shake my head in frustration. "I'll let Pika and Aye know what's going on. No one will allow anything to happen to her."

"Why the fuck didn't I see this shit earlier?" I ask myself aloud.

"No one saw it." I know he's right, but even knowing he's right, I want to put her ass on a plane and send her somewhere safe, where I can deal with this shit without her being in the middle of it. "We're watching him. He has eyes on him, and Lane isn't stupid. Even if what he's done is stupid, he's not a dumbass He won't take a chance."

"Fuck," I clip, when I really want to roar my frustration.

"I know this situation isn't ideal, but right now, we need to roll with it. When he makes his next move, I'll make mine and put an end to it."

"No, fuck no. I don't know what his plan was, but he drugged her, could have fucking hurt her. He makes a move, I'm putting him down," I rumble, letting the weight of my words sink in then continue. "We don't show our hand, don't change shit, and when I talk to Maggie, I'll tell her to keep her guard up, but to play it cool. We don't know his plan, but we also don't know if he's taking orders from someone else right now."

"You think Paulie's in on this shit?" he asks, and I shrug, having no fucking idea if he is, but I wouldn't be surprised to find out he has something to do with it.

"Paulie has deep pockets. Money makes people do crazy shit, so it could have started out as him taking an order then turned into him wanting Maggie. Right now, I'm walking fucking blind, but I'm not willing to risk Maggie in this fucked-up game. When you talk to Pika, Aye, and Teo, you make sure they know that Lane isn't fed anything he can pass along to someone else."

"I'll talk to them."

"I'll talk to Mags."

"Your woman's crazy. She may try to take him out herself," he mutters, and I catch the smile in his voice.

"Don't say that shit. You know she will, and that's the last thing we need right now."

"True, but it could be fun to watch." He laughs, but I don't find anything funny about this, not right now. My woman is strong, but she is going to be hurt that someone else she trusted is not someone worthy of that faith. "We'll get this sorted," he mutters, reading me, and I nod.

"Fill the guys in tonight. When Kai and Kenton get in, tell them we'll talk in the morning. I'm going to talk to Maggie then, too. She needs sleep, and I want her to have at least one good night of it before more bullshit is piled on her that will keep her from resting easy," I tell him then storm into the house, making sure to keep my face impassive as I nod at the guys, who are still sitting around the table as I pass.

When I make it to the room Maggie and I are sharing, she's still out, but now she's tucked a pillow to her chest with one leg out of the covers and thrown over it. Getting undressed, I shut off the light, get into bed, and pull the pillow from her grasp, shoving it behind my head.

The second I'm settled, before I can pull her into me, her body moves. Her leg slides over both of mine as her arm moves across my waist, and her head nestles into the crook of my arm. I never did this shit with a woman before Maggie. The idea of having someone so close all night would have annoyed me. Maggie didn't have the option of sleeping any other way. I wouldn't allow it. I not only want her close; I need her close.

Running my hand through her hair, I stare at the clock across the room, the green lights reading a little after ten. It's early. Kai and Kenton will be in soon with their women. We were supposed to start talks tonight, but that shit will have to wait. Tomorrow is going to suck in more than one way, and I want to give Maggie one more night of just this—her in my arms, the world outside of us not creeping in.

Closing my eyes, I let out a breath, thinking that if her parents want to be there when we get married, they'll have to meet us as soon as we hit town when this shit is done. Because I'm pulling over at the first wedding chapel I see.

With something to look forward to, I smile and fall asleep.

Chapter 11

Maggie

Locked up

WAKING WITH MY cheek pressed to Sven's chest, my hand resting over his heart, and my leg over both of his, I blink my eyes open slowly. Looking past my hand and the expanse of Sven's chest, I see lavender walls and beautiful dark furniture. Blinking again, I realize I slept through our arrival at Kai's house and had been put to bed without ever waking up.

"You awake?" Sven asks, shifting my hair out of my face and off my neck and settling his hand on my back.

"No," I whisper, wishing I wasn't, since I know that once we leave this bed, I will have to deal with everything going on outside of it, including the fact that Sven and his friends are going up against one of the biggest monsters in Vegas. A monster that put out a hit on him, and succeeded in shooting him in the chest not even a month ago.

"Wish I could let you sleep, baby, but we have some shit to talk about, and I want to make sure you're good before we walk out of this room," he says, running his hand down my back and settling it on the curve of my waist.

Lifting my head, I place my chin to his chest and meet his eyes then ask, "What is it?" seeing the worry he's trying to hide as he scans my face.

"I'm gonna ask you something, and I want you to really think about it before you answer."

"Okay," I breathe, a little scared by the tone of his voice and the way his body has gotten tight under mine.

"There is no right or wrong answer, and I swear, baby, no matter my reaction right now, I'm not pissed at you, okay?" he asks as his hand on my hip squeezes gently.

As I try to sit up, his arm holds me closer, keeping me in place, and he jerks his head no. "You stay right here."

"You're freaking me out," I whisper, trying to catch my breath that has suddenly turned choppy.

His face softens and his hand comes up to run along my jaw. "Has Lane ever said anything to you, made you feel uncomfortable in any way?" he asks, and my body stills.

"Don't," I whisper, shaking my head and knowing what he's alluding to.

"Maggie."

"I would never—"

"I know that, baby," he cuts me off. "That's not what I'm after. I need to know if you have ever noticed him acting strangely when you're around?"

"What's going on?" I ask, Lane has never made me uncomfortable, but so much has happened over the last few weeks that I wouldn't notice if he was acting strange.

Rolling us, he settles his body over mine and his hands move to hold my face as he dips his closer. "I'm going on my gut. I have no proof right now, but I think he's the one who drugged you."

"You thought it was Eva," I remind him.

He nods then mutters quietly, "I did, but now I don't."

"Why?"

"I don't know. That's what I need to find out."

Licking my lips and studying his jaw, I repeat, "You...you think he drugged me?"

"I do," he agrees softly, and I look into his eyes and know he's the one person I can really trust in this whole world, the one person who will never lie to me or lead me astray.

"Why?" I ask again, and his forehead drops to rest against mine as his fingers move along my jaw.

"No idea, baby. Zack said Lane flipped yesterday when we were upstairs. Last night was the first time I saw something in his eyes I didn't like. Right now, it's just a feeling, but my gut has never led me in the wrong direction before, so I'm going with it."

"He's here," I say softly, and his face moves away from mine. "I…what am I supposed to do?"

"One: don't be you."

"What?" I frown and he smiles.

"You know I love you, but you cannot do anything that will lead him to believe we're on to him."

"But—"

"No." His thumb covers my mouth. "I didn't tell you this so you would form some ridiculous plan, one I would most likely have to rescue you from. I'm telling you so you'll keep your eyes open. If you're in a room with him alone, you make your escape. He corners you, again, find an escape. He says anything, does anything, you tell me or one of the other men in the house immediately. You do not engage him." He pauses, dropping his face closer, along with his voice. "Ever."

"I won't," I whisper.

"Good," he whispers back, and my hand timidly moves to the scar on his chest and I run my finger over it, changing the subject.

"I slept through meeting everyone last night."

"The only ones here when we got here were Kai's men, Pika, and Aye. Everyone else showed up after I came to bed."

"Oh," I mutter, and he smiles then bends lower and runs his lips across mine softly.

"Morgan gets a phone call today," he tells me, something I mentioned a few days ago, and I'm actually surprised he remembers. I know he and Morgan didn't get off on the right foot. Plus, her 'talk' with him didn't exactly make her his favorite person.

"She gets released in two weeks," I mutter, running my hand

through his hair. Nothing in life is ever guaranteed, but I have a feeling Morgan staying clean is going to stick. I couldn't go see her for obvious reasons, but my parents had seen her and said she was looking healthy and happy. She gained weight and was coming to terms with some of the things she had done, and the counselors were helping her get down to the root of the problem while helping her find other ways to cope with her feelings.

It was no surprise to me that the doctors told her what I had told her a million fracking times—that being around Amy is no good for her—and that until she has a better hold on her sobriety, she needed to stay as far away from her as possible. I can't wait to see her for myself to tell her how proud I am of her.

We had a few phone calls, and when Sven was in the hospital, she wanted to check herself out of rehab to be with me. I felt like I had my sister back, and more so, I felt like I had my family back. My parents, who hate Vegas, stayed with Sven and me the week after he was released from the hospital. They took care of everything while they were with us, from groceries, cooking, and running errands, to dealing with the club when someone needed to be there. I didn't even ask them for any of it; they just gave it, no questions asked.

"She can stay at the house," Sven says from above me, pulling me from my thoughts, and my eyes go to him.

Dropping my hand to his shoulder, I feel my face go soft as I ask, "Really?"

His head tilts to the side and he studies me for a second before saying, "Of course. She needs a place to crash. As long as she's clean, she's always welcome."

"Thank you, honey," I whisper, watching his eyes go soft as I run my hand down his back. "I think her plan is to say with Mom and Dad for awhile. I don't know if she'll go back to Vegas."

"Smart," he mutters, dropping forward and kissing me once more.

"I'm proud of her," I tell him, something he knows, and his face goes softer. His thumbs move over my cheeks as he mutters, "You should be."

"Thank you again for having my back."

"Always, Maggie," he whispers, and hearing the sincerity in his tone, I lift up and press my mouth hard to his, needing him to know how much that means to me. By the time we pull away, we're both breathing heavily, and I know it's time to get up and face the outside world again, even though I wish we could hide away.

TAKING A SIP of coffee, my eyes take in the room. The house, like the room Sven and I stayed in last night, is beautiful, with high vaulted ceilings, huge picture windows that look out over the desert, and furniture that is not only comfortable, but also well made and gorgeous.

Scanning the room again, I stop and watch Kai hold his son, Maxim, close to his chest as he feeds him, and then I watch as his eyes soften and a smile twitches his lips when Myla throws back her blonde head, laughing at something Frank says to her. Kai and Myla fit perfectly; she's the soft to his hard, and you can tell just by watching him that he knows what kind of beauty he has in his grasp and that he would die before allowing something or someone to take that from him.

Pulling my gaze from them, my eyes land on Autumn and I smile, and she returns it then tips her head back toward her husband, Kenton, when he leans over the back of the couch. He bends toward her, placing his mouth close to her ear so he can whisper something to her. Watching a smile form on her lips, I curiously wonder what he said, and then I watch her mouth soften and her eyes pull back to meet his. His hand moves to her lower jaw and his mouth drops to touch hers.

Dragging my eyes from them, I take another sip of coffee. I learned from Sven when he introduced me to everyone that his best friend, Asher, is also Kenton's cousin. I could see this, since I had seen pictures of Asher and knew that he was very good-looking, just not as gorgeous as Sven. Though I'm sure me being in love with Sven has some effect on that decision, still, the family resemblance was there.

"You okay?" Sven asks, taking a seat next to me, and I turn my head to look at him.

"Yes, everyone is really nice, and Myla and Autumn are both very sweet," I tell him quietly as he places his hand around the back of my neck so he can pull me closer.

"They're good women," he mutters back just as quietly.

"Kai and Kenton are both really nice too—a little scary, but really nice," I confide, and he smiles then leans in to press a kiss to my forehead, not replying to that comment. "What is going to happen now?" I ask on a whisper, pulling back to search his face. Having eaten a huge breakfast with everyone laughing and joking, this whole thing feels like a few friends getting together for a weekend of hanging out. It doesn't at all feel like the men in this room are going to be discussing and taking out a man even the FBI fears.

"We're letting you guys settle while we wait for Justin."

"Who's Justin?"

"Remember I told you I had a friend follow you to your parents?" he asks, and I nod. "That was Justin."

"I never met him."

"Nope, but you will. He should be here in a bit," he mutters as his eyes go past me over my shoulder. I watch them narrow slightly, and then he pulls me closer by the back of my neck so he can kiss me. It's not a soft kiss; it's a kiss that has me almost dropping my coffee as I fall into him.

When he pulls away, I look at him, and his eyes hold mine for a second before moving back over my shoulder. Using my coffee as an excuse, I lift it toward my mouth then look to my right, where his eyes are pointed. Zack and Teo are standing near Kenton, and both of them have their eyes to the left. Turning that way, I watch Lane's retreating back as he leaves the room.

"What was that?" I ask Sven.

His eyes come to me and he shakes his head, but I can see annoyance there as he mutters, "Nothing for you to worry about." The whole 'don't worry your pretty little head' act is going to get old quickly. Even knowing the reason behind it, I still find it annoying.

Pulling my eyes from him, I scan the room and find Myla watching me. I smile at her, and she smiles back, but her eyes move from me to the door behind me, and I wonder if she saw what just happened with Lane. Then I move my eyes from her and see Autumn with the same curious look on her face. When her gaze comes to me, I know she's trying to tell me something; I just have no idea what it is.

"You girls are not getting involved," Sven rumbles, and I jump, turning my head to look at him.

"What?"

"You are not getting involved," he repeats, and I hold his stare then snap, "I know that."

Shaking his head, he rolls his eyes toward the ceiling. I have no idea what that means, so I ignore it and go back to drinking my coffee.

WATCHING A MAN walk into the room looking like one of the Vikings from the show on TV, I sit back on the couch and hold Maxim closer to me. Sven, Kenton, and Kai disappeared an hour ago, leaving the girls and me alone so they could go "talk". When they left, I asked Myla if I could hold her son, and she instantly handed him over. I couldn't remember ever holding a baby, but holding him, looking into his sweet tiny face, seeing how small and delicate he is, I know I want that for Sven and myself—more now than ever before.

"Um…" I mutter, looking at the guy and wondering if I should ask him who he is or how the hell he got inside.

But Autumn gets up from her seat, runs across the room and into his arms, and cries, "Justin!" as she slams against him.

Relaxing back in the chair at his name and the way Autumn greets him, I hear him mumble, "Hey, Sweetcheeks," as he dips his head, placing a kiss on her cheek. Then, his huge arms wrap around her in a tight hug as he lifts her off the ground.

"What's with the beard?" she asks, tugging on the end of his bushy facial hair that matches the rest of his appearance. He's hot—in a scary kind of way, but no less hot.

"My lady needs a comfortable place to sit, and I'm accommodating." He grins, and she smacks his chest then rolls her eyes, but I burst out into a fit of giggles, and so does Myla, who is sitting next to me.

"Girls, this is Justin. Justin, this is Maggie and Myla," she says, turning toward us with his arm around her shoulders.

"Nice to meet you both." He smiles and we both say hi.

"Is there a reason your hands are on my wife?" Kenton asks, coming into the room, pulling a grinning Autumn away from Justin, and tucking her into his front.

"You know she loves me more." Justin smiles, and Kenton narrows his eyes then surprises me by pulling him in for a one-armed hug.

"Glad you could make it, man," he mutters, patting his back hard.

"Wouldn't miss it. Where is everyone?" Justin asks, taking a step back.

"We're in the kitchen, though it doesn't surprise me that you found the women before you found us."

"Pussy magnet." He taps his nose, and Autumn hits him in his chest as I start to laugh again hearing Myla giggle at the same time.

"I don't know how Aubrey puts up with you," Autumn says, quietly shaking her head.

'She loves me." Justin grins, then looks at Kenton and mutters, "Let's go. I got some information to share, and then I need to talk to Sven alone."

That comment has my ears perking up, and I wonder what he needs to tell Sven or what he needs to tell him alone.

"You good, babe?" Kenton asks Autumn, and she nods then looks at Justin and takes a step closer to him.

"Are you coming back with us when we leave?" she asks him quietly, and when he gives her a soft smile and nods, I see her body relax. "Good," she whispers, and his face softens even more.

"I miss my girls." he tells her quietly, and her face softens even more.

"I know they miss you, too." She mumbles and he taps her under her chin with his knuckle, and then his eyes come to Myla and me.

"Nice to meet you, ladies." He winks, and I have the urge to roll my eyes, but I fight it and watch Kenton and Justin leave the room while Autumn comes back to the couch, taking a seat next to me.

"So what's the deal with that Lane guy?" Autumn asks quietly, leaning closer to me. Swallowing, I wonder what I should say, or if I should say anything at all, since I really don't know what's going on with him. "He was watching you with Sven throughout breakfast, and then more when we all came in here to sit down after we ate. I thought he was going to pull you away from Sven when he kissed you."

"Um..." I breathe, because that is not good at all.

"Pika had a crush on me," Myla whispers, and I look at her. "I was clueless. I thought we were friends. I had never thought of him that way, and I didn't even know he felt anything for me until Kai pointed it out."

"Really?" I ask.

"Really," she answers, smiling down at Maxim when he stretches his tiny arms over his head and pouts out his lips.

"I...I don't know what's going on with him. A few weeks ago, I was drugged," I whisper, and both women gasp at the same time. "Sven thought it was one of the bartenders at the club, but now he thinks different."

"Well, from the outside, not knowing your story, I would have sworn you and Lane had history," Autumn whispers quietly.

"We don't. I don't even recall him ever hitting on me, to be honest," I tell them, wondering if Sven has this all wrong.

"You may not have history, honey, but his reaction was not a normal one. He was pissed."

"That may be so, but it still makes no sense," I tell them, wondering if I should just try to talk to him and see what is going on for myself. If he does have feelings for me, I may be able to just tell him that I don't feel the same way, and we can put this weirdness behind us and focus on what's really happening.

"I can see what you're thinking, and I don't think that's smart," Myla whispers, gaining my attention. "If Sven is anything like Kai, and I have a feeling he is a lot like him, he won't like it, and by not like it, I mean he will probably be pissed and lose his mind."

"I don't know. If it were me, I would probably just ask him what's going on," Autumn mutters. "Even though Kenton would most likely kill me after I did it."

"My point exactly," Myla murmurs, looking down at Maxim when he starts to fuss, and I carefully move him into her arms then sit back on the couch.

"I'm not going to do anything. Sven made it clear this morning that he wants this to play out," I tell them, even though I don't know if that's the right thing to do.

"I think that's smart," Myla replies, but Autumn's eyes meet mine and I can see she doesn't feel the same. Now I feel like I have a good angel and a bad one on my shoulders.

"I'll give it a couple days," I mutter, and my good angel, Myla, sighs. My bad angel, Autumn, smiles and I bite my lip.

"I NEED TO go to the store," Autumn says, plopping down on the couch next to me, and I turn to look at her, noticing she's dressed for the day in jeans, a black tank, and cute black sandals that have a large silver and turquoise jewel twisted between the leather straps on the top of her foot. When I got up this morning, I didn't even bother getting dressed. I showered, and put on a pair of yoga pants and a hoodie. Yesterday and the day before that, we spent the entire day sitting on the couch. If I was going to sit on the couch today, I was going to do it comfortably.

"That's not going to happen," I mutter, tucking my sock-covered feet under my bottom and looking back at the TV. It's been two days since we got here, and the guys have been gone most of the time, leaving us with Zack, Teo, and Pika. Sven has been keeping an eye on Lane by keeping him close. I'm not sure if this is smart, but when I tried to bring it up, he made it clear he was doing what he was doing for a reason only known to him and that he didn't want me to worry about it. Honestly, I was surprised every time Lane walked back into the house.

"I'm going with or without permission," she tells me, and I turn to look at her again and notice she looks serious.

"What's going on?" I ask, turning my body toward her.

"I'm late," she whispers.

"Late for wh—" I pause when her words register. "You're late?" I repeat, taking her hand.

"We've been trying for awhile." She shakes her head. "With everything happening, I didn't even think…then this morning—" She closes her eyes and drops her voice. "Kenton said something about the date, and I did some math in my head and I'm late…two weeks late."

"Holy shit! We need to go to the store," I whisper-hiss, and she smiles then her eyes fill with tears. "This is awesome," I tell her softly.

"I know, but I don't want to get my hopes up. It could just be stress."

"So we'll find a way to get you a test, and then you'll know for sure."

"How do we go about doing that?" she asks, and I look across the room at Pika and Zack, who are sitting in front of a computer and talking quietly. Then I remember Teo went out for a run a few minutes ago, and Myla has been upstairs with Maxim most of the morning, because he's teething and not feeling well.

"You're close with Justin, right?" I ask, glancing at the guys again to make sure they're still busy.

"Very." She nods, squeezing my hand.

"The guys trust him. Maybe he can take us to the store."

"Kenton doesn't want me leaving the house at all, not for any reason. He even used his I'm the boss tone when he told me so I know he's serious."

"I hate that voice." I scrunch up my face, knowing Sven uses that same tone all the time and it's annoying.

"It's annoying," she agrees vocalizing my thoughts making me smile.

"OKAY, SO IF not Justin then we need to come up with a plan," I mutter.

And we do come up with a plan…even though it's not a good one *at all*.

AS SOON AS we pull up in front of the drug store, I put the car in park, look at Autumn, and smile big, whispering, "We did it."

"I know." She grins.

Biting my lip, I look at her then remind her, "Now we have to get back, so let's run in, get the test, and get out."

"They don't even know we're gone."

She's right…or I hope she is, anyway. We left when the guys were busy upstairs. We triggered the door alarm earlier while we were still in the house, and opened the gate so we could leave without being noticed. Then we put pillows in each of our beds so it would look like we were laying down for a nap. No one followed us when we left, so for now, we are good—or once again, I hope so.

"Let's go." I laugh, opening my door, and then scream when a large hand presses down on the top of my head, shoving me back in my seat before slamming the door.

"Oh no," Autumn whispers, and I look over at her then through the window and see Justin.

"Crud," I whisper as the backdoor opens and Justin slides inside, shutting the door.

"Hello, ladies." He smiles, crossing his arms over his chest.

"What are you doing here?" Autumn asks, and his eyes go to her.

"Sweetcheeks, do you really think you guys can outsmart us?" he prompts, and my heart starts to pound as I look around for Sven, expecting him to walk up to the car.

"Don't worry, Maggie. Sven isn't here," he mutters, and I let out a long breath.

"Though he does know you two dipped out."

"Great." I drop my forehead to the steering wheel and pound it there a few times.

"How did you know we were gone?" Autumn asks, glaring at him.

"Zack spotted you before you even got off the property. I was heading back to the house when he phoned and told me you took off. I pulled over, and you two drove right past me." That was alarming. I was making sure we weren't being followed, and still missed him. "I followed you, wanting to see what the fuck you were up to."

"Oh, well me and Maggie just need to run into the store real quick. We'll be right back," she tells him.

"Not happening, Sweetcheeks." He shakes his head, crossing his arms over his chest.

"It'll take less than five minutes," she argues.

"Not happening. Start the car up, Maggie. We're going back," he tells me, but I pretend I didn't hear and keep the keys in my hand.

"I need to go into the store, Justin, and you're not going to stop me," she replies, putting her hand on the handle.

"Open that door, Sweetcheeks, and I swear I'll shoot you."

"You won't," she hisses.

"I will, because unlike you, I remember what happened to you. If something like that happens again, Kenton will lose his shit," he says quietly, and I bite my lip, because I know from the history Sven shared with me that Autumn was shot at close range by one of Paulie's hit men a little over a year ago, and she almost died. Kenton would lose his mind if something like that happened again; any man who loved a woman would.

"Fine, then you go in and buy the damn test," she cries, and his smile drops.

"What test?" he asks, studying her.

"This is so irritating," she screams.

"What test, Autumn?" he repeats, and she turns in her seat so she can face him.

"A pregnancy test," she hisses.

His face softens as he asks, "Seriously?"

"I don't know. That's why I need a test."

"Fuck." He rubs the back of his head. "I'll buy it. Lock the doors as soon as I'm out. And Maggie?" he calls, and I focus on him. "If you see anything, take off. Don't wait around. Just drive back to the house."

"Got it." I nod and he opens the door. Putting the keys back in, I start the car up and put it in reverse, just in case.

"We're in so much trouble," I inform Autumn as we watch Justin walk into the store.

"Yeah," she agrees. "You can say it was my idea."

"It was your idea." I laugh, and she chuckles, too, and then I press my lips together as we watch Justin walk out of the store with three hot pink boxes in his hand. Pointing at me, he comes around to the driver's side.

"I'll drive," he tells me, opening my door.

"I can drive." I glare at him.

"No offense, Buns, but get your ass in the back."

"Buns?" I whisper irately as he leans over me, unhooking my belt.

"Backseat," he repeats, and I glare at him, but then give up my death-look when I see I'm not going to win and climb over the middle console into the backseat.

"Just so you know, I'm an excellent driver," I inform him when I catch his eyes in the rearview mirror.

"Sure you are, Buns." He laughs.

"I am," I mutter, crossing my arms over my chest and glaring at him again.

"I should have had you get me some water," Autumn says, and I pull my eyes from the rearview mirror and watch her scan a piece of paper with directions on it.

"We're not stopping again, Sweetcheeks. Kenton and Sven are both pissed. I should have had you both back to the house ten minutes ago."

"That's why I need the water. I could drink it, pee on this stick, and then hopefully show him it's positive and soften him up a bit," she says, and I laugh.

"It will be okay. I mean, we're safe, right? They should be okay."

I hear Justin snort, but I ignore that and hold Autumn's eyes as she mouths,

Thank you.

Anytime, I mouth back then turn my head and look out the window, hoping we are not in too much trouble.

"Are you out of your fucking mind?" Sven roars, opening the back of the car as soon as the car comes to a stop.

"I don't believe so," I grumble, surprised that even though his eyes are not angry but *pissed*, he still gently takes my hand and helps me out of the car.

"Now is not a time to be cute, Maggie," he says, dipping his face close to mine.

"I'm not being cute, honey," I reply then look over at Autumn to make sure she's okay. I notice that at some point, she must've taken the pregnancy tests out of the boxes and shoved them in her back pocket, since I can see the white ends sticking out.

"This isn't a joke," he whispers harshly, and I place my hand against his chest, feeling his heart pounding hard before I get up on my tiptoes.

"I'm sorry," I say calmly. "Swear it won't happen again."

His hands hold mine to his chest and he shakes his head. "I know it won't happen again, because I'm handcuffing you to the bed."

"You're not."

"Yeah, I am," he rumbles, dipping his head and kissing me hard.

"We had something important to do," I say breathlessly when he pulls his mouth from mine.

"The only important thing you need to do right now is to listen and stay put."

"When do we get to go home?" I ask quietly after a moment, and his face softens.

"I don't know, baby. Hopefully soon, but until then, I need you to be here."

"I know, and I won't leave again."

"I know you won't."

"You're not handcuffing me to the bed."

"We'll see," he mutters, looking over my head.

"You good?" he asks, and I turn to look at Autumn and Kenton, who are standing much the same way as Sven and me.

"Yeah, man," Kenton mutters then looks over the hood of the car at Justin. "Thanks for getting them back here."

"No problemo, Boss." Justin grins then looks at Sven. "You need to teach Buns how to drive. Chick cannot drive, man." He shakes his head and I narrow my eyes on him.

"Do not call me Buns, and I'm a great driver. I passed the test in one shot," I inform him haughtily.

"Instructor was probably more interested in you than keeping the population of Vegas safe," he grumbles, still grinning.

"Whatever," I mutter back, because the instructor did ask me for my number after he passed me, but I wasn't going to share that with Justin.

"Thought so."

"You're very annoying."

"He is," Autumn agrees, walking over to punch him in the arm, and then she wraps her arms around his waist, giving him a squeeze before going back to Kenton and kissing his chin as his arms wrap around her.

"You guys ready to get back to Kai?" Justin asks, and I want to pout that Sven's leaving again, but I hold it in since I know he doesn't need that right now.

"Yeah, man," Kenton agrees, and I look up at Sven when his arms give me a squeeze.

"Do not leave the house for any reason."

"What if there's a fire?"

"Stay inside."

"What if there's a fire?" I repeat, and his eyes close then his forehead drops to mine.

"Please stay inside, baby."

"Fine." I close my eyes, holding him a little tighter, and then I lift up, placing my mouth against his, whispering there, "Be safe and come back soon."

"Soon as I can." He kisses me softly once more then lets me go to get into the Suburban, with Kenton behind the wheel and Justin getting into the back.

"I can't wait until this is done," Autumn says, taking my hand as we watch the guys pull away.

"Me neither," I agree, smiling as Sven points at the house in a silent demand. "Let's go in before he comes back and cuffs me to the bed," I say, smiling when she laughs.

"Not sure what you were thinking, but next time you two do some shit like that, I'm locking you in the closet," Zack says as soon as we enter the house.

"I'm sorry," I tell him, and his nostrils flare.

"You're not, but do something like that again and you will be."

"Zack," I whisper, taking a step toward him.

Holding up his hands, his eyes hold mine. "I adore you Maggie, but I'm pissed at you right now."

"I know, and I promise I will be on my best behavior from now on."

"I know you will be, because—no joke—I will lock your ass in a closet if I have to."

"I believe you."

"You should."

"I do," I agree, trying to fight a smile, but he catches it anyway.

"My man is so fucked," he mutters, and I run to him and wrap my arms around his back, giving him a squeeze.

"Don't lock me in the closet. I'm afraid of the dark."

"Liar," he grumbles, squeezing me back, letting me know we're okay. Taking a step back, I look over his shoulder at Pika, who is standing with his arms crossed over his chest and leaning against the wall.

"I'm sorry."

"You're safe. It's all good, but like Zack said, we've got no problem locking you two away."

"You won't have to do that," I assure him, and he nods then pulls himself off the wall and leaves the room.

"I'm going to my room for a bit," Autumn says, and I turn to look at her.

"Sure, I'll be in the living room if you need me." I smile, and she nods before heading up the stairs.

Looking back at Zack, I ask, "Wanna watch *Born in the Wild?*"

"Fuck no." He shakes his head as his face loses some of its color.

"Well, if you change your mind, I'll be in the living room." I grin then head in there, make myself comfortable on the couch, and eventually fall asleep watching a woman give birth to a baby in the woods.

Chapter 12
Sven
Truth

"**T**HIS ISN'T EXACTLY a job you can put an ad out for," Kai rumbles, and my eyes move through my office and over to him. Since my club is closed down for the time being, we have been meeting up here, leaving the girls at the house with Zack, Pika, and Teo.

"Yeah, but you know as well as I do that someone else is going to step in the second Paulie is no longer a part of the equation," I reply, sitting back in my chair. "I don't know shit about the business you're in, but I do know business, and anytime someone steps out of a possession, there's always someone there to take over, and I can't imagine this will be any different."

"You're right. Someone else will step in, but I'm not sure our move should be leading someone else into the seat," Kai says, placing his drink on my desk.

"I didn't say I agreed with Justin's idea. I do think we need a way to guarantee we won't be collateral damage. If that comes in the form of making an alliance with someone else, then I'm all for it."

"Aedan," Justin puts in, and I turn to look at him. "Guy is fucked, but he is also not fucking crazy," he says, referring to the Irish high-ranking drug dealer he's been working with.

"He's killed a lot of fucking people." Kenton frowns.

"He has," Justin agrees. "Aedan made a name for himself at twenty-three when he took out his boss, that boss being Armando Levy, the biggest drug lord Vegas had ever seen. A man no one—not even the

FBI—had the balls to stand up to," Justin says then looks at Kai. "You know his story. You know he took out Armando because he was kidnapping women, getting them addicted to blow, and then putting them on the tracks."

"You're making him sound like a fucking choirboy," Kenton chides, leaning back in his chair.

"I'm not saying he's a fucking angel of mercy. I'm saying he has a moral compass, which is more than what Paulie has," Justin replies, sweeping the room, looking at each of us. "Regardless of what we do, what steps we take, there will be someone who takes over. There is no way to prevent that. The only thing we can do is put someone in that seat who isn't going to come back for us."

"You can't guarantee he won't, Justin," Kai mutters, standing from his chair to pace the room.

"I can. He is not a fan of Paulie's."

"Why the fuck do we need to be involved in helping him into that seat?" Kenton asks, and Justin looks at him.

"There are four main families in Vegas. Those four families control what happens in this town—who pimps, who sells dope, and who sells guns. Three of those families are tied to Paulie. Only one family is not, and that's Aedan's."

"Justin has a point," I conclude, and Kai scowls at me. Sitting forward, I put my hands on my desk and lean in. "Listen, I don't give a fuck who does what in Vegas. The only thing I want is to live a life where I don't have to look over my shoulder. Searching for some fuckwad who thinks he's gonna make alliances by taking me out."

"We all can agree on that." Kai nods then looks to Justin. "Set up a meeting. Tell him I want to speak with him about business. We won't mention what's going on until we get a feel for him."

"On it," he mutters, pulling out his phone and stepping out of the office to make the call.

"Were Maggie and Autumn okay?" Kai asks, and I look at Kenton, seeing his expression is the same as mine.

"Autumn said she needed to go to the drug store, so she and Maggie came up with a plan to do that."

"She could have asked one of the guys to get whatever she needed," Kai says, and I feel my lips twitch.

"Don't know much about Myla, but Maggie's always down for causing chaos. Pretty sure she thrives on driving me crazy."

"Autumn's the same. I'm surprised she didn't hatch an escape plan sooner, actually." Kenton chuckles.

"Thank god Maxim is teething, Myla's been locked in our room." Kai mutters as Justin comes back into the office.

"Meeting's set, tomorrow at two, he's meeting us here."

"Good," I nod, rubbing my jaw.

"Now we need to talk about Lane," Justin adds, taking a seat across from me once more.

"He still downstairs?" I ask, and he nods.

"Yep, and I don't think this will surprise you, but I ran his phone record. He's been keeping in contact with one of Paulie's guys."

"Fuck," I clip, standing from my chair and turning to the window behind me. Looking down at the club floor, I see that Lane and Aye are sitting at the bar.

"I don't know what they are talking about when they do talk, but the calls are constant—one a night over the last two months. I also watched the tape again," he says quietly, and I turn to face him. "In one clip, he acted like he was pushing someone off of Maggie at the bar. That's when he slipped the substance he used in her drink."

"It's taking everything in me not to fucking kill him," I whisper.

"He's our in," Justin says, and I let out a breath.

"He's going to get us where we need to be with Paulie, so when we take him out, it's not expected. We are going to use him as a pawn and play him at his own game.

"He's sleeping down the hall from my woman," I remind him quietly.

"He can't make a move without one of us knowing about it."

"I want this shit done," I growl. I'm so fucking frustrated by this situation, and knowing my suspicions about Lane are justified, the anger and betrayal I've been feeling is choking me.

"I'm not happy that he knows where the women are, Justin," Kai breaks in, and Justin pulls his eyes off me to look at Kai, who's still standing with his arms crossed over his chest.

"You have Zack, Pika, and Teo at the house, a security system that rivals the Pentagon's, and enough guns to start a small war. The girls are safe, and if I thought for one second they weren't, I would have you move them to Dino's," Justin says, holding his gaze.

"How do you know Dino?" Kia asks, raising a brow.

"Been here off and on over the last few months working with Aedan. I know more than I want to," Justin answers, making me wonder what the fuck he's been up to and why he's working with Aedan to begin with. Justin doesn't do work for just anyone, and I can't imagine him helping out a drug dealer. That isn't his style. He wants the world to be a better place.

"How close are you with Aedan?" Kai asks, studying him.

"Wouldn't trust him with my lift, but right now, he's an ally," he replies immediately, and Kai studies him for a moment more before nodding and taking a step back.

"Let's head back to the house. Myla's been with Maxim the last few days without a break," Kai says, pulling his phone out of his pocket.

"Works for me. I need to make sure Autumn hasn't escaped out the window, or found a way to talk Myla or Maggie into helping her dig a hole back to Tennessee," Kenton interjects, standing from his chair as I roll my shoulder and press the palm of my hand into it as I stand.

"You good, man?" Kenton asks, watching me.

"Yeah," I mutter, dropping my arm to my side.

"If you need to step back, we'll understand," Kai assures, and my gaze goes to him.

"Not fucking happening. The bullet that hit me could have hit Maggie. I could have let all this shit go before. Now—fuck no. I'm in until this mess is cleaned up and Paulie is six feet under, preferably buried with Lane next to him," I tell him, and he jerks his head once in agreement then heads for the door.

As soon as we reach the club floor, Aye slides off his barstool. "Are we heading back to the house?" he asks while tucking his gun into the back of his jeans.

"We are. I'll fill you in on what's going down when we get there," Kai tells him, and he nods following him out.

"I'll ride with you," Justin tells Lane as we step outside. "We need to stop so I can pick up my bike before we head back to the house."

"Sure," Lane replies with a nod, following him across the lot.

"It'll be over soon," Kenton says, and I pull my eyes from Lane's back and look at him as I move to the passenger side door of the Suburban, opening it up and settling myself inside.

"Yeah," I rumble, slamming the door closed.

"Soon," he repeats.

"Not soon enough." I pull out my cell and reply to a text from Ace, letting him know my lawyer will be in contact tomorrow with the contracts for the club.

"I didn't want to come back," he mutters, backing out of the parking space, and my eyes move to him. "I sure as fuck didn't want Autumn to be here, but I knew I couldn't leave her in Tennessee and risk someone going after her there."

"I wanted to send Maggie away, but didn't for the same reason," I agree, shoving my cell into my pocket.

"Never thought I'd see the day you'd crash and burn over a woman." He laughs, pulling out onto the main road. "I don't know anyone who thought you'd settle."

"I didn't plan for her." I run my hands down my face.

"You deserve to have that. To have her," he says quietly, stopping at a red light and looks at me. "I'm glad for you, man."

I jerk up my chin, and he shakes his head then pulls off when the light changes to green.

"I THOUGHT WE were meeting alone," Aedan says, taking a seat on the couch in my office with his eyes moving from Kai to Justin. "You know I don't like surprises," he informs him, raising a brow.

"I have a feeling you're gonna like this one," Justin says, sitting on the edge of the coffee table across from him. Having never met Aedan, I didn't expect to see a thirty-something man dressed like a biker walk into my club. Most made men in Vegas dress just like what they are, men of money and power. Aedan, in jeans, a white shirt, and black motorcycle boots, doesn't look like he fits in with any of them.

"That's doubtful," he mutters then waves his hand around. "Let's get this over with. I have shit to do."

"First, what's your relationship with Paulie?" Kai asks from the middle of the room, where he planted himself with his arms crossed over his chest as soon as we all settled in.

"Not sure why that's any of your fucking business, Hawaii," Aedan replies, looking at Kai, his body alert.

Kai looks at Justin for a moment before moving his eyes back to Aedan. "Ok, let's do this. I know Paulie's been making moves to take you out," he says, and Aedan's glare moves to Justin.

"You tell him that shit?" he asks, sitting forward, pinning Justin in place with his gaze.

"You know I didn't have to tell anyone shit," Justin replies quietly with an edge to his tone. "Everyone knows Paulie's got a hard-on for you. It's no secret."

"Fuck Paulie," Aedan says, pulling his eyes from Justin to scan the room. "I took this meeting out of respect, but now I'm getting pissed. Tell me what this is about. I don't have time to play twenty-questions or feel like I'm being interrogated."

"All we need to know is where your relationships stands with Paulie." I stand and his attention moves to me. "I don't have time for bullshit. Justin here believes you want Paulie gone. Is that true or not?" I ask, and his eyes narrow on me.

"Paulie's a piece of shit, just like his son was. No one's sad the world he's built is slipping through his fingers, and more than a few are waiting for him to fall," he says and then stands. "Like I said, I came here out of respect, but like you, I don't have time for bullshit" he says, walking toward the door but then stops when Kai speaks.

"I'm assuming you know the story of my wife and the property she owns in Vegas." My eyes go to him, but his are on Aedan, and I know he's referring to the property Myla's parents left to her before their deaths, properties worth millions, maybe even billions. Paulie's son, before his death, planned to kidnap and marry Myla in order to gain control of that property, and Kai was almost killed because of it.

"I've heard about it," Aedan confirms, turning to face him, crossing his arms over his chest.

"It's yours," Kai says quietly, and the room starts to buzz with an undercurrent of energy.

"What?" Aedan asks with his brows pulled together.

"That property and the land it's on is yours...with one condition."

"What the fuck, Kai?" Kenton asks, looking at him.

"I don't need it, and Myla doesn't need it. That land killed her family, and it's about time she got something good from it. She wants to live free, and I want that for her, my son, and our unborn child."

"Jesus," I mutter, staring at Kai.

"What's your condition?" Aedan questions.

"You help us remove Paulie." He pauses then rumbles, "Permanently. No one can know the men in this room were involved in his removal, and if there is ever any backlash, that shit's on you."

"Why the fuck don't you just take him out and keep your property?" Aedan asks the question I want to ask for myself.

"I told you—that property is a guarantee you'll hold up your end of the bargain. I know you have honor. I just don't know how deep it runs, and if someone is questioning your worth, thinking of taking you out, let's just say that land will give you the power you need to hold onto your position," Kai says, and Aedan moves back into the room and takes a seat on the couch once more, looking confused and a little shocked.

"There are easier ways than this," he says rubbing his jaw. "I've been in talks with a few of Paulie's associates. A lot of them are looking to cut ties," he adds, looking around the room and ending on Kai. "I'm not sure if you know Rauel,"

"I know of him," Kai confirms.

"Then you know he controls most of the drugs that come into the United States. Paulie's been one of the only people Rauel will deal with. He trusts no one. He's paranoid and cautious. That was, until Rauel found out Paulie's son was skimming off the top. You see, Rauel had a son around Paulie's son's age, and when Rauel found out his son was stealing from him, he killed him himself, with no remorse. Rauel lost respect for Paulie when he didn't personally deal with his son. If you want a takeover, I have no doubt Rauel would follow you faster than anyone."

"That isn't my life anymore," Kai says quietly, studying Aedan. "I made a promise years ago to my great-grandfather that I would put our family on a path to redemption, and I intend to keep that promise."

"You're giving me something for a job I was going to do anyway," Aedan replies just as quietly. "Paulie's son raped my sister; then, he beat the shit out of her and left her for dead," he says, and the room goes silent. No one even breathes. "Paulie didn't give a fuck when I brought what happened to his attention, and unluckily for me, someone got to his son before I did. I don't need your property. I'll help you no marker needed."

"Aubrey," Kenton rumbles with his eyes on Justin, and my eyes go to him, seeing him looking at his lap with his hands fisted tightly and his jaw hard. "Why the fuck didn't you tell me this shit?" Kenton asks, and Justin lifts his head to look at him.

"You know I couldn't do that," he whispers harshly.

"I wanted her to have an abortion," Aedan says, looking at Kenton. "He fucking raped her. She never even had a boyfriend, and he fucking raped her and put his kid in her. My sister ran away. I did that. I pushed her too hard, and when Justin found out there were people looking for her, he contacted me, and I told him to keep who she is to himself. Aubrey's safe. No one knows she exists, and I want to keep it that way. My sister has too much heart for this life, and she's happy where she is and has made it clear she's not leaving Justin. Not that I'm happy about that part, but I want her to have what she wants. She deserves to be happy."

My eyes move to Justin, wondering what the fuck is really going on and who the fuck Aubrey is to him.

"You know I'll always take care of her," Justin assures, looking at Aedan.

"I know," he mutters then looks around the room. "Paulie knows people are gunning for him. He's not stupid, and ending him won't be easy. Since his son's death, his security has doubled and he's no longer taking meetings."

"We have an in," Justin says, and Aedan's eyes move to him.

"It seems there's a lot you haven't shared," he says quietly, studying Justin.

"You know the important shit," Justin replies just as low.

Aedan lets out a long breath and asks, "So what's the plan?"

"I've been doing some digging. Paulie has a mistress. He's been seeing her for the last four years. His wife doesn't know about her, but I'm guessing if she did, she wouldn't be happy," Justin says, and I cut in.

"I don't know what you heard, but Paulie's been stepping out on his wife for a long time. No way a woman, *any* woman, could miss it. My guess is she just doesn't give a fuck what he does, as long as she gets to live the high life."

"You're right. She couldn't care less about the others. But this woman is different, and I have a feeling she won't like what's been going on," he says, pulling up a picture on his phone of a young girl with long blonde hair, blue eyes, and giant fake tits. "Her name is Anita Lynn. She's twenty-six. Paulie met her at a club she was stripping at and moved her into a better place right away, only to move her into a bigger place four months later. Her house is twice the size of the one he shares with his wife, and he just recently found out she is pregnant with his child. Paulie's been moving money around so that when he asks his wife of the last thirty-two years for a divorce, she won't be able to take him to the cleaners."

"You're right. She won't like that," Kenton murmurs, handing Justin his phone back.

"Lane is our in to Paulie, but before we take him out, we are going to rattle his gilded cage. If things with his wife go how I think they will, she'll send him packing. This will be unexpected, so his guards will be scrambling to cover him. That's when we'll strike, using Lane to contact his man and tell us where Paulie is."

"Sounds a little too easy," I mutter, and Justin's eyes move to me.

"Most wars are ended in silence," he says quietly, and I see Aedan's head shake and his lips twitch.

"Justin is one scary motherfucker. I don't even question it anymore." He shrugs then stands. "I need to get back to business. As soon as you guys have a plan in place, call me. My brothers won't ask questions, and you'll have more backup," he offers, patting Justin's back then shaking each of our hands before walking out of the office.

"I can't believe you didn't tell me that Aedan is Aubrey's brother," Kenton gripes, and Justin stands.

"It's not important. You know what she is to me, and that's all that matters," Justin says, standing and putting a gun into the back of his jeans.

"I didn't even know you had a girlfriend." I frown, crossing my arms over my chest.

"I don't have a girlfriend," he mutters then grins. "I have a wife."

"What the fuck?" I whisper.

"Why isn't she here?" Kai asks, studying him.

"She's never coming back to Vegas. She's with my mom and dad. My dad, who owns more guns than even you. She's safe with *our daughter* at my parents' home."

"Did I fall down the fucking rabbit hole?" I ask, looking around, hearing Kenton chuckle at my side.

"This information is making me second-guess your relationship with Aedan," Kai says, and Justin's eyes move to him and his back straightens.

"I personally don't give a fuck about the guy. My wife was scared out of her fucking head when she ran from him and her family. I know he loves his sister, but he will always put business first, and that shit isn't okay with me. If you doubt my loyalty, then that shit's on you. I have proven on more than one occasion where my loyalties lie."

"No one in this room is questioning your loyalty," I assert calmly, and watch his body visibly relax. "But you know, Justin, even if you don't have a relationship with Aedan, you're tied to him, and that is something we should have heard about before now."

"Aubrey doesn't exist for anyone. She's been through enough. We all have one goal, and that's to take Paulie out. I think you can each understand now why this job is just as important to me as it is to any of you," he says, moving toward the door. "Now, if we're done gossiping, let's get back to the house. I have some shit to take care of before we take Lane on a trip out to Dino's."

"Lane's mine." I look at each of them, making sure they understand. "He drugged Maggie. I don't know what his plan for her was, but I'm not naive enough to think he didn't plan on taking advantage of her," I finish, feeling the anger I've been holding in expand with each breath.

"He's yours," Justin affirms quietly, and I can see in his eyes that he knows what I'm feeling, but when he speaks, I can hear the pain in his words and recognize that he, more than anyone, knows what could have happened. "Paulie Jr. drugged Aubrey. She..." He shakes his head, running his hands over his hair and dropping his eyes to the floor, and his voice catches when he speaks. "She went out with some girlfriends, and he drugged her after she didn't give him the attention he wanted. I'm grateful the drug erased her memory of what happened, but she still knew after she woke up in the hospital that she had been violated. If I had known what happened to her when I killed that motherfucker, I would have tortured him before taking his life. His death was too quick, and far too painless."

"Jesus," Kenton whispers, while Kai growls, "Motherfucker," under his breath.

"I'm sorry, man," I say, but the words aren't enough.

"It didn't happen to me, but I promised my wife it wouldn't happen to anyone else. That drug—the drug Paulie used on her and the one Lane used on Maggie—they were the same. I've never heard of it used outside that circle."

"That's why you're here?"

"That's why I'm here," he agrees then looks through us before heading out the door.

"THIS PLACE CREEPS me the fuck out," Justin says from the driver's seat as we head down a sandy dirt road in the middle of the desert toward a house. I can barely make it out through the headlights and dust Kai and Kenton's SUV is spitting up in front of ours.

"Exactly what is this place?" I ask, and Justin looks at me, the lights of the dash bouncing off his face.

"Imagine a horror movie, and then add the mob to that shit, and this is what you would come up with," he explains, and I look over my shoulder at Lane tied up in the backseat, and even in the dark, I notice his eyes are filled with fear.

"You picked the wrong side," I tell him quietly, hearing him groan through the gag and duck tape covering his mouth.

Pulling up to the dark house, I watch a large man wearing a wife-beater, jeans, and boots, with a shotgun resting over his shoulder, walk up to the passenger side of Kai's SUV. Seeing him nod and walk off toward the house, he comes back out a few minutes later, getting on a four-wheeler. Following behind him and the SUV in front of us, we drive out for miles, ending in the middle of the dark desert. Getting out when we stop, I look around then watch as the guy, Dino, heads a few feet away and pulls open a hatch.

"What the fuck?" I hiss, seeing that down a set of stairs set into the ground is a concrete room. The walls are covered with different tools, with a metal-framed chair set in the middle bolted to the ground.

"Told you this was the shit scary movies are made of," Justin whispers from my side, and I look at him then open the back door, drag Lane out, and then yank him down the stairs into the room.

Pushing him into the metal chair in the middle of the room, I rip the tape off his mouth and pull out the gag, tossing it to the floor.

"I can't believe you betrayed me," I murmur, cutting the plastic ties holding his wrists together. As soon as he's free, he does what I knew he would do. His arm swings out. Ducking under his fist, I lift my elbow, ramming it up under his chin. His head flies back and his teeth gnash together so hard, I wouldn't be surprised if a few broke. Grabbing a long leather strap off the wall, I wrap it around his throat and pull back. His hands rip at the strap trying to pull it off, but I hold it tighter.

"What the fuck we're you thinking?" I ask close to his ear, as his face turns purple.

"Pretty sure he can't answer if he can't breathe" Kenton says blandly from my side, so I loosen the strap and listen as Lane sucks in hair while Justin secures his hands to frame of the chair.

"You're gonna die." He laughs, rolling his head on his shoulders. "You're all gonna die."

"What did they offer you?" I ask and his eyes focus on mine, a creepy smile lighting his eyes.

"You're dead," He licks his lips, and I notice blood coating his teeth. "I was going to make her my whore," he whispers and my blood turns cold. "Take her from the club, say I dropped her at home, take her away, so you wouldn't have been able to find her. She would have been mine." He laughs. "I would have fucked her in every hole in her fucking body, and when I was finished, I would have passed her along to someone else to use," he says and I search the walls of the room looking for something worthy of him. My eyes stop on a pair of lawn sheers with dark silver blades and long black handles.

"That was your plan when you drugged her?" I ask nodding to the wall. Kai's eyes flare as he pulls the sheers down, passing them to Justin who hands them to me.

"I wouldn't have taken her when she was drugged." He smiles his creepy smile again as I test the weight of the sheers. "I would have waited until she knew it was me fucking her in the ass."

Nodding, I flip the sheers over and use both hands to cut off his fingers one by one. Roaring in agony, his face pales as his blood drains onto the floor. Dipping my face closer to his, I mutter, "Now I'm gonna cut off your cock." Seeing fear in his eyes, I smile. By the time I'm done with him, he's unconscious and we've learned everything we could from him including who his contact with Paulie is.

"ARE YOU FUCKING shitting me?" Justin roars into his phone as he slams the door to the Suburban. Stepping around the back, I watch him pace then feel Kenton and Kai come up next to me.

"What's going on?" Kenton asks, and I look at him and shrug then back at Justin when he pulls back his arm, tossing his phone off into the distance.

"His wife fucking killed him!" he roars, reaching his hand up and pulling his hair.

"What?" I ask, taking a step toward him.

"That was Aedan. Police swarmed Paulie's house ten minutes after Aedan and his boys heard a shot. They just watched the police drag Paulie's wife in a pair of cuffs to the back of a squad car. One of his boys was able to get close and heard the cops say she killed her husband-- shot him in the fucking head at close range."

"Are you fucking kidding me?" Kenton asks, and Justin's swings around toward him.

"No," he clips then closes his eyes. "What the fuck?"

"This is good," Kai mutters, and Justin's eyes open to meet his. "It's done. We didn't even have to get our hands dirty. I don't know about you, but I have enough black on my soul."

"All this shit was for nothing. I could have fucking sent her that shit weeks ago. I've been away from my wife for weeks dealing with this shit. You guys came out here to deal with it, and now—"

"It's done," I repeat Kai's words, cutting him off. "Aedan gets what he wants, and we leave all this shit behind us. I got my vengeance, and now I'm going to get my girl, take her home, and then tell her in the morning that we're getting married. At the end of the day, we all got what we wanted. None of the other shit matters."

"Sven's right, Justin," Kenton says quietly. "Paulie and his son are both dead. You know where they were making the drugs thanks to Lane, and the cops are shutting the lab down, probably as we speak. It's time to go home. You know Aubrey and Jenna need you there with them."

Visibly swallowing, he fists his hands at his sides and I now understand what changed about him. It's not that he suddenly became hard. He suddenly found himself caring for two people who he feels he needs to protect from the world. "Your girls are lucky to have you, man," I whisper, meeting his gaze. "But I guarantee they just need *you*. Believe me when I say that."

Nodding, his head drops forward and he pulls in a breath. "Do you want to help me find my phone?" he asks after a moment, and we all laugh, but then we spend the next forty minutes searching for his cell. Once we find it, the sun is starting to rise and we head back to Kai's. All of the girls are awake, so we stay for breakfast then say our goodbyes and head home.

Chapter 13

Sven

True happiness

"I'M MARRYING MAGGIE. If you want to walk her down the aisle, you need to be at the Harmony Chapel in an hour," I tell Maggie's dad as soon as he picks up the phone.

"I'm guessing I can't talk you into waiting a few months?"

"Nope," I deny, smiling at the ground under my feet.

"Does my daughter even know she's getting married?" he asks, and I laugh, looking toward the store I sent Maggie into after she told me there was no way she is getting married without at least wearing a dress.

"She knows," I mumble, hearing him laugh.

"We'll be there," he replies, hanging up.

Shoving my cell into my pocket, I look through the window, seeing Maggie talking to one of the sales girls. Knowing she's okay I walk to the building next-door and go inside to pick up one more item before we make our way to the chapel.

Watching Maggie walk toward me with her arm entwined with her father's I feel my heart beat kick up. She looks more beautiful than I have ever seen her. Her strapless white dress hugs each of her curves perfectly; her eyes are shinning with love, and the smile on her face, fuck that smile is a smile I would kill for.

"You look beautiful," I whisper, taking her from her father at the top of the aisle.

"You look very handsome yourself," she whispers back.

Pressing a brief kiss to her lips, I nod at her dad then turn her toward the minister to make her my wife.

"WE COULD HAVE at least had dinner with my parents," Maggie complains as I guide her into the private elevator blindfolded.

"We could have," I agree picking her up when the elevator comes to a stop. "But then I would have sat with a hard on all through dinner, thinking of all the ways I want to remove this dress," I explain, nibbling her ear as her arms wrap around my shoulders.

"Where are we?" she asks as I set her on her feet.

"We don't have time to take a honeymoon right now." I pull off her blindfold, watching her face light up. "I figured we could spend a few days here naked instead."

Biting her lips she spins in a circle taking in the penthouse. "Oh my god," she whispers in awe, walking to the swimming pool in the middle of the room.

"Naked in this place with you for a few days is better than any honeymoon I could have dreamt up." She grins, walking backward and I start to prowl after her. Then I laugh when she takes off running, catching up with her when she traps herself in the bedroom, I push her down onto the bed. Lifting my weight off her, I search her eyes then lower my mouth over hers. I will never be worthy of the love I see in her eyes, but every fucking day I will try to earn it.

Maggie

HEADING TO THE bed from the bathroom, I stop in my tracks as my eyes land on my sleeping husband. I don't know how many times I've seen him shirtless, but I know it's more times than I can count. I've also memorized the way he looks naked, how he feels pressed against me, how he tastes, what it feels like when he holds me. I've memorized everything about him, but the visual I have now is one I want forever.

I used to think love was a fairy tale, an impossible dream, but having what I have with Sven, I know that not only is it possible, but it's something that happens when you least expect it. It takes you for a ride you may not be ready for, but it leaves you steady on your feet when you get off.

Moving quietly to the bed, I put my knees on the mattress and run my finger over the thick platinum band on Sven's finger, admiring what it is and what it stands for.

"Why are you up?" he asks, opening one eye to peek at me while his fingers wrap around mine.

"I couldn't sleep," I tell him, falling to my side and scooting closer to him.

"You couldn't?" he asks, getting up on his elbow while his fingers run down between my breasts.

"No." I smile, parting my thighs.

"Eager, are we?" He grins, leaning down to kiss me as his fingers roll over my clit, making my hips jerk.

"I like my husband's fingers," I breathe, running my own through his hair.

"Just my fingers?" he asks, sliding one then two deep, rolling them over my G-spot, causing me to gasp.

"I don't know. I also like your mouth and your...you know."

Chuckling, he scoots down the bed, swings one of my legs over his shoulder, and licks while his fingers pump. "I think you should tell me what your favorite is out of the three." He licks me again and my hands move to hold him in place. By the time he's done, my eyes are heavy, and if I had to tell anyone what my favorite was, I wouldn't be able to, because he's a master with all three.

Kenton

ROLLING OVER, I place my hand out on the mattress and come up with air. "What the fuck?" Opening my eyes, I lift my head and see the bed is empty, but the light in the attached bathroom is on, and I can hear whimpering coming from in there. Getting out of bed, I don't even bother finding my pants. I pick my gun up off the side table and slowly make my way to the bathroom door, which is open a crack, where I can see Autumn through the mirror, standing naked in front of the sink with tears in her eyes. "Baby, what the fuck?" I ask, swinging the door fully open, watching her jump when our gazes connect.

"I...I can't believe it," she whispers, smiling while more tears fill her beautiful eyes.

"Believe what?" I ask quietly, setting my gun on the counter so I can take her into my arms.

"This," she whispers, reaching behind me then tucking her arms between us.

Dropping my eyes to her hands, my heart skips a beat as I realize she has a pregnancy test in her grasp, a pregnancy test with the word *Pregnant* clear as day on the small oval screen. I pull my eyes from the test to look at her.

"Jesus," I whisper, closing my eyes and dropping my forehead to rest against hers.

"I hope that's a good 'Jesus,'" she whispers back, and my eyes open to meet hers.

"Never been happier, baby. I swear, I think you give me happy, and then you top that shit with something else every fucking time," I tell her, and a loud sob tears up her throat as she drops her forehead to my chest and wraps her arms tight around me. Holding her to me, I rest my cheek on the top of her head.

"We need to call your mom and Aunt Viv."

Chuckling, I pull her head from my chest so I can see her eyes and shake my head. "We're not calling my mom, or anyone else for that matter."

"But she'll be so excited." She pouts, and I lean in, kissing her softly.

"She'll still be excited when you tell her later," I mutter as I turn her, lifting her onto the counter.

"But I want to tell her now."

"Sorry, baby, we're celebrating. Then you're gonna be too tired to call her, so like I said, that call's going to have to wait," I inform her, pushing her knees apart as I tweak her nipple, hearing her gasp. Gripping the back of her head with one hand, I thrust my tongue into her mouth, while my other hand leaves her breast, slides up her inner thigh, and my fingers roll over her clit.

"I'll call them tomorrow," she agrees, wrapping her legs around my hips as her head tips back so I can take her mouth again. Lifting her off the counter, I carry her to the bed. Planting her on the mattress, I end our kiss and make my way down her body, stopping along the way to kiss each nipple and her lower stomach, settling myself between her legs.

Swiping my tongue up her center, her thighs tighten around my head and the heels of her feet press into my back, lifting her higher into my mouth. I drink down her first orgasm and settle myself between her folds for her second, where I release my own deep inside her.

Kai

"Is he asleep?" Myla asks, walking into Maxim's room wearing her nightgown, her wet hair down around her shoulders.

"He is. How are you feeling?" I ask, pushing my fingers through her hair, tilting her head back.

"Good." She smiles softly, running her hands up my chest.

"How's my daughter?" I ask, sliding my hands around her waist, pulling her closer to me while travelling them down to cup her bottom.

"We could be having another boy," she murmurs smiling softly.

"But we're not," I say, nuzzling her neck while bending her back as I slide my hands down the back of her thighs, lifting her up.

Wrapping her legs around my waist, her hands move from my shoulders to grip around the back of my neck as her mouth trails lazily up the side, ending at my ear, where her warm breath whispers, "I need you inside of me."

Pressing her to the wall in the hallway, I push her panties to the side and flick her clit. "Are you going to feed me?" I ask on a rumble, feeling her wetness soak my fingers as I push two inside her, rubbing her G-spot.

"I'll do whatever you want," she breathes, riding my hand as her heels dig into the back of my thighs.

"I like that answer." I lick over her mouth then bite down on her bottom lip. Pulling her away from the wall, I walk to our bedroom, kicking the door closed behind us. Once I carry my wife to the bed, I take my time, giving her everything before taking even more.

WALKING DOWN THE beach toward Myla and Maxim, I smile as I listen to my wife's laughter and my son's giggle as the waves crash into them, sitting in the sand near the shore.

"Come on, Daddy." Myla smiles, turning her head toward me as I close the distance between us. Settling myself behind her, I grin when Maxim splashes his hand in the water and babbles.

"Are you happy, Makamae?" I ask, pressing my lips against her neck. Her hand comes up to wrap around the side of my head as her own turns to catch my eyes.

"This is my happiness, Kai—this moment, and a million others just like it that you've given me."

Looking into her beautiful eyes, I know she's right, and now, the rest of our days will be spent just like this.

Epilogue

Maggie

A year and a whole lot of happiness later

S MELLING BACON, MY stomach growls and I try to fight it. I really do, but this baby has a mind of its own, and I swear it only wants meat. Sitting up in bed, I push my hair out of my face, place my hand over my large, round stomach, and ask, "Why couldn't you like tofu?" like he understands me. I feel a sharp kick right to my bladder, and I pull in a deep breath.

I didn't even have to take a pregnancy test to know I was pregnant. One day, I woke up and the thought of tofu made me queasy, while the idea of a hamburger made me salivate. That morning, I told Sven I was pregnant. He told me I was crazy. We had only been trying to conceive for a month, and even if I was pregnant, I wasn't far enough along to come up positive with a test. A week after my food cravings didn't diminish, I went and bought a test. It was still a week until my period was due, but I took the test anyway, and it came up with two pink lines—one slightly darker than the other, proving I was right.

Awkwardly rolling out of bed, I put my feet to the floor and push myself off the mattress then waddle to the bathroom, brushing my teeth, and taking care of business as quickly as a nine-months pregnant woman can. Pulling my robe from the back of the door, I slip it on and tie the waist then move out of the room.

Sven got his wish and we moved to Tennessee a month after all the drama went down. It didn't take me long *at all* to fall in the love with the town he called home, or the people he considered his family. When we moved to town, we stayed in Susan and James Mayson's house while our home was built.

Our plan hadn't been to stay with them. We planned to rent a house for a few months, but after Susan heard this news, she went all mom-mode on Sven and me, and insisted we stay with her and James, that they had plenty of room. I obviously tried to convince them otherwise, not wanting to be an inconvenience, but I learned quickly that when Susan wanted something, she got it, and she wanted us to stay with them.

I never knew people like the Maysons existed before. People who are good through and through, people who would do anything for those they consider family, and Sven and I were just that to them. Mayson Construction built our home, and most days, Sven could be found helping the men he considered brothers with the job of building our house. It made it that much more special when it was complete, and he knew his hard work went into the place our kids would grow up.

Walking down the long hall from our bedroom, past Sven's office, I head through the great room, with its floor to ceiling windows and view of the large pond in the backyard, and into the big open kitchen where Sven is standing shirtless in front of the stove with the phone to his ear.

Spotting me, he grins then mutters, "I gotta go Ace." And he drops the phone to the counter. Ace bought the club from Sven and funny enough he and Eva got together; I don't know how it happened, but she turned him into a one-woman man.

"Was wondering how long it would take you to get here," Sven says, using a fork to scoop out bacon from the frying pan onto a plate covered with a paper towel.

"You know it's not actually me who likes bacon—it's your son—right?" I ask, moving around the long counter and stealing a slice of crispy bacon from the plate.

"I'm glad my boy likes meat," Sven mutters, wrapping his hand around the side of my neck, leaning in, kissing my mouth, whispering, "Morning," and then dropping his hands to my stomach and bending down.

"I say we make a no-tofu rule for the house. What do you say?" he asks my belly, and our son kicks hard at the sound of his dad's voice. "I'm taking that as a yes." He smiles, looking up at me.

"I'm eating tofu. I'm only not eating tofu right now, because he makes me sick every time I try," I tell him, something he already knows.

"Whatever you say, baby." He grins as I reach for another piece of bacon. "You excited to see Morgan?"

"Yes, but I think she's just coming so she can decorate and hog Maddox when he gets here."

"She's gonna have to fight me for my boy."

I know he's telling the truth, as his eyes light with a fire that's only there when he talks about his family, especially his son. He's excited to be a dad, and I have no doubt he will be hands-on. I honestly think I'll have a hard time getting our kid away from him.

"I really can't wait to see my mom and dad," I tell him quietly as he rubs my tummy. My relationship with my parents changed drastically. They are no longer absent, but fully involved in not only my life, but also my sister's. They even bought a small RV so they can travel to Tennessee to visit Sven and me, and to Colorado, where Morgan now lives with her fiancé.

After Morgan got out of rehab, she stayed with my parents for a few months then took a job in Colorado at a rehab facility for troubled youth. The owner of the facility, Greg, took one look at my sister and fell in love—as he puts it. They're happy, and best of all, my sister is doing amazing in her recovery, and I really believe her helping young kids find the right path has been good for her.

"What time are they arriving?" he asks, kissing my forehead before moving away to the fridge.

"I think tomorrow sometime, but if Dad has his way, it could be late tonight," I tell him, and he looks over his shoulder and grins.

"I'm guessing your mom is still on her 'Kama Sutra across the US' kick?" he asks, coming out of the fridge with eggs and a block of cheese.

"It's so weird," I mutter, shaking my head.

"She's got a lot of followers." He smiles, setting the carton of eggs on the counter. He isn't wrong; my mom started a few social media pages and has close to forty thousand followers. When she and my dad travel, they stop along the way, and my mom teaches classes on the Kama Sutra, though she still hasn't talked Sven into taking one. She tries every time we see her.

"It's still weird," I repeat, listening to him laugh.

"I still have the book she gave me on her last visit. I think we should try out a few of the positions."

"This is kind of in the way," I tell him, wrapping my arms around my large belly.

"I'm sure there's something in there we could try." He grins, and I feel the place between my legs tingle at the thought. One thing for sure—the heat between us hasn't died down, not even a little bit, and I have no doubt it never will.

"QUIET, LITTLE MAN. Momma's sleeping," I hear Sven whisper, and I keep my position in the bed but open my eyes and watch him pick up Maddox from his bassinet and carry him out of the room. Sitting up, I slip out of bed and head down the hall, making sure to stay quiet as I follow behind them. Standing in the doorway of the living room, I watch as Sven walks to the kitchen to make a bottle then walks to stand in the middle of the room with Maddox in his arms, swaying him from side-to-side as he feeds him.

Biting my lip to keep from crying, I listen as Sven tells our son the story of how we met then smile when he adds that he thought I was crazy. I have no regrets. Looking back at every single moment, the bad ones included, I have no regrets about any of it, because I know the foundation we built when we became an 'us' is solid; nothing will ever break us.

Moving back to the bedroom, I stop in the hall and look at one of the pictures I had framed right after Maddox was born. Sven is standing with his parents, his mom next to his father, both looking happy and smiling at their grandson. His mom will never be normal, but looking at them as a family, I know Sven needed that connection, and even more so, I know his parents needed it, and I'm just glad they all have it now.

Moving down the hall, I get back into bed and pull the blanket up over my shoulder, and I try to fight it, but I fall asleep.

Sven

"SHIT, MAGS." I run my fingers through the hair on either side of her head while her hand works in sync with her mouth, taking me down her throat. "Fuck, come here," I growl, but she shakes her head with my cock still in her mouth. "Now," I demand, raising my hips off the bed as she takes me deeper, pushing me closer to the edge. Putting my hands under her armpits, I jerk her away from my cock, flip her to her back, push her legs apart, and then slam inside her. "I come inside of you, not in your mouth," I remind her, moving my thumb to her clit and rolling my finger over it.

"Yes, inside of me," she whimpers, wrapping her legs around my back.

"You're so wet, baby. Jesus, you love sucking me off, don't you?" I ask, rolling her clit faster.

"Yes," she hisses, and my mouth travels down her neck, nipping the skin as I go, ending on her breast. Her nails dig into my back and I pull her nipple into my mouth, biting down on the tip and feeling the walls of her pussy contract around me. "Sven!" she cries, and I lift my head to watch her come apart under me as I thrust faster, her orgasm pulling mine from me.

Planting myself against her cervix, I cover her mouth with mine and groan down her throat as I lose myself deep inside her. Feeling her limbs wrap around me, I pull my head back and run my fingers through her hair then roll us, settling her against me while I attempt to catch my breath.

"I love you," she murmurs, kissing my chest, and I tilt my head down toward her and give her a squeeze.

"Love you too, baby," I tell her, dragging the blanket up over us as she presses her face into my chest and tucks her hands between us. Hearing her breathing even out, I know she's asleep. Kissing her forehead, I pull her closer still.

Looking at the TV monitor next to the bed, I watch my son's chest rise and fall steadily for a moment, and then rest my chin on the top of my wife's head, close my eyes, and fall asleep knowing I'm living the impossible dream.

INFATUATION

Justin and Aubrey

Prologue

HEARING THE RATTLE of an old car and the sound of squeaky breaks, I get up from my couch and go to the window and pull back the curtain, just enough to see outside without drawing attention to myself. It's dark but the light from the street lamp in the parking lot has cast a glow on the car beneath it. The rusty beat-up powder blue Buick needed to go to the junkyard a few years ago. The bumper is hanging on by ropes someone tied around it and the trunk. The back right taillight is covered in red tape, and I know from seeing the car in daylight that there is more rust on it than there is paint.

The driver's side door opens and my heart pounds against my rib cage, the same thing it does every time I see her.

Watching her get out of the car, I grin as she closes the door only to have it swing open again. Taking a step back, she kicks the door with so much force that the car rocks from side to side. I'm sure she just added another dent to the car, not that anyone will notice or that it will matter.

Blowing a piece of her long blonde hair out of her face, I watch it flutter in the light as she leans her head back to rest her hands on her round stomach.

She must be at least seven months pregnant if not more. Then again, I could be wrong. Her small size makes her stomach look huge. I would guess she's around five one. She has a slim body except for her breasts, which are about a handful and her stomach, which looks like a basketball tucked under her shirt.

Watching her walk toward the building with her face free of makeup and her long blonde hair pulled over one shoulder and her simple jeans and tee, I wonder how the fuck she came to live with Shelly. She doesn't look like Shelly's friends, who I know because every time Shelly has a party, which is most nights, her friends and whatever men they pick up are usually outside standing around the front of the building smoking and drinking. Shelly wears too much makeup and not enough clothes, and her friends are the same. Then there's her. She doesn't fit, which makes her more interesting.

As she gets closer, I notice the dark circles under her eyes and the exhaustion in her features. Every time I see her, she's either coming from work or going to work. Okay, I should say every time I spy on her, since I've never actually spoken to her and she has no idea I even exist. She pauses right outside her door and her head drops. Even though she's in profile, I can see the annoyance and deflation on her face. As she opens the door, loud music streams outside and a room full of people can be seen inside.

I'm sure her roommate isn't helping her level of exhaustion. The urge to protect her—to do something—has me moving to my computer.

Twenty minutes later, I go to the window and watch a group of ten people along with Shelly leave the apartment across from mine. Smiling, I go to the couch to sit down, put on my headphones, and start up Call of Duty.

Chapter 1

H EADING FOR MY Rover, I look to the left when I hear, "You stupid piece of crap, open now." Then I watch my neighbor pull and tug on her car door, trying to get it open as she yells at it.

"Need some help?" Startled, she jumps back. Her eyes get big and her cheeks turn a shade of dusty rose.

"Um…no…no, I got it," she says putting one foot on the door and pulling harder than she was before.

"Let me help," I tell her gently, ignoring her protest as I move her out of the way, then pull on the door expecting it to open for me. But then I feel like an ass when it doesn't budge. When I pull it again, still nothing. How fucking hard did she kick it shut last night? "It's stuck," I mutter, and then hear giggling coming from her that rings through my ears and brings my dick to life. Turning to look at her, I pull in a swift breath. I knew she was going to be beautiful up close, but I didn't realize how fucking gorgeous she would be. Her blonde hair is up in some kind of bun on top of her head, drawing attention to her big blue eyes, soft feminine face, and totally fucking kissable lips.

"I may have kicked it a little too hard last night," she whispers ducking her head, but I want her eyes on me—I need her eyes on me.

"What's your name?" Her eyes fly up to meet mine, and I'm sure my question sounded like a demand mixed with a growl, but there is nothing I can do about it now.

"Me?" she asks looking around, and I find myself smiling at her.

"You honey, what's your name?"

"I don't know if I should tell you that," she mumbles and my head tilts to the side to study her.

"You don't know if you should tell me your name?" I ask after a moment.

"Well, I don't know you."

Chuckling, I move away from the door toward her, then stop when her body stills and her eyes fill with fear. My jaw tics and I feel my heart squeeze. Who ever put that fear in her would answer to me, but first I wanted—no needed—to know her name.

"My name's Justin. I live in apartment two ten." I tilt my head toward the building hoping she'll feel more comfortable knowing I'm her neighbor.

"Justin," she whispers swinging her eyes from me to the building and back again.

"Justin," I confirm.

Licking her bottom lip, she takes a step toward me then stops. "I'm Aubrey. I live with Shelly."

"Nice to meet you, Aubrey."

"You, too," she mutters then takes a step back. "Shelly said you're nice."

That was surprising because I've only spoken to Shelly a hand full of times since she moved in. Then again, she probably thought I was nice, considering I didn't call the cops on her every time she was having a party.

"Where are you going?"

"I need to go to the post office then to work." She pulls out a cell phone from her pocket and looks at the time. "Crap, I'm totally gonna be late to work," she mutters to herself and I notice her phone is the kind you buy at the store for twenty dollars—the kind of phone I used for a throw away when I was working a case and didn't want anyone to track it.

"Let's try your other doors," I say and her cheeks get even darker. She presses her lips together and tucks her phone into her pocket.

"Your other doors don't work either," I guess from the look on her face.

"No, only the driver's door. The other doors were welded shut because they kept opening on the fly.

"Jesus," I mutter running a hand over my head. I didn't think she would approve of me taking her car to the junkyard where it belonged and buying her a new car, at least not yet anyway.

"I'm sure you have better things to do with your time than stand out here with me. I'll just go in and ask Shelly if I can use her Triple A. Hopefully they can pull it open for me."

"I was heading to the post office," I lie. "Why don't you go with me, and I'll drop you to work after."

"That's really sweet but—"

"Honey…" I cut her off. "It's gonna take at least twenty or more minutes for someone to show up, and you already said you're gonna be late for work."

Looking at me then her car, I can tell she's torn. "Okay, if you're sure you don't mind."

"Not at all." I take her arm and lead her over to my Rover and click the alarm off before opening the door for her. I make sure she's settled before I slam the door closed. Jogging around the back, I get in behind the wheel and feel myself relax.

"This is a nice car." Looking over at her, I smile then press the button that starts it up.

"This was a gift from a friend of mine," I tell her and her eyes get big.

"A gift?"

"Well, kinda a bribe gift. A friend of mine in Hawaii tried to bribe me into coming to work for him."

"You're in Tennessee," she points out softly.

"Didn't say I took the bribe."

"But you have this car."

"Yep," I agree with a smile while backing out of my parking space.

"He didn't get mad?"

"Nah, he knew before he tried to bribe me that I wouldn't leave my job."

"Then why did he try?" she asks sounding adorably confused.

"Why does anyone do anything?"

"Good point." She laughs and that laugh does some funny shit to my chest.

Getting to the post office, I wonder what the fuck I'm going to do since I have nothing to mail and no reason to be here. Helping her out, I lead her inside then stand in line.

"Stamps," I mutter to myself. She turns and tilts her head back to look at me then asks, "What?"

"Stamps… Um, I need stamps," I tell her, knowing I'm normally much better at making up shit on the fly.

"Oh." She shrugs then goes to the open teller and tells him that she needs a money order. Hearing her say the amount of four hundred dollars, I'm more than a little surprised; her car is a piece of shit and the clothes she has on, though she makes them look good, are worn and old. And she's pregnant—very pregnant. She must need that money. I have no idea how much a kid costs, but four hundred dollars would go a long way to help her.

Once I'm done paying for my stamps, I move to the side and wait for her. When she's finished, she graces me with a bright smile. I take her hand and lead her outside to the Rover, helping her in before moving around the hood and getting in behind the wheel.

"Where do you work?" I ask as I start the engine.

"I… Do you know Dolly's on West Elm?" she asks quietly, and my head swings her direction. Dolly's is a strip club, one of the bigger ones in town. Beating back the anger I feel, I mutter, "Yeah, I know it."

"I… I… That's where I work."

Well, that answered the question of how she knew Shelly, since Shelly works that club, and a few others around town.

"You're pregnant," I point out the obvious, not that she's not beautiful and not that some men don't get off on pregnant women, but I can't imagine her working at a club like that.

"I work in the back. I help with the books, and sometimes on the weekends, I do the girls' makeup and hair if it's slow. Johnny, my boss, has been sweet about helping me out," she mummers and I turn my head to look at her and see she's staring out the window, her chin wobbling.

"Please don't cry," I say quietly reaching over to take her hand.

"I won't. I don't cry." She turns her head to look at me and the broken look in her gaze causes my heart to stutter in my chest.

"Have dinner with me tonight," I blurt and her hand jerks in mine. Her eyes grow in surprise.

"You... You want to have dinner with me?" she whispers.

"I'm the king of Hamburger Helper." I smile and her bottom lip goes between her teeth for a moment before she whispers, "Okay,"

"Okay?" I ask just to confirm, feeling my pulse quicken.

"Yes, Justin, okay." Hearing my name leave her mouth does that same shit to my chest, making it feel funny once more, and I feel myself grin as I pull out of the parking space and head toward Dolly's.

Chapter 2

M OVING FROM THE kitchen to the living room carrying two bowls of Hamburger Helper, one of the only things I know how to cook, I stop in my tracks when I spot Aubrey asleep on my couch with her head on the armrest, her feet tucked up near her ass, and her hand resting over her belly. Letting out a breath, I move to the couch, setting both bowls on the coffee table. When I picked her up from work, she looked exhausted, but happy to see me all the same. I knew she had to be tired, so when I got her to my place, I showed her around and then told her to rest while I cooked. Pulling the blanket off the back of the couch, I lay it over her then take her dinner back to the kitchen and set it in the microwave, figuring she can have it when she wakes up.

Turning the TV on, I lower the volume and sit back eating. Hearing whimpering coming from Audrey, I set my bowl aside once more and turn to face her. Whatever she's dreaming about isn't good. Her body is writhing and her breathing is labored.

"Audrey." I grab her hand and her foot swings out kicking me in the stomach as she sits up yelling.

"Noooooo!"

"Jesus," I breathe, as her eyes focus on me and her hands cover her mouth.

"I'm so... oh God, I'm so sorry," she whispers. "Did I hurt you?"

"No, are you okay?" I ask studying her, and her face pales as she scoots away from me. "I will never hurt you," I tell her watching her hands clench into fists. "Never," I repeat.

"I need to go. I'm so sorry..." She gets up off the couch, grabbing her sweatshirt. Before I can stop her, she's gone, slamming the door behind her.

"Fuck." I rub my hands down my face and see that on the floor in front of the couch are her sneakers. Smiling, I get up off the couch and head to the door carrying her shoes with me.

Knocking on Shelly's apartment door, I wait only a moment for it to open and am a little surprised when Aubrey pokes her head out.

"You forgot your shoes," I tell her softly holding them out to her.

"Thank you," she whispers, taking them from me and ducking her head.

"I still have your dinner, if you want it."

"I… I'm not hungry," she says looking up at me. Her stomach takes that moment to gurgle loudly and I raise a brow. "Okay, I'm hungry but I…" Her cheeks get pink and I take a step closer to her.

"Don't be embarrassed. One day you can tell me about it, but right now, I'd like it if you had dinner with me."

"Are you sure?" she asks studying me.

"Absolutely."

Nodding, she steps out of her apartment and closes the door behind her. I notice she's slipped on a pair of flip-flops. Taking her hand, I lead her back up the stairs to my place then settle her on the couch before going to the kitchen to nuke her food and grab her a glass of orange juice. When I get back into the living room, I can tell she's still nervous, but I know there is nothing I can do about that right now. It will take time for her to trust me.

"Tell me a little about yourself," I say handing her, her food while setting her cup on the table.

"There isn't much to tell." She shrugs, but I know she lying as her hands fidget.

"How long have you been here?" I ask, setting my feet on the coffee table lounging back.

"About seven months," she says between bites. "I was just nine weeks pregnant when I got here and now I'm almost due."

"Where's the father?" I ask quietly, and her bottom lip goes between her teeth and her eyes meet mine.

"Hopefully dead," she whispers, catching me off-guard by the fierceness of that statement.

"Does he know?" I whisper back and her head shakes from side to side.

Studying her for a moment, I see that there is something there, something ugly and it takes everything in me not to drag her to my lap and hold her while she tells me about it.

"Eat babe," I mutter nodding toward her bowl. "You can save that story for another day," I tell her, and her chin wobbles as she nods and digs into her food.

Turning up the volume on the TV, I sit back and watch the show while keeping an eye on her.

"You are the king of Hamburger Helper," she says and I turn my head to look at her and smile as she sets her bowl on the coffee table.

"My mom tried to teach me to cook, but the only things that stuck were that and mac and cheese with hotdogs. I suck in the kitchen otherwise," I tell her, watching as she tucks her feet under her.

"My parents are Irish and they both love to cook. Thankfully they shared their talent with me."

"Where are they now?"

"Vegas, well all of my family lives there. My mom and dad along with my brother and a few cousins."

"You came to Tennessee alone?"

"Yeah, they didn't want me to keep my baby," she whispers, placing her hands over her stomach. "I hate her dad, but that wasn't her fault. Plus, she's half of me and innocent. It may sound crazy, but when I found out I was pregnant, I knew that regardless of how she was made, I loved her more than anything else in this world, and I would never let anyone take her from me."

"You keep saying she, is she a girl?"

"Yeah, she's a girl." She smiles then reaches out and grabs my hand pulling it to her stomach. Letting her lead the way, her hand presses down on mine and I feel movement under her shirt as the baby undoubtedly moves around. Looking up at her, I feel my face go soft as I watch a beautiful smile spread across her face, and her eyes light with excitement. Without thinking, I use my free hand to push a piece of her hair behind her ear. Her sharp intake of breath has me leaning close enough to feel her breath against my mouth.

"I really want to kiss you, Aubrey," I whisper and her eyes close briefly before she leans forward, resting her mouth against mine. Kissing her softly I pull away then slide my hand behind her neck, tip her head down and touch my mouth to her forehead.

Acknowledgments

First I want to give thanks to God without him none of this would be possible.

Second I want to thank my husband. I love you now and always.

To my editors. Kayla, you know I adore you woman. Thank you for all your hard work and for being an editing rock star. PREMA EDITING thank you for your hard work I can't wait to work with you in the future.

Thank you to TRSOR you girls are always so hard working, I will forever be thankful for everything you do.

To every Blog and reader thank you for taking the time to read and share my books. There would never be enough ink in the world to acknowledge you all but I will forever be grateful to each of you.

XOXO Aurora

Other books by this Author

The Until Series
Until November – Now Available
Until Trevor – Now Available
Until Lilly – Now Available
Until Nico – Now Available
Second Chance Holiday – Now Available

Underground Kings Series
Assumption – Now Available
Obligation – Now Available
Distraction – Now Available

Until Her Series
Until July – Now Available
Until June – *COMING SOON*

Until Him Series
Until Jax – Now Available
Until Sage – *COMING SOON*

Alpha Law
Justified – Now Available
Liability – Now Available
Verdict – *COMING SOON*

Shooting Stars series
Fighting to breathe – Now available
Wide open spaces – *COMING SOON*
Paranormal – Sea of Veracity – *COMING SOON*

About The Author

NEW YORK TIMES & USA TODAY BESTSELLING AUTHOR
Aurora Rose Reynolds started writing so that the over the top alpha men
that lived in her head would leave her alone. When she's not writing or
reading she spends her days with her very own real life alpha who loves
her as much as the men in her books love their women and their Great
Dane Blue that always keeps her on her toes.

For more information on books that are in the works or just to say hello,
follow me on Facebook:

facebook.com/pages/Aurora-Rose-Reynolds/474845965932269

Goodreads:

goodreads.com/author/show/7215619.Aurora_Rose_Reynolds

Twitter:

@Auroraroser

E-mail Aurora she would love to hear from you:

Auroraroser@gmail.com

And don't forget to stop by her website to find out about new releases,
or to order signed books.

AuroraRoseReynolds.com

52245565R00128

Made in the USA
Charleston, SC
13 February 2016